자귀나무꽃이 필 때

자귀나무꽃이 필 때

발행일	2023년 11월 14일		
지은이	정민주		
펴낸이	손형국		
펴낸곳	(주)북랩		
편집인	선일영	편집	윤용민, 배진용, 김다빈, 김부경
디자인	이현수, 김민하, 임진형, 안유경, 한수희	제작	박기성, 구성우, 이창영, 배상진
마케팅	김회란, 박진관		
출판등록	2004. 12. 1(제2012-000051호)		
주소	서울특별시 금천구 가산디지털 1로 168, 우림라이온스밸리 B동 B113~114호, C동 B101호		
홈페이지	www.book.co.kr		
전화번호	(02)2026-5777	팩스	(02)3159-9637

ISBN   979-11-93499-44-3 03810 (종이책)   979-11-93499-45-0 05810 (전자책)

(주)북랩 성공출판의 파트너

북랩 홈페이지와 패밀리 사이트에서 다양한 출판 솔루션을 만나 보세요!

홈페이지 book.co.kr   •   **블로그** blog.naver.com/essaybook   •   **출판문의** book@book.co.kr

작가 연락처 문의 ▶ ask.book.co.kr

작가 연락처는 개인정보이므로 북랩에서 알려드릴 수 없습니다.

이 책은 전라남도, (재)전라남도문화재단의 후원을 받아 발간되었습니다.

자귀나무꽃이
필 때

When Silk Tree Flowers Blossom

정민주 지음·번역
Written and Translated by Minju Jeong

 북랩

청춘에게

목차

001 멈춰버린 자동차 / 10

002 모태 솔로 / 16

003 할아버지가 된 레오나르도 디카프리오 / 25

004 자귀나무꽃이 필 때 / 37

005 꿈과 야망 / 47

006 어느 멋진 날 / 55

007 운명의 장난 / 65

008 먼지가 되어 / 75

009 시절 인연 / 92

010 협주곡 / 98

011 피아노 치는 남자와 자귀나무꽃 / 110

작가의 말 / 118

001   A Stalled Car / 122

002   Forever Alone / 129

003   Leonardo DiCaprio Becomes an Old Man / 141

004   When Silk Tree Flowers Blossom / 157

005   Dreams and Ambitions / 170

006   One Fine Day / 181

007   Mischief of Destiny / 194

008   Turning to Dust / 206

009   Fate in Time / 228

010   Concerto / 236

011   A Man Playing the Piano and Silk Tree Flowers / 252

The Author's Words / 262

001

멈춰버린 자동차

2월의 어느 토요일 아침, 권철수는 노트북과 전날 밤늦게까지 보았던 업무 관련 서류들을 자신의 중고 자가용의 조수석에 놓고 운전석에 앉았다. 입춘이 지났지만, 여전히 한겨울처럼 추워 그는 차가운 손을 호 불고 시동을 걸었다. 시동이 걸리지 않았다. 가끔 이럴 때가 있다. 두세 번 시도하면 시동이 걸리고 곧잘 잘 달려준 차였기에 그날도 그러려니 했다. 하지만 몇 번을 더 시도해도 여전히 시동이 걸리지 않았다. 자신을 위해 지난 십 년간 달려 준 자가용이 완전히 멈춘 것이다.

권철수는 겨우겨우 힘을 내어 이끌어 갔던 자신의 인생도 그날 아침 멈춰버린 자가용처럼 잠시 멈추게 될 거라는 것을 그때는 모르고 있었다. 중고차 거래업자에게 전화를 걸었다. 차의 뒷좌석에 미처 정리하지 못하고 쌓여있는 이미 끝난 사건들의 검토보고서들과 판결문 초고 서류들을 현재 진행 중인 사건들의 서류와 함께 가방 안으로 쑤셔 넣었다. 뒷좌석에 몇 년째, 몇 달째 놓여있던 법 관련 책들도 가방 안에 넣었다. 노트북과 무거운 가방을 양쪽 어깨에 메고 자신의 원룸으로 가서 바닥에 쏟았다.

"엉망이군."

원룸 바닥에 쏟아진 서류들과 책, 노트북 가방을 보며 이 한마디를 내뱉었다. 현재 진행 중인 사건의 검토보고서와 판결문 초고 서류들만 골라서 가방에 넣은 후 노트북 가방과 함께 들고 원룸을 나왔다. 곧 중고차 거래업자가 도착했고 자동차 매각 절차를 밟았다. 거주하고 있는 경기도 욕망시의 시청 차량등록과에서 자가용 이전 절차를 끝냈다.

지하철을 타기 위해 택시를 타고 가장 가까운 역으로 갔다. 걸어서 10분 거리지만 걷는 것을 싫어하는 철수는 가까운 거리도 자가용이나 택시를 이용했다. 지하철을 타고 서울중앙지방법원이 있는 교대역으로 향했다. 지하철에는 자리가 없었다. 그는 가방을 지하철 바닥에 내려놓고 한숨과 함께 다시 한번 "엉망이야."라는 말을 내뱉었다. 철수는 언젠가부터 항상 자신의 삶이 엉망이라고 생각하고 있었다. 지난 십 년간 잘나가던 차가 오늘 멈추어 버린 것도 아쉽지만 토요일의 귀한 아침 시간을 몽땅 중고차 거래소를 찾고 차를 파는 절차에 써 버린 것도 아쉽게 생각하고 있었다.

욕망시에 있는 수원지방법원 욕망 지원에서 재판연구원으로 근무하고 있는 철수는 한 달에 한두 번은 주말에 자신의 차로 서울로 나왔다. 그중에서도 대법원과 서울중앙지방법원 그리고 예술의 전당이 있는 서초구를 방문하는 것은 그의 몇 년 된 습관이었다. 서초구를 방문할 때면 대법원과 서울중앙지방법원 부근의 카페에서 자신의 업무를 처리했다. 또 정기적으로 예술의 전당의 소식을 받아보며 흥미 있는 예술 공연을 보러오기도 했다.

하지만 오늘은 차를 매각했기 때문에 지하철을 갈아타며 교대역에 도착했다. 120kg이 넘는 뚱뚱한 몸으로 1시간 넘게 지하철에서 서 있었고, 두 가방을 양쪽 어깨에 메고 걸어야 해서 극도로 지쳐있었다. 입춘이 오긴 했지만, 체감온도는 여전히 한겨울인데도 그는 땀을 흘리고 있었다.

철수는 교대역을 나오자마자 주변 공기를 들이마셨다. 그는 이곳에 방문할 때마다 주중에 쌓였던 직무 스트레스가 풀렸고 생기와 활력을 느꼈다. 자신의 꿈과 야망의 도시 서울, 그곳에서도 대한민국의 대표적인 두 법원과 예술의 전당이 있는 부유한 동네인 서초구에 올 때 약간의 정서적 치유와 뿌듯함을 느꼈다. 그리고 언젠가는 자신도 꼭 서울 시민이 되겠다고, 이 부촌에 살겠다고 다짐했다.

그가 종종 가는 단골 카페 주변은 쇼핑몰과 식당, 카페가 밀집한 곳이어서 횡단보도에 신호등이 있지만, 주말에는 너무 많은 사람과 차량이 오고 가기에 사고의 위험이 있었다. 교통사고의 위험을 줄이기 위해 주말에는 그곳에 아르바이트생이 고용되었다. 아르바이트생은 차량과 사람들이 서로 부딪치지 않고 원활하게 지나가도록 LED 신호봉을 들고 차량과 사람들의 흐름을 정리했다. 아르바이트생은 자주 바뀌었다. 하지만 지난 4계절 동안 철수는 비쩍 마른 남자 아르바이트생을 이곳에 방문할 때마다 보았다, 그가 아마 최장기로 일하는 아르바이트생이 아닐까 생각했다. 여름에는 땀을 삐질삐질 흘리며 창이 큰 모자를 쓰고 뜨거운 태양 볕 아래에서 일했고, 비가 오는 날은 비옷을 입고 비를 맞으며 일하고, 추운 겨울인 지금은 두꺼운 감색 파카를 입고 감색 털모자를 쓰고 교통정리를 하고 있었다. 청년은 그날도 여느 때처럼 무표정한 얼굴이었다. 그는 차량이 다 지나가도록 신호봉으로 사람들을 막았다. 신호등에 사람들이 많이 모이면 신호봉으로 신호를 주며 지나가는 차량을 멈추게 했다. 그리고 횡단보도 중앙으로 가서 LED 신호봉을 옆으로 뻗으며 호루라기를 크게 불고 사람들이 지나가도록 신호를 주었다.

철수는 그날 차가 없이 와서 교대역 주변이 익숙하지 않아 종종 길을 잃었다. 그때마다 처음부터 다시 시작하기 위해 이 횡단보도로 돌아왔다. 이 횡단보도는 그가 방향을 잡는데 기준이 되어 주었다.

횡단보도를 건넌 후 단골 카페로 들어갔다. 배경음악으로 피아노 음악이 은은히 흘러나왔다. 한겨울인데도 땀을 흘리며 혼자서 무언가에 몰두하고 있는 철수를 젊은 여자들이 힐끗힐끗 쳐다보았다. 사람들의 수다로 시끄러운 카페에서 혼자 무언가를 열심히 공부하며 작성하고 있는 모습이 그들에게 독특하게 보였다. 뭐 특별한 일은 아니었다. 이런 일은 한두 번이 아니었기에 그들의 시선을 무시하고 계속 집중했지만, 그날따라 계속해서 앉아 있기가 힘들었다. 몸이 힘들고 식은땀이 났다. 결국 더는 집중하지 못하고 카페를 나왔다.

그는 그 붐비는 횡단보도에 멈추어 섰다. 신호등이 빨간색에서 초록

색으로 바뀌었다. 신호봉을 들고 있던 마른 청년이 신호봉을 옆으로 뻗고 호루라기를 불었다. 사람들이 우르르 지나가기 시작했다. 철수도 그 무리 속에서 걸었지만, 점점 힘이 빠졌다. 제대로 걸을 수가 없었다. 겨우겨우 느릿느릿 지나갔다. 신호봉을 들고 있던 그 마른 청년이 그를 주목했다. 그는 그날 오후 여러 차례 이 횡단보도를 건너던 사람이었다. 사람들이 다 지나가고 신호가 빨간색으로 바뀐 지 한참이 지났는데도 여전히 느릿느릿 걷는 이 뚱뚱한 중년의 남자가 짜증스러웠다. 횡단보도 옆에 멈춰 섰던 차량이 경적을 울리기 시작했다. 이 뚱뚱한 중년의 남자가 인도에 도착할 때까지 그 마른 청년은 못마땅한 눈길을 그에게 보내며 그를 향해 한마디 내뱉었다.

"미친놈 아니야?"

청년은 호루라기를 크게 불었고 곧 차들은 속도를 내며 무섭게 달리기 시작했다. 철수는 미친놈처럼 보일 수도 있겠다고 생각하고 무시하고 걸었다. 하지만 그것보다는 배가 체한 듯하고 점점 머리가 어지러워져서 그의 말에 신경을 쓸 수가 없었다는 것이 더 정확하겠다. 귀에서 계속 '삐~' 소리가 났다.

바로 앞에 보이는 이비인후과가 있는 건물로 들어갔다. 이비인후과에 간신히 다다랐지만, 토요일의 진료 시간이 끝나 문이 닫혀 있었다. 그는 점점 매스꺼움을 느꼈다. 머리가 빙빙 돌고 팔이 저렸다. 온몸에서 식은땀이 났다. 서 있을 수도 없고 걸을 수도 없어서 쓰러졌고 계속 구토를 했다. 귀에서는 여전히 '삐~' 소리가 지속되었다. 가슴속은 답답하고 무언가가 그를 짓누르는 듯했다. 가장 참을 수 없는 것은 머리가 빙빙 돈다는 것이었다. 눈앞의 세상이 빙빙 돌고 고통은 견딜 수 없을 만큼 심해졌다. 건물 관리인이 그를 보고 응급차를 불렀다. 곧 도착한 응급 구조원들이 그를 들것에 눕혀 구급차로 옮겼다.

"환자분, 가방 안에서 지갑을 꺼내 신분증을 보고 신분 확인을 해도 될까요? 아니면 환자분이 직접 말씀해 주시겠어요?" 한 응급구조사가 친절하지만 위급하게 물어보았다. 대답조차 할 수 없었다. 온몸이 저리고 식은땀이 났다. 구토가 심해지며 머리가 빙빙 돌았다. 정신을 잃었다.

002

모태 솔로

철수는 욕망시에 있는 수원지방법원 욕망 지원에서 계약직 재판연구원으로 십 년째 근무하고 있다. 판사를 도와 기록을 검토하고 검토보고서와 판결문 초고를 작성하는 등의 업무를 수행한다. 판사의 업무를 도와주면서 판사의 수많은 판결 양과 신속한 판결 속도에 감탄했다. 또 사람들이 재판 결과를 이해하고 수용할 수 있도록 판결문을 잘 작성하는 판사에게 경외감을 느끼고 있었다. 판사라는 자신의 못다 이룬 꿈에 한숨을 쉬다가도 동시에 판사는 정말 아무나 하는 게 아니구나 하는 두 가지 감정이 교차했다.

지방 태생인 그는 고등학교 졸업 후 서울의 입시학원에서 1년을 재수하고 서울대 법학과에 진학했다. 20대 시절 아르바이트하며 학비와 생계비를 스스로 벌어 학업을 마쳤다. 군 복무와 대학 과정을 마친 후에도 아르바이트하며 30대 초반까지 보냈다. 그 후, 벌어놓은 돈으로 자신의 꿈이자 야망인 판사가 되기 위해 사법시험 공부를 시작했다. 노량진으로 가서 처음 두 해는 전업 수험생으로 사법고시에만 매달렸다. 학원 수강비, 독서실비, 고시원비, 식비, 수험서 비용 등 매달 나가는 돈이 엄청났다. 첫해 1차 시험에서 합격했다. 그다음 해 2차 시험에도 합격했지만 3차에서 고배를 마셨다. 그간 벌어놓은 모든 돈을 투자하며 전업 수험생으로 2년을 준비해 온 시험인데 3차에서 떨어졌을 때는 허탈했다. 하지만 당시 사시 공부는 기본 몇 년에서 10년까지 하는 것이 일반적이었기에 곧 마음을 다잡았다. 벌어놓은 모든 돈이 떨어지자 다시 아르바이트하며 4년을 더 사법시험 준비에 매달렸지만 합격하지 못했다. 조금만 더 하면 합격할 수 있다는 생각 때문에 고시 공부를 손에서 놓을 수가 없었다. 마치 마약과 같았다.

생활고에 시달리던 그는 결국 눈을 낮추어 일반 법원 공무원 시험으로 전향했다. 2년을 더 공부하여 나이 사십에 욕망시의 수원지방법원 욕망 지원에 계약직 재판연구원으로 채용되었다. 채용된 후에도 판사의 꿈을 접을 수 없어서 매달 들어오는 월급으로 인터넷 수강을 하며 2017년까지 사법시험 공부를 지속했다. 퇴근 후의 시간과 휴일을 공부에 반납하며 사십 대 중반까지 보낸 것이다.

다른 청년들처럼 데이트하거나 연애를 하는 것은 꿈도 꾸지 못했다. 주의가 산만해지지 않도록 연애와 결혼, 운동, 취미활동 등 모든 것을 성공한 후, 즉 사법시험에 합격하여 판사가 된 후에 하자고 미루며 오직 일과 공부에만 몰두하였다. 덕분에 가난이 청년 시기 내내 그를 따라다녔다. 또한 마음속에 쓴 뿌리가 자랐다. 이루지 못한 판사의 꿈, 성공한 후에 하자고 미루어 온 소망들, 가난, 경쟁, 그리고 수많은 실패와 고생들이 세월과 함께 좌절과 낙심으로 변해 마음속에 쌓여갔다. 자신의 인생에 대한 실망감과 세상에 대한 분노가 자라고 있었지만, 정작 자신은 그것을 깨닫지 못했다.

2017년을 마지막으로 사법시험이 폐지된 후, 이제 그에게 성공은 판사가 되는 것에서 계약 임기 이삼 년이 끝날 때마다 재계약이 성사되는 것이 되었다. 계약직 자리를 유지하기 위해 애쓰며 부장판사와 동료들의 비위를 맞추고 자신을 드러내지 않고 살았다. 어느 순간, 그는 자신의 본모습을 잃게 되었다. 언젠가부터 화가 거세당한 사람처럼 살고 있었다. 웬만해서는 화내지 않았다. 묵묵히 말없이 일만 해서 심지어 어느 때는 자신이 말하는 법을 잃어버렸다고 생각할 정도였다. 구내식당에서 식사할 때는 다한증으로 땀이 비 오듯 쏟아져서 늘 수건을 챙겨서 땀을 닦으며 밥을 먹었다. 법원 직원들은 그와 바라보며 밥을 먹는 것을 피했다. 밥맛이 떨어지고 불쾌하기 때문이다. 직원들과 밥을 먹을 때는 동료들의 시야가 덜 닿는 맨 끝으로 가서 수건으로 땀을 닦으며 밥을 먹었다.

이런 계약직의 삶은 그가 모든 것을 투자해 노량진에서 공부하던 마흔 살까지 생각조차 해보지 못한 미래였다. 그에게는 이런 삶이 그의 높은 이상과는 아주 다른 열등한 삶처럼 느껴졌다. 그는 외면적으로 성실하게 일하고 무능한 직원들이 벌려놓은 문제들을 조용히 해결해주는 능력 있는 재판연구원이지만 내면적으로는 이렇게밖에 살 수 없는 자신에게 분노하고 있었다. 그동안 쌓였던 여러 가지 감정과 스트레스를 밖으로 표출하지 않고 마음속에 억누르며 살아갔다.

계약직이기는 해도 법원에서 일한다는 타이틀 때문에, 그가 가입한 결혼 중개 회사에서 가끔 선 자리가 들어왔다. 하지만 120kg이 넘는 뚱뚱한 사내가 알이 두꺼운 안경을 쓰고 숨을 거칠게 내쉬며 앉아 있는 것을 보고 상대 여성들은 상당히 당황했다. 나쁜 시력으로 안경알이 두꺼워서 눈은 실제의 눈보다 더욱 작아 보였다. 안경 너머로 보이는 눈은 초점이 없고 멍했다. 이는 지난 수십 년간 이어진 사법시험과 공무원 시험 준비, 그리고 재판연구원 업무로 수험서, 책, 컴퓨터, 서류 등을 오래 쳐다보며 공부하고 검토하는 삶을 살았기 때문이지만 중매 시장에 나온 여성들은 이를 알 턱이 없었다. 심지어 약을 한 사람들의 눈처럼 보인다는 오해를 사기도 했다. 게다가 선 시장에 내놓은 프로필 사진은 그가 이렇게까지 심하게 살찌기 전에 찍은 사진이어서 사진만 보고 나온 여자들은 깜짝 놀랄 수밖에 없었다.

그는 말하는 것도, 행동하는 것도, 웃는 것도, 반응하는 것도 상당히 느렸다. 여자가 질문을 던지면 약 3초가 흐른 뒤에 서서히 입술을 떼었다. 그리고 아주 짧은 단답형으로 대답하고 다시 침묵했다. 여자들은 그런 그가 답답했다. 게다가 같이 음식이라도 먹으면 그는 계속 땀을 흘렸고 수건이나 식당의 냅킨으로 두피와 얼굴, 목덜미에 연신 흘러내리는 땀을 닦았다. 아무리 닦아도 그의 얼굴과 목덜미는 분수라도 되는 듯이 계속 땀을 뿜어냈고 그의 윗옷은 축축하게 젖었다. 그 모습을 보고 있노라면 먹던 음식도 토하고 싶은 심정이었지만 여자들은 예의상 그럴 수 없었다. 여자들은 먹은 음식이 입 밖으로 나오지 못하게 꿀딱 삼키며 목구멍 안으로 구겨 넣었고 그 후로는 더는 음식을 먹지 않았다. 그가 한때는 '레오나르도 디카프리오[1]'라고 불렸고 여성들의 마음을 즉시 사로잡을 만큼 잘생기고, 지적이고 언변도 좋고 매력 넘치던 젊은 청년이었다는 것을 어떤 여자도 생각하지 못했다.

그는 매번 소개팅과 선에서 퇴짜를 맞았다. 두세 번 더 만남으로 이어진 적이 거의 없었다. 게다가 안정된 직장을 가진 남자를 찾는 여자들에게는 그의 계약직의 직책도 감점 요소였다. 법원 미혼 여자 동료들도 그를 동료 이상으로 생각하지 않았다. 이런저런 이유로 여자들과 지속적인 만남으로 이어지지도 않고 계속 돈만 쓰게 되어 만남에 대해 회의감이 들었다. 여자들에게 산 밥과 찻값만 모았더라도 천만 원이 넘었을 것이다. 결국 그는 만남조차 거부하게 되었다.

돈을 쏟아도 고작 한두 번의 만남으로 끝나버렸지만, 철수는 아쉬워하지 않았다. 아무리 그가 모태 솔로이고 여자 결핍의 삶을 살아왔다고는 해도 엄연히 이상형은 존재했다. 여자와의 만남에 실패할수록 그는 성공에 더욱 집착하게 되었고 퇴근 후면 분초를 아끼며 사법시험 공부에 매진했다. 사법시험에 합격만 하면 모든 것이 다 해결될 것만 같았다. 또한 이상형에 더욱 집착하게 되었다. 그의 이상형은 어리고 예쁜 것은 기본이고, 하얀 피부에, 긴 생머리를 늘어뜨린, 손가락이 길고 가느다란 피아노 치는 여자였다. 언젠가는 자신도 꼭 성공해서 이상형의 여자와 연애하고 결혼해서 아들딸 낳고 행복하게 살 거라는 꿈과 희망을 품으며 목표에 매진했다. 그는 나이가 들어도 여전히 어

---

1 미국의 배우. 영화 《타이타닉》을 통해 세계 최고의 인기 스타 중 한 명이 되었다. 1990년대 할리우드 청춘스타의 아이콘이었으며 꽃미남의 대명사로 회자한다.

리고 예쁜 여자를 고집했다. 그것은 청년 시절을 누리지 못한 채 고생으로 보내버린 것에 대한 일종의 보상심리 때문이었다.

서울 서초동에서 쓰러진 후, 병원에서 뇌경색으로 당분간 일할 수 없다는 진단이 내려졌다. 법원 계약직 직원이었지만 10년간 병가나 결근을 한 번도 내지 않고 열심히 일했고, 성과와 기여도가 커서 5개월의 유급 병가 휴직이 허락되었다. 그는 5개월 후 다시 복직하기로 하고 고향으로 내려가기 위해 짐을 정리했다. 거주해 오던 경기도 욕망시의 빌라 원룸에서 지내는 것보다 고향으로 내려가서 건강을 돌보는 것이 더 낫겠다고 판단한 것이다.

그의 빌라 원룸 양쪽 벽면에는, 큰 갈색 책장 두 개가 천장 높이까지 우뚝 솟아 벽을 덮고 있었다. 책장에는 법 관련 서적들과 수험서들이 빼곡히 꽂혀 있었다. 좁은 원룸에 우뚝 솟은 이 책장들은 도심의 거대한 건물을 생각나게 했고 가슴을 턱 막히게 했다. 하지만 노량진에서 고시 공부를 했던 그에게는 이런 답답함은 익숙했다. 창문이 있는 벽에는 갈색 독서실 책상 하나가 덩그러니 놓여있었다. 2012년 경기도 욕망시의 지방법원에서 재판연구원으로 고용이 된 해에 구매하여 2017년까지 앉았던 책상이다. 2017년 12월 31일 사법시험 폐지[2]와 함께 저 자리에 앉지 않게 된 것이 벌써 오 년이 되었다. 이제 저 책상도 법 관련 책과 수험서들도 필요가 없었다. 하지만 버릴 수가 없었다.

---

2 전통의 법조인 검정 선발 방식이었던 사법시험이 2017년 시험을 끝으로 역사 속으로 사라지고 이후 법조인 양성은 법학전문대학원에 맡겨진다.

저 책상과 책들이 사라진다면, 자신의 젊은 시절도 함께 사라질 것 같았다. 그것들은 자신의 청년기를 대변해주는 물건들이었다.

사법시험 폐지는 그의 마음속의 기둥 하나를 뽑아가는 것 같았다. 시험 합격 하나만을 바라보며 연애도 행복도 다 미루고 젊음이라는 시간과 에너지, 그리고 돈을 사법시험이라는 제단 위에 희생 제물로 바치며 달려 오지 않았던가! 삼십 대를, 그리고 사십 대가 되어서는 퇴근 후 저녁 시간과 주말, 그리고 모든 공휴일을 몽땅 산 제물로 바치지 않았던가! 인생이 허무했다. 자신의 어리석은 신념과 야망에 속아왔다는 생각이 들었다.

2018년부터 판사가 되기 위해서는 법학전문대학원에 들어가 3년의 과정을 이수하고 변호사 시험을 봐야 하는데 야간 과정이 없기에 또 꿈을 좇아서 직장을 그만두고 법학전문대학원에 들어가는 도박을 하고 싶지 않았다. 비슷한 과정을 이미 충분히 겪었기 때문에 다시 처음으로 돌아가 그 과정을 반복하고 싶지 않았다.

힘든 일상에서 성공하고야 말겠다며 커피를 온몸에 쏟아부으며 카페인의 기운을 빌려 하루 20시간 가까이 일하고 공부하던 독기는 사라져 버렸다. 이것이 목표가 사라져서 일어난 변화인지 아니면 나이가 들어서 그러한 것인지 확실히 알지 못했지만, 자신을 지탱해 온 독기와 열정이 사라져 버린 것에 대해 늘 아쉬워했다. 성공하지 못한 채 나이 들어버린 자신을 용서하기가 힘들었다. 가장 귀한 젊음과 건강을 헛된 것을 추구하며 쏟아버리게 몰아온 자신의 환경이 원망스러웠다.

사회가 정의하는 획일화된 성공관과 자신의 잘못된 신념에 속아 어리석게 젊음을 탕진해버린 것이 한탄스러웠다. 계약직으로서 앞일에 대한 두려움도 심해졌다.

예전에는 바쁜 일상으로 한 번도 느껴보지 못했던 허무함, 공허감 그리고 외로움이라는 감정들이 찾아왔다. 지인들이 술을 마시자고 부르면 이 감정들에서 벗어나기 위해 거절하지 않고 나갔다. 유머 감각도 없고 말수도 없고 음식을 먹을 때 땀을 비 오듯 쏟으며 수건으로 연신 닦아 내리는 자신을 불러주는 지인들에게 감사했다. 술집에서 사람들이 모여 적당히 취하며 웃고 떠드는 분위기가 외로움과 공허한 감정을 가져갔고 대신 즐거움을 주었다. 이제는 지인들과의 술자리가 그에게 유일한 낙이 되어버렸다. 자신을 짓누르는 힘든 현실과 갑갑한 생각에서 잠시 빠져나올 수 있는 탈출구였고, 또 다음 날 그의 밥줄인 직장에 출근하여 경쟁과 사내 정치의 일상으로 뛰어들어 충성할 수 있게 해주는 힘이었다. 약속이 없는 날이면 원룸의 방바닥에 멍하니 앉아서 새로 구매한 텔레비전을 쳐다보았다. 그런 나날이 이어졌다.

사법시험을 준비하던 때부터 이어진 오랜 좌식 생활과 운동 부족으로 그는 복부비만에 시달렸다. 복부에 쌓여만 가는 지방 덩어리는 그를 임신한 남자처럼 보이게 했다. 뚱뚱해지니 걷기도 힘들었다. 늘 앉아 있고만 싶었다. 조금만 걸어도 숨이 차서 헐떡였다. 걷기도 힘든데 무슨 운동을 하고 싶겠는가! 그는 늘 앉아 있었고 가까운 거리도 차를 몰고 갔다.

언젠가부터 퇴근 후, 술에 취해 원룸에 들어오면 뱃살을 몸에서 떼어 늘 이불장 서랍에 곱게 개어서 넣어두는 상상을 했다. 뱃살은 그의 지난 삶의 방증이었다. 청춘의 특권과 즐거움을 뒤로 미룬 채 목표를 향해 독서실 책상에 앉아서 공부하던 삶…. 퇴근해서도 쉬지도 못하고 법 책을 원룸 방바닥과 식탁 위에까지 쏟아두고 자정이 넘어서까지 공부하던 삶…. 직장에서도 늘 책상에 앉아서 쉬지 않고 집중하며 열심히 업무를 하던 삶…. 자신의 의견을 드러내지 않고, 늘 부장과 동료들에게 맞추어주던 삶…. 무례한 사람들에게 성격을 죽이고 냉정을 유지하며 친절하게 문제를 해결하던 삶…. 아이러니하게도 뱃살은 이렇게 노력하며 고생했던 철수의 삶의 구현이었다.

003

할아버지가 된
레오나르도 디카프리오

고향의 친형 집으로 요양하러 가기 위해 가져갈 물건들을 챙겼다. 원룸 한쪽 구석에 물건들을 이것저것 담아둔 작은 플라스틱 서랍장 두 개가 있었다. 원룸의 세 벽을 차지하고 있는 육중한 두 책장과 독서실 책상과는 크기와 차지하고 있는 공간 면에서 대조를 이루고 있지만, 색깔이 노란색과 하늘색으로 어둡고 답답한 원룸을 그나마 밝게 해주는 유일한 가구였다. 서랍을 하나씩 열어보았다. 한때 그의 정서와 소망을 표현하던 물건들이 뒤죽박죽 섞여 있었다. 그 물건들도 그의 청춘 시절처럼 그의 관심과 돌봄을 받지 못한 채 방치되어 있었다. 서랍장과 벽 사이, 그리고 서랍장과 서랍장 사이 빈틈에서도 오랫동안 처박혔던 사진들, CD들이 보였다. 빛도 들어가지 않고 세월의 먼지만 가득 쌓여있는 구석에서 사진과 CD를 꺼냈다. 20대 때의 사진이었다. 서울대 레오나르도 디카프리오라고 불렸던 젊고 청순하고 잘생긴 권철수가 하얀 이를 드러내고 환하게 웃고 있었다. CD는 피아노곡집이었다. CD 표지에는 그 CD를 샀던 날짜와 장소, 그리고 간단한 메모가 적혀있었다. 그 앨범을 처음 샀던 시기로 기억을 더듬었다.

그가 피아노 음악에 처음 매료된 것은 아르바이트를 두세 개씩 하며 열심히 돈을 모으던 19년 전, 31살 때였다. 그날도 여느 때처럼 아르바이트를 끝내고 지하철을 탔다. 그날은 운이 좋았다. 지하철에서 자리를 잡은 것이다. 그가 거주하는 고시원까지는 한 시간 정도의 거리이니 그 시간 동안 피곤한 몸을 쉬게 할 수 있었다. 잠이 스르르 들었다.

어디선가 음악 소리가 들려왔다. 철수는 꿈을 꾸는 것 같았다. 구깃구깃 찌들었던 뇌가 서서히 풀리는 느낌이었다. 뇌가 촉촉해졌다. 향긋한 바람이 뇌를 스치고 지나갔다. 뇌세포 하나하나가 살아나고 춤을 추는 것 같았다. 깊이 빠졌던 잠에서 서서히 깨어 눈을 떴다. 그 음악은 한 행상이 틀어놓은 CD 플레이어에서 나오는 소리였다. 행상은 피아노 음악을 틀어놓고 지하철 이용객들에게 피아노 음악 CD를 팔고 있었다. 철수는 만 원을 주고 CD 하나를 샀다. 피아노 음악이 그의 찌든 뇌를 소생시켜주기도 했지만, 그 음악 덕분에 내려야 할 역을 지나치지 않고 잠에서 깰 수 있었기 때문이다.

그 뒤로 아르바이트가 끝나면 지하철에서 또는 고시원에서 휴대용 CD 플레이어에 이어폰을 꽂고 피아노 음악을 듣곤 했다. 하지만 바쁜 일상에 묻혀 곧 음악 없는 삶으로 돌아갔다. 피아노곡 CD와 CD 플레이어는 다른 물건들과 함께 아무 빛도 들어가지 않는, 철수의 손이 닿지 않는 곳에 오랫동안 방치되었다.

철수는 그 CD와 CD 플레이어를 가방 안에 챙겨 넣고 5개월간 자신의 건강을 돌보기 위해 고향 친형 집으로 내려갔다. 친형은 동생 철수를 안아주었다. 생기있고 활발했던 동생이 자신의 본연의 모습을 잃고 세월과 함께 점점 다른 사람이 되어가더니 이제는 병을 얻어 돌아온 것이 마음 아팠다.

"지금 당분간 쉬는 것이 오히려 전화위복이 될 거야. 너의 마음과 육체가 아프다고 그렇게 신호들을 보냈는데도 무시하고 살아서 이렇게 병이 커졌지만, 앞으로는 무시하지 말고 너의 육체와 마음에 귀를 기울이렴. 회복될 거야." 그는 철수를 따뜻한 말로 위로했다. 형수는 철수의 회복을 돕기 위해 채소와 과일 등 건강식 위주로 철수의 식사에 신경을 써주었다.

현재 고등학교 2학년인 두 남매 쌍둥이 조카들은 그를 '법원 할아버지'라고 불렀다. 쌍둥이들이 보기에 그는 그들의 아버지보다 동생이지만 10살은 더 많아 보였다. 옛날 가족사진 속의 젊고 잘생긴 삼촌은 온데간데없고 나이 들고, 흰머리가 가득하고 배가 볼록한 뚱뚱한 아저씨가 삼촌이라고 하며 명절 때마다 나타났다. 게다가 매해 고향으로 내려올 때 보는 삼촌은 더 뚱뚱해지고 더 늙어있었다. 옛날 가족사진에 존재하는 청초하고 젊은 날씬한 몸매의 남자가 삼촌과 동일인이라고는 도저히 믿을 수 없었다. 영화배우처럼 잘생긴 삼촌은 가족사진 속에서만 존재했다.

하지만 쌍둥이들이 철수에게 좋아하는 면도 있었다. 철수는 형 집에 방문할 때마다 회를 몇십만 원어치 사 왔다. 철수가 오는 날은 그들이 다양한 회를 마음껏 먹을 수 있는 날이었다. 게다가 그는 술에 취하면 마음이 기뻐져서 쌍둥이들에게 용돈으로 몇만 원씩 주었다. 때로는 몇십만 원을 주기도 했다. 쌍둥이들은 삼촌이 술에 취하기만 하면 돈을 주는 것이 기뻐서 삼촌이 맥주 마시기를 기다렸다. 빈 잔이 보이기라도 하면 얼른 채워주었다. 철수는 회와 돈 때문이라도 자신에게 들러붙는 쌍둥이들이 귀여웠다. 이번에는 건강 때문에 술을 마시지는 않았지만, 조카들에게 넉넉히 용돈을 주었다.

고향 형 집에 머무르는 동안, 그는 직장에 다니던 때의 습관처럼 아침에 일찍 깨었다. 하지만 눈만 떴을 뿐 아무것도 할 수 없었다. 무의미함과 무기력증이 그를 거세게 짓눌렀다. 그 거센 짓눌림을 이기고 일어나기란 정말 힘들었다. 자신이 지금까지 무엇을 위해 살아왔나, 쓸데없고 아무것도 아닌 것들에 자신의 귀한 젊음과 건강을 다 써버렸다는 생각이 들었다.

쌍둥이들이 피아노 CD 음악을 삼촌이 산책하며 들을 수 있도록 MP3로 다운받아 주었다. 쌍둥이들이 준 MP3를 호주머니에 넣고 이어폰을 귀에 꽂고 동네 공원을 산책하며 하루하루를 보냈다.

피아노 음악을 들으며 산책 중인 어느 날 아침, 은행에서 철수에게 적금 만기일이라는 문자가 왔다. 형 집에 오고 나서 몇 주 동안 풀지 않았던 여행용 가방을 열었다. 그 안에서 통장 지갑을 꺼냈다. 적금통장과 예금통장들을 하나씩 열어보았다. 거기에는 지난 십 년간 재판연구원으로 일하며 차곡차곡 모아 놓은 돈이 숫자로 찍혀있었다. 통장에는 어느덧 숫자가 하나씩 더 늘어갔지만, 그 숫자가 늘어간다고 해서 그의 삶이 달라진 것은 없었다. 그저 통장에 적힌 숫자에 불과했다. 이 숫자로 할 수 있는 게 없었다. 아니, 하고 싶은 것이 무엇인지 몰랐을지도…. 아니, 하고 싶은 것이 있었다. 서울에 아파트를 사는 것이었다. 그는 늘 서울로 갈 기회를 호시탐탐 노리고 있었다. 자신의 주민등록증에 서울특별시라는 글을 새기고 싶었다. 그러나 서울에서 이 돈은 아파트 보증금밖에 되지 못했다. 자신이 아무리 열심히 살아도 서울에 집을 살 수 없다는 것을 알았을 때, 하고 싶었던 것들도, 갖고 싶은 것들도 의미가 없게 돼버렸다. 철수는 만기가 된 통장과 신분증을 들고 은행으로 갔다. 예·적금을 갱신했다.

철수는 은행 일을 보고 바로 약속 장소로 갔다. 서울대 법학과 2년 선배 오영식과 14년 후배 이연우를 만나기 위해서였다. 연우는 10년 전에 서울대 법학과 향우회에서 알게 된 고향 후배였다. 고향에 올 때마다 그들을 만나긴 하지만 마지막으로 만난 때가 두 해 전이었다. 약속 장소는 연우가 최근에 개업한 맥줏집이었다.

이연우. 그는 철수보다 열네 살이 어렸다. 부드럽고 중성적으로 들리는 이름과는 다르게 키가 크고 우락부락하며 얼굴에 수염이 잔뜩 나 있다. 철수만큼은 아니지만, 그도 역시 뚱뚱했고, 여자들에게 '산적'이라는 소리를 듣곤 했다. 그도 철수처럼 여자들에게 인기가 없었다. 성격도 나이 든 철수와 비슷하여 자신의 속내를 말하지 않고 경청만 했다. 하지만 속내를 드러내지 않고 경청하는 동기는 철수와는 달랐다. 철수는 사회생활을 하면서 조직 속에서 살아남기 위해 자신을 드러내지 않고 억압하며 조직에 맞추어 가는 거라면, 연우는 자신의 야망 때문이었다. 자신보다 오래 살아온 형들의 말을 듣고 있으면 얻는 것도 깨닫는 것도 많았다. 형들의 생각과 행위에 대해 옳다 그르다 등의 자기 생각은 조금도 말하지 않았다. 그저 듣기만 했다. 그들의 인생사를 들으며 그들을 반면교사 삼아 그들과는 다른 생각을 하고 다른 선택을 했다.

계산대에 서 있던 연우는 자신의 맥줏집 입구로 들어오는 철수를 향해 활짝 미소를 지었다. 먼저 와서 테이블에 앉아 있던 영식도 입구로 들어오는 철수를 향해 손을 흔들었다.

"형, 오랜만이에요. 몇 년 만인 거죠?" 연우가 반갑게 악수하며 인사했다.

"……이삼 년……된 거 같아."

"맞아요. 이 년 전에 추석에 한 번 왔다 갔으니까."

세 명 중 유일하게 철수만이 전공의 끈을 놓지 않고 전공과 관련된 일을 하고 있었기에 연우는 내심 철수를 부러워했다. 하지만 매해, 점점 더 살이 쪄가고 눈이 멍해져 가는 철수를 볼 때마다 그쪽 길로 들어서지 않은 것이 오히려 다행이라고 생각했다. 오히려 전공과 상관없이 술집에서 서빙, 고깃집에서 고기 굽기, 편의점 아르바이트, 배달 기사와 같이 다양한 아르바이트를 하며 살아가는 자기 인생이 오히려 낫다고 생각했다. 체형도 성격도 비슷한 철수를 볼 때마다 자신도 법 관련 일을 하면 저 형처럼 변하지 않으리라는 보장을 할 수 없었기 때문이다. 연우는 아르바이트하면서 매달 철수 정도의 월급은 벌고 있었고 지역의 이런저런 모임에도 참석하면서 유대관계도 넓히고 있어 자신의 삶에 만족하고 있었다. 이제는 평생을 함께할 여자친구도 생기고, 맥줏집도 개업해서 자기 사업을 시작했기 때문에 남들을 부러워하는 마음도 없어졌다. 철수처럼 경쟁이 심한 직업과 많은 돈과 노력이 드는 서울과 수도권 지역을 고집하며 에너지와 세월을 낭비하지 않고 진입장벽이 낮은 지역 사회에서 자신의 입지를 견고히 해나갔다.

"연우야, 축하한다. 드디어 사업을 시작하는구나. 사람들도 많고 장사가 잘되는구나." 연우와 철수가 영식이 있는 테이블로 오자 영식이 말했다.

오영식. 철수의 서울대 법학과 2년 선배이자 고향 형이다. 그도 대학 졸업 후 철수와 함께 판검사가 되기 위해 전업 수험생으로 2년을 노량진에서 공부한 적이 있었다. 두 해 모두 떨어지자 공부에 자신의 젊은 날을 썩히고 싶지 않았고 공무원 생활도 자신과 맞지 않다고 생각하여 그만두었다. 전직 치과 의사인 아버지의 경제적 지원 덕에 젊을 때 직업을 갖지 않아도 고생 없이 넉넉하게 돈을 쓰며 살 수 있었다. 사업으로 성공하고 싶었던 그는 사업자금으로 아버지에게서 돈을 몇 차례 가져다 썼다. 명석하고 재기발랄한 성격 덕에 한때 사업이 성공 가도를 달렸지만 언젠가부터 사업이 뜻대로 되지 않았다. 결국 그의 아버지는 경제적 지원을 멈췄다. 지원이 끊기자 자신이 몰던 외제 차를 하나씩 팔아 근근이 연명하다가 돈이 떨어져 사십이 넘어 고향 부모님

곁으로 돌아왔다. 하지만 부모님은 늙고 지쳐있었고 노환까지 겹쳐 이리저리 많이 아프게 되었다. 부모님의 재산이 병원비와 요양 비용으로 많이 나가서 영식에게 유산을 얼마나 남겨줄지도 미지수였다. 영식은 부모에게 인정받지도 못한 채 부모에게 매여 그들의 건강을 돌보고 심부름을 하며 사는 자신의 신세를 연우와 철수에게 종종 하소연하며 풀었다. 젊을 적 외제 차를 끌며 여러 여자를 만나고 다양한 스포츠도 하면서 젊음을 즐겼지만, 이제는 오십이 넘어 당뇨로 인해 오래 걷지도 못했다. 외제 차도 다 팔아버려서 외출할 때마다 택시를 타고 다녔다. 버스를 타는 것은 아직 그의 자존심이 허락하지 않았다.

"······형님, 일찍······도착······하셨네요?" 철수가 영식의 옆에 앉으며 말했다.

"택시 타고 오면 금방 와."

"영식 형님, 잠수 깨고 나오셔서 기쁩니다. 형님이 잠적하시면 무슨 일이 생길지 늘 염려돼요." 연우가 말했다.

"염려는 무슨···. 나 잘 사니까 걱정하지 말고. 철수 근황이 궁금해 전화해보니 고향에 내려왔다 해서 얼굴 보려고 나온 거야."

"네. 철수 형님이 내려오셔서 영식 형님이 다시 수면 위로 올라오셨으니 다 철수 형님 덕분이에요."

"······잠수를······타?"

"영식 형님은 가끔 잠적해요. 연락이 두절되죠. 형님, 제가 뭐 서운하게 한 게 있습니까? 앞으로 잠적하지 마세요. 전화번호도 바꾸지 마시고."

"미안하다. 앞으로 잠수 안 탈게. 약속하마."

"그런데 철수 형, 더 뚱뚱해졌습니다. 임신한 남자 같아요. 심하게 뚱뚱해졌네요."

연우는 맥주를 영식과 철수의 잔에 따라주며 철수의 지방이 가득한 배를 턱으로 가리켰다.

"……아……며칠간 뱃살……떼어내지 않아서……."

"산적, 너도 마찬가지야. 철수보다 덜 뚱뚱하다고 넌 예외라 생각하지 마. 너희들 근육은 없고 배만 동그랗게 되어있는데 그거 복부 지방이야. 거기서 나쁜 염증 신호를 보내지. 이게 뇌세포를 안 좋게 만들고 신경 자체를 노화시키는 거야. 운동해. 움직여서 태워야 해. 안 그러면 너희들 일찍 죽을 거야. 뇌가 망쳐진단 말이야. 너희들 잠도 불규칙적으로 자고, 술·담배하고, 영양가 없는 음식을 먹고 그러니 뇌세포가 몇십만 개씩 죽고 있고 재생도 못 하고 있잖아. 뇌에 영양분이 없고 노폐물이 쌓이면 뇌가 죽는 거야. 너희들 배가 말해준다. 너희들 뇌세포 이미 많이 죽은 거야. 이거, 늙으면 너희들 치매로 이어져."

술·담배를 하지 않는 영식의 말에 모두 수긍하며 조용히 들었다. 셋 중에서 나이가 가장 많은 쉰둘인 영식은 유일하게 담배를 피지 않았다. 과거에는 술을 즐겼지만, 당뇨에 걸리고부터는 술은 가끔 맥주 한두 잔만 마실 뿐 더는 마시지 않았다. 영식은 건강을 지키기 위해 이리저리 의학 잡학을 혼자서 공부했다. 또한 노부모를 모시고 살고 있어서 건강에 대한 상식이 필요했다. 서울대 법학과 향우회에서 연우를 알게 되던 날부터 그는 고향에서 연우와 어울렸다. 화산분화구 같은 얼굴 피부를 가진 뚱뚱한 연우의 건강을 염려하며 그에게 건강 상식들을 말해주고 그가 건강을 챙기도록 잔소리도 했다.

"그런데, 철수 형, 뱃살을 떼어내신다니요?"

"……떼어내면 좀……편해져……. 숨쉬기도 쉬워지고……."

"철수…애가 가끔은 헛소리를 하더라고."

인내심 있게 철수의 느린 말을 듣고 있던 영식이 말했다.

곧 아르바이트생이 안주로 통닭 한 마리와 어묵탕을 가지고 왔다. 아르바이트생은 비닐장갑을 끼더니 연우와 철수, 영식 앞에서 통닭의 살들을 먹기 좋게 조심스럽게 떼어주었다. 철수는 뚫어지게 그 통닭을 쳐다보았다. 아르바이트생이 뜯어서 옆에 쌓아 둔 뽀얀 닭의 살들이 서랍장 안에 떼어서 쌓아둔 자신의 뱃살과 닮았다고 생각했다. 아르바이트생이 살들을 다 떼어내자 철수는 게걸스럽게 먹기 시작했다. 땀방울이 온몸에 맺혔다. 연우는 아르바이트생에게 수건을 가져오라고 했다. 영식은 맥주를 들이켰다.

"철수형, 맥주 안 드세요?"

"……주치의가……술을 끊어야 한다고……무섭게 경고하더라. ……서울 서초에서 쓰러지고부터……술……끊었어."

"그런데 드시면서 왜 그렇게 땀을 흘리세요?"

연우는 아르바이트생이 가져온 수건을 받아 철수에게 내밀었다.

"……그게……과체중이 되면서……먹기만 하면 땀이 나더라."

"연우야, 근데 아르바이트생 정말 잘생겼다. 여기 아르바이트생들 인물 보고 뽑니?" 영식이 말했다.

"맞아요. 아무나 뽑지 않아요. 주 고객층이 외모에 민감한 이삼십 대이다 보니 잘생기고 성실한 아르바이트생들을 뽑아요."

"연우 너 사업 수단이 좋구나. 맞아, 아르바이트생이 잘생기고 이쁘면 알바생 보려고 한 번 더 오겠지. 그러면서 단골 확보하는 거고. 철수도 이삼십 대에 미모가 뛰어났는데 말이야. '서울대 레오나르도 디카프리오'였잖아. 철수 보려고 여학생들이 일부러 철수가 듣는 교양과목을 들었지. 철수 때문에 동아리에 가입하는 여학생들도 수십 명이었고. 그때 철수가 받은 러브레터를 담아보니 세 박스였어. 믿어지냐? 거대한 종이 상자로 세 박스! 여학생들이 또박또박 예쁘게 쓴 편지와 엽서들 말이야. 너의 아르바이트생들 미모는 리즈 시절 철수를 따라올 수 없어. 그런 애가 이렇게 변했단 말이지." 영식이 닭고기를 먹고 있는 철수의 등을 툭 치며 말했다.

"러브레터들은 다 어떻게 했어요? 보관하고 있나요? 보여주시면 형이 한때는 레오나르도 디카프리오였다는 말을 믿을게요." 연우가 철수에게 말했다.

"철수야, 그 러브레터 어떻게 했냐? 가지고 있지?" 영식이 물었다.

"……버렸어요."

"왜?" 영식의 눈이 휘둥그레졌다.

"……힘들 때마다……가끔……보곤 했는데 그게 날 과거에 묶어두어……내 미래에, 내 성공에 방해……될까 봐……."

"언제 버렸어?" 영식이 물었다.

"……대학 졸업하자마자……."

"형님, 하하하. 개그 하신 거죠? 증명할 길이 없네요. 하하하." 연우가 박장대소했다.

"쯧쯧…. 참 너다운 생각이다." 영식이 혀를 차며 머리를 흔들었다.

"대학 때 사진이 있을 거야. 과거 앨범 좀 뒤져봐야겠다."

"근데, 철수 형. 무슨 위 절제 수술 같은 거 했나요? 뱃살을 떼어내다니요?"

"애가 가끔은 헛소리를 하더라고. 성격도 많이 변했고. 옛날의 날렵하고 명철하던 외모와 성격은 어디로 가고 대신 멍하고 말도 없고 느리고 또 가끔은 이렇게 헛소리를 해."

침묵하고 있는 철수를 대신해 영식이 말했다. 철수는 영식의 말에 살짝 미소만 지었다. 어차피 아무도 믿지 않기 때문에 굳이 더 말해봤자 입만 아플 뿐이다.

004
자귀나무꽃이 필 때

여름이 시작되는 6월의 첫날 아침, 철수는 여느 때처럼 MP3로 피아노 음악을 들으며 산책했다. 그날은 그간 가보지 않은 길로 걸었다. 그 길을 걷다가 한 피아노 학원과 마주쳤다. 젊었을 때부터 피아노 치는 여자와 결혼하고 싶다는 로망이 있었지만, 피아노는커녕 악기를 다룰 줄 아는 여자는 그와 연이 닿지 않았다. 이제는 자신이 직접 피아노를 쳐보고 싶었다. 철수는 피아노 학원으로 들어갔다.

아침에는 은퇴한 어르신 두 명이 배우고 있었고, 오후에는 유치원생들과 초등학생들이 넘쳐났다. 저녁에는 중학생 몇 명과 피아노 학과를 희망하는 입시생 두어 명이 다니고 있었다. 성인들만 존재하는 세상에서 살아온 그에게 이 작은 생명체들이 생소하게 보였다. 그들의 재잘거림과 생명력이 그에게 활기를 주었다.

피아노 학원 선생님, 송혜은. 그녀는 31살의 상냥하고 친절한 여성이었다. 얼굴은 연예인 얼굴처럼 광이 났고 피부는 희었다. 그녀의 손도, 그녀의 팔도, 그녀의 목덜미도…. 그녀에게는 햇볕에 그을린 자국은 하나도 없었다. 긴 생머리는 차분함을 더해주었다. 피아노 치는 여자 하면 긴 손가락이 연상되지만, 그녀의 손은 작고 뭉뚝했다. 흰 손톱은 보이지 않게 바짝 깎았다. 작고 뭉뚝한 손가락이 피아노 건반 위에서 바쁘게 움직였다.

'저렇게 작은 손으로도 피아노를 칠 수 있구나.'

그녀의 손가락은 그의 고정관념을 깼다. 그가 이상적으로 생각한 긴 손가락은 아니었지만, 오히려 귀여워 보였다. 특히, 그녀의 양쪽 엄지 손가락은 정말 작고 뭉뚝했다.

그녀가 옆에 앉아서 교습할 때, 그녀에게서 늘 향긋한 냄새가 났다. 그의 눈에는 그녀가 여신처럼 보였다. 그가 평생 꿈꿨던 이상형의 여자가 바로 옆에 앉아서 친절하게 피아노를 가르쳐 주고 있다. 다른 사람들이 말을 할 때는 투박스럽고 짜증스럽게만 들리는 지방색 강한 사투리도 그녀가 말할 때는 전혀 귀에 거슬리지 않았다. 오히려 귀여웠다.

철수가 오랜 세월 꿈꾸던 여성은 31살의 모습으로, 그녀를 꿈꾸고 기다려 온 그는 50살의 모습으로 만나 지금 피아노 의자에 나란히 앉아 있다. 꿈속의 이상형을 텔레비전 속의 연예인들처럼 바라만 보지 않고, 현실 세계에서 피아노 의자 위에 나란히 앉아 마주 보며 대화하고 있다. 이건 기적이다!

피아노 선생님의 레슨이 그를 매일 조금씩 구하고 있었다. 이 음악 수업이 없었다면 그는 계속 무기력과 허탈감 속에 살아가고 있었을 것이다. 그는 수없이 많은 여자에게서 퇴짜를 맞아봤고 자신이 여자들에게 인기가 없다는 것을 알고 있었기에 그녀에게 '피아노 선생님'이라는 순수한 감정 이상은 품지 않았다. 게다가 그녀는 자신보다 19살이나 어리기 때문에 그녀에게 그 이상의 감정을 품는다는 것은 생각할 수조차 없었다.

선볼 때 외에는 여자와 평생 대화해본 적이 없는 그가 젊고 아름다운 이상형의 여자와 대화를 할 수 있다는 것은 그의 오십 인생에 처음 있는 일이었다. 젊고 아름다운 여자가 매일 자신과 대화해주다니! 기적이 일어났다고밖에 할 수 없었다.

직장의 상하 위계질서 안에서 명령을 전달받고 보고하던 형식의 소통에서 벗어나 평등 선상에서 어떤 억압이나 스트레스 없이 대화하고 소통할 수 있다는 것도 그에게는 치유였다.

철수에게 매일의 이 순간은 너무나 소중한 시간이었다. 누구에게도 뺏기기 싫은 소중한 시간이었다. 이 순간들이 영원하기를 바랐다. 그녀는 젊고 아름답고 매력적이기에 곧 젊고 훌륭한 청년을 만나서 결혼할 것이다. 자신은 오십 평생 모태 솔로로 살아왔고 이제는 늙고 뚱뚱하고 매력이 없어졌기에 앞으로도 누군가를 사귀기는 힘들겠다고 생각했다. 그래서 그녀 옆에서 평생 그녀의 친절한 피아노 교습을 받으며 이렇게 대화하며 살 수만 있다면 그는 그것으로 만족하고 감사할 것 같았다.

피아노를 배우기 시작한 지 몇 주가 지나고 어느 날 문득 피아노 학원에 가는 길에 무인 사진관을 발견했다. 사진관의 한쪽 벽은 크고 넓은 전신거울로 이루어져 있었다. 이 길을 그전에도 여러 번 오고 갔지만 워낙 외모에 무심하게 살아왔기 때문에 거울의 존재를 모른 채 지나쳤었다. 철수는 거울에 자신의 모습을 비춰보았다. 거기에는 뚱뚱한 나이 든 아저씨, 즉 조카들의 말대로 '법원 할아버지'가 서 있었다.

'저……괴물은 누구……야?'

수십 년 만에 처음으로 본 자신의 전신 모습은 참으로 충격적이었다. 어쩌다가 이런 뚱뚱한 괴물이 되어버린 거지? 왜 이렇게 나이가 들어버린 거지? 도대체 지난 세월 내게 무슨 일이 있었던 거야? 이삼십 대 청년 시절의 싱그럽고 아름다웠던 젊음은 어디로 간 거야? 그는 거울에 비친 자신의 모습을 더는 볼 수가 없었다. 부정하고 싶었다. 두려웠다.

철수는 피아노 학원으로 향했다. 가는 길에 한 은행 지점이 있다. 그 은행 앞을 지나면 횡단보도가 있고 그 횡단보도를 건너면 바로 피아노 학원이 있다. 언젠가부터 그 은행 지점을 지날 때마다 향기가 났다. 향기가 좋았지만, 그 향기가 어디서 오는지는 알 수 없었다.

피아노 선생님은 언제나 그렇듯이 환한 미소로 철수를 맞이하였고 철수의 꾸준함과 성실함을 칭찬하였다. 아침에는 은퇴하고 취미로 피아노를 배우는 어르신 두 명이 각 실에서 연습했다. 연습이 끝나면 어르신들은 소파에 앉아 담소를 나누고 철수도 거기에 끼어 그들의 대화를 듣곤 했다.

"내가 10년 전 직장 다닐 때, 퇴근 후에 1년을 배웠거든. 물론 그때는 다른 선생님에게 배웠지만. 그때 그만두고 10년이 지나고 다시 배우는 거야. 다시 배운 지 이제 1년이 되었는데 10년 전에 배운 거 다까먹었어. 기초부터 다시 시작하고 있어. 그때 그만두지 말고 계속했어야 했는데. 저기, 아저씨 그만두지 말고 계속하세요." 그들은 말없이 듣고 있는 철수에게 한마디 했다.

"……네."

10년이라…. 이제 철수가 복직하고 은퇴할 수 있을 때까지 10년이 남았다. 그 10년 동안 계약직 자리에서 구조조정으로 해고되지 않고 계속 버틸 수 있다면 말이다.

피아노 학원에 다니기 시작한 지 두 번째 달인 7월 중순. 오 개월의 병가가 끝나가지만, 욕망시의 법원으로 돌아가기가 망설여졌다. 피아노 선생님에게 교습을 받는 하루하루가 그에게는 소중했고 이 시간을 포기하고 싶지 않았다. 지속하고 싶었다. 레슨 시간을 통해 젊고 아름다운 이상형의 피아노 선생님을 마주 보며 대화할 수 있다는 것은 그의 하루 중 가장 큰 기쁨이었다. 욕망시로 돌아가서 그곳에서 다른 피아노 선생님에게 배울 수도 있지만, 그들은 이 피아노 선생님이 아니다. 세상에는 젊고 아름다운 여선생들이 많지만, 그들은 그녀가 아니다. 그녀는 동화 〈어린 왕자〉에서 어린 왕자의 고향 행성에 있는 장미꽃과 같았다. 세상에는 수없이 많은 아름다운 장미가 존재하지만 어린 왕자의 행성에 있는 한 송이 장미가 그에게 특별한 것처럼, 피아노 선생님은 철수에게 특별했다. 그녀와 헤어지는 시간을 최대한 늦추고 싶었다. 다시 욕망시로 돌아가면 그는 일에 파묻혀서 지낼 것이고, 그녀는 시간과 함께 그에게서 잊힐 것이다. 그녀를 잊고 싶지 않았다.

이제는 매일 아침 정해진 시간에 피아노 학원에 가는 것이 직장에 다니는 것처럼 일과가 되었다. 욕망시에 있을 때는 늘 가까운 곳도 자신의 차나 택시를 타고 다녔지만 차를 처분하고 고향으로 내려와서는 피아노 학원까지 걸어 다녔다. 학원 가는 길에 있는 무인 사진관 앞에 그는 늘 멈추어 섰다. 사진관의 전신거울 앞에 멈춰서서 자신의 모습을 비춰보며 고양이처럼 그루밍했다. 그루밍을 마치고 좀 더 걸으면 한 은행 지점이 있다. 은행 앞을 지나면 횡단보도가 있고 그 횡단보도를 건너면 바로 피아노 학원이 있다. 그 은행 지점을 지날 때마다 은은한 향기가 났고, 곧 피아노 선생님을 볼 수 있다는 설렘으로 철수의 가슴은 심하게 두근거렸다.

그러던 어느 날, 여름의 뜨거운 태양의 열기로 그 향기가 더욱 강렬해졌다. 철수는 피아노 학원 가는 길에 은행 앞을 지나가다가 그 강렬한 향기를 무시할 수 없어 뒤를 돌아보았다. 도대체 이 향기가 어디에서 오는 것일까? 그는 그 향기가 어디서 오는 것인지 살폈다. 그가 서두르며 지나쳐 온 인도 위에는 신비로운 색채를 가진 예쁜 술[3]들이 부채모양으로 곳곳에 떨어져 있었다. 꽃이었다. 꽃처럼 생기지 않았지만 분명 꽃이었다. 전형적인 꽃의 모양과 다른 모양의 꽃. 아랫부분의 흰

---

3 끈, 띠, 책상보, 옷 따위에 장식으로 다는 여러 가닥의 실

색에서 윗부분의 분홍색 같기도 하고 보라색 같기도 한 색으로 그러데이션을 이루고 있어서 신비감을 더했다. 이 꽃들이 어디에서 떨어졌는지 알기 위해 고개를 들어 위를 쳐다보았다. 은행 점포 앞에 심겨 있는 나무 중 하나였다. 달콤하고 강렬한 향을 내는 나무였다. 푸르고 울창한 가지 속에서 흰색에서 진분홍색으로 그러데이션을 이루는 꽃을 피우는, 향기까지 그윽한 신비로운 나무였다. 이 신비로운 나무가 피아노 학원 가는 길에 심겨 있었다니…. 학원 가는 길에 이 길을 늘 지나갔지만 한 번도 이 나무의 존재를 눈여겨본 적이 없었다.

'이……나무의……이름이……뭘까?'

철수는 걸음을 멈추고 그 신비로운 나무를 한참 바라보았다. 그는 인도에 떨어진 부채모양의 꽃들을 주웠다. 그리고 코에 가까이 대고 향기를 맡으며 학원으로 걸어갔다.

그는 그 뒤로 매일 아침 그 나무에서 떨어진 부채모양의 꽃들을 한 움큼 집어 작은 꽃다발을 만들고 항상 피아노 위에 올려두고 피아노 연습을 했다.

철수가 보도 위에서 진분홍 꽃을 줍는 것을 매일 지켜보던, 나이 지긋한 노상 주차장 주차 관리인이 철수에게 무어라 말을 걸었다. 철수는 혹시나 해서 물었다.

"……선생님, 이 나무……이름이……뭔지……아세요?"

"아, 소 쌀밥 나무예요! 소들이 정말 잘 먹지요. 정말 좋아해요!"

"……그렇군요."

'소 쌀밥 나무라⋯⋯. 소들이 정말 좋아한다⋯⋯. 내가 '소'띠인데⋯⋯.'

"또 자귀나무라고도 해요. 부부 금실을 상징하는 나무이지요. 그래서 합환(合歡)목, 부부목, 사랑목이라고도 해요."

"⋯⋯그렇군요."

"지금 한창 피는 시기지요. 여름에 꽃이 피는 나무예요. 6월부터 8월까지."

철수는 미소를 지었다. 이 신비로운 나무의 이름을 드디어 알게 되었다. 신비로운 향과 형태만큼이나 이름도 신비롭다. 이름의 의미도 신비롭다. 가슴이 또다시 설렌다. 그는 다시 자귀나무꽃의 향기를 맡았다. 가슴이 두근거렸다. 조금만 더 걸으면 곧 피아노 선생님을 볼 수 있다는 생각이 강렬한 자귀나무꽃의 향과 섞여서 그의 심장을 거세게 요동치게 했고 정신을 혼미하게 했다.

8월이 시작되기 전, 철수는 해고를 각오하고 복직을 6개월을 더 미루었다. 아직 그의 건강이 회복되지도 않았지만, 더 큰 이유는 피아노 선생님을 떠나고 싶지 않았기 때문이었다. 다행히 욕망시에 있는 수원지방법원 욕망 지원에서는 6개월 후로 그의 복직을 미루어주었다. 비록 무급 병가이지만 그는 6개월 후에 다시 복직할 수 있게 되어 직장을 잃지 않게 된 것이다.

철수는 평생 꿈꾸었던 이상 속의 그녀를 만났고 레슨 시간을 통해 매일 그녀와 대화하고 있다. 그녀의 존재가 그를 천국에 있게 했다. 비록 혼자 좋아하는 짝사랑이기는 하지만 그녀가 있기에 그는 늘 설레었고 마음이 안정되어 갔다. 허무함과 외로움도 점차 사라져갔다. 천국이 이곳이기에 다른 곳으로 갈 필요가 없음을 알게 되었다.

그는 젊어지고 싶었다. 삼십 대 초반 이후 처음으로 외모를 꾸미고자 하는 마음이 생겼다. 이십 년 가까이 피우던 담배를 끊었다. 미용실에 가서 덥수룩한 머리를 자르고, 희끗희끗해진 머리를 까맣게 염색했다. 새 옷을 샀다. 구두를 반짝반짝 닦았다. 매일 피아노 학원 가는 길에 무인 사진관의 전신거울 앞에서 자신을 비춰보는 것이 새로운 습관이 되었다. 고양이들이 그루밍하듯이 전신거울 앞에서 자신도 모르게 머리를 만지며 매무새를 가다듬었다. 그리고 매일 아침 자귀나무 꽃을 주워 피아노 위에 올려두고 연습했다.

헬스장에 등록해 매일 운동을 했다. 수십 년간 방치한 자신의 몸을 돌보기 시작했다. 피아노 선생님에게 매력적으로 보이길 원했다. 임산부처럼 불룩 튀어나온 복부 지방을 빼고 날렵하고 멋진 왕(王)자를 자신의 복부에 만들고 싶었다. 트레이너의 도움을 받아 헬스장의 여러 운동 기구들을 사용해 상체, 하체, 복근 운동을 했다. 매일 운동 전후 체중계에 올라가 몸무게가 조금씩 감량되는 것을 확인했다. 식단도 신경을 썼다. 인스턴트 식품과 술과 고기 위주의 식단에서 단백질과 채소, 과일 위주의 식단으로 바꾸었다.

하지만 볼록 튀어나온 뱃살은 내장 지방으로 쉽게 빠지지 않았다. 그는 자기 전에 그날그날 솟아오른 뱃살을 떼어내는 것밖에 할 도리가 없었다. 옷장 서랍을 열었다. 기존에 떼어냈던 뱃살들이 하나의 형태를 이루어 두꺼운 겨울옷처럼 곱게 개어져 있었다. 철수는 뱃살을 떼어내어 서랍 속의 기존 뱃살에 떨어뜨렸다. 지방 덩어리들이 서로 붙어서 이제 하나가 되었다. 철수는 서랍 문을 조심스럽게 닫았다.

영식과 연우는 나날이 활기 있고 밝아져 가며 살이 조금씩 빠지는 철수를 보고 의아해했다. 그가 시작한 피아노와 운동이 그를 이렇게까지 변화시키다니 하며 놀라워했다. 예술과 체육활동, 취미활동, 그리고 충분한 휴식이 인간에게 미치는 영향에 대해 만날 때마다 토론했다. 하지만 진실은 철수만이 알고 있었다. 그건 음악으로 자신을 표현해서만도, 취미로 정신적 억압을 풀어내고 운동으로 살을 조금씩 빼서만도, 병가를 내서 육체와 정신을 푹 쉬게 해주었기 때문만도 아니었다. 그것들은 부차적인 이유일 뿐이었다. 철수를 변화시켜 가는 것은 사랑의 힘이었다. 짝사랑! 사랑처럼 보이지 않는 사랑! 비록 짝사랑이기는 하지만, 사랑이라는 감정이 그를 새롭게 하고 있었다.

005

꿈과 야망

　철수와 연우, 그리고 영식은 종종 연우의 맥줏집에서 만났다. 철수는 술을 마시지 않고 다른 음료로 대신했다. 연우의 맥줏집은 늘 젊은 손님들로 붐볐다. 영식은 연우의 맥줏집에 가는 것이 즐거웠다. 노부모를 뒤치다꺼리하는 일상에서 탈출하여 맥줏집에서 젊은 이삼십 대 청춘들을 보고 있노라면 힘이 났다. 그도 당뇨 때문에 술을 금하였지만, 이곳에 오면 맥주가 달아 기꺼이 즐겁게 마셨다.

　"기분 좋게 마시면 약이 되지. 그런데 철수, 너 이번에 병가 연장했다며?"

　"……네. 내년 초까지……연장했어요……."

　"그러고 보면 형은 정말 열심히 일했나 봐요. 한낱 계약직 직원에게 1년이라는 병가 휴직을 주고." 연우가 말했다.

　"잘 됐다. 자꾸 뱃살 떼어낸다고, 뽀얀 뱃살이 산처럼 커졌다고 헛소리해 대더니…. 넌 좀 쉬어야 해."

　"근데, 형. 뱃살은…나도 뚱뚱해서 내장 지방 때문에 힘들긴 한데 형의 뱃살 이야기가 좀 들어봅시다."

"……언젠가부터……먹기만 하면……오랜 좌식 생활과……업무 스트레스로……복부에 지방이 쌓이더라……. 불편해서……업무를 하기가 힘들었어. 자기 전에 뱃살을……떼어냈지. 하지만 소용이 없어……. 또 매일 내장 지방이 쌓여서……저녁에 밥을 먹거나 술을 마시고 나면……배가 산처럼 볼록해지더라고. 그래서 매일 저녁……뱃살을 떼어내게……됐지."

"그럼 그 떼어낸 뱃살은 어떻게 하셨어요?"

"……욕망시에서는……원룸 이불장……에 넣어놨고 여기 시골[4]로……와서는……친형 집의 옷장 서랍에……넣어놨지."

"거의 매일 떼어내셨다면 크기가 어마어마하겠어요?"

"……서랍이……수용하지 못할……정도가 되면……방바닥까지……흘러 나와……쌓이겠지."

"철수야 버릴 생각은 안 하냐?" 영식이 물었다.

"……처음에는……내 뱃살이……혐오스러웠는데……점점 쌓여서……거대해져 가는……뱃살을……보면……또 다른 한편으로는……내가 이렇게 열심히 애쓰며 살아왔구나……나 자신에게……측은한 감정이……들더라고요. 내가 불쌍……하더라고요. 애쓰며 살아온……내 청춘의 방증 같은 거라서……버릴 수 없더라고요……."

"철수야, 넌 일을 너무 많이 했어. 병가도 연장하게 되었으니 일 생각 하지 말고 푹 쉬어라. 철수가 젊은 시절 야망에 눈이 멀어서 사회적 지위를 자신의 정체성으로 삼다 보니 이렇게 돼버렸네. 쯧쯧…안타깝

---

4 서울과 경기도에 사는 일부 사람들은 지방 도시를 시골이라 부른다.

다…. 외모도 못난 괴물처럼 변해버리고…가끔 이제는 헛소리까지 하고…." 철수의 느린 말을 인내심 있게 듣고 있던 영식이 말했다.

"아이고 형님. 형님은 부모님이라는 든든한 배경도 있고 물려받을 유산도 있어서 그런 말씀을 쉽게 하시겠지만 철수형과 저는 다르죠. 우리는 우리가 벌어서 먹고살고 노후 대책도 마련해야 하고. 철수형이나 저나 흙수저로 태어난 청춘들은 쉴 틈이 어디 있습니까." 조용히 듣고 있던 연우가 말했다.

"……다음 달부터……아침과 오후에……친형의 편의점에서……아르바이트하며 형의 일을……도와주기로……했어. 몸이 아파서……잠시……쉬며 형의 편의점 아르바이트를 하겠지만……완쾌되면 다시……성공을……."

철수가 말을 끝내기도 전에 연우가 끼어들었다.

"철수 형님. 형이 평생을 데이트도 안 하고, 즐기고 누리지를 못하니까 성공감을 느끼지 못하는 거예요. 그래서 '좀 더, 좀 더'하며 결핍감만 느끼는 거라고요. 좀 즐기고 사십시오. 여자도 만나고. 저 얼마 전에 연애 시작했잖아요. 눈 낮추니까 여자가 보이더라고요. 내 외모는 산적 같은데 이쁘고 어린 여자만 원하니까 애인이 안 생겼던 거죠. 그 여자 저보다 6살이 많아요. 하지만 좋은 여자죠."

"좋은 여자지. 너에게 맥줏집도 개업시켜 주고…. 그런데, 내 앞에서는 연애 강의는 하지 마라. 난 결혼할 생각이 없으니." 결혼에 대해 거부감이 많은 영식이 연우의 말을 막았다.

"이건, 영식 형님에게 하는 말이 아니고요. 철수 형님에게 하는 말입니다. 형님 목표는 이루기 쉽게 적당히 낮춰서 잡으세요. 형님, 2차까지 종종 합격해서 포기하기 쉽지 않았겠지만, 그래도 사법시험 포기하고 욕망시 법원에 계약직 직원으로 들어가신 것 잘하신 겁니다. 목표는 그렇게 낮게 잡아야 해요. 2017년도에 사법시험 폐지 안 됐으면 계속 근무하면서 퇴근하고도 또 휴일에도 독서실에 박혀서 공부만 하고 살았을 테고. 그러다 보면 정신과 마음이 더 피폐해지고, 즐기지도 못하니 성격도 더 어두워지고. 고시 폐인 되는 거죠. 눈 낮추고 법원 계약직 들어가서 돈도 모으고 그나마 소개팅도 들어오고 사람처럼 살아가는 거 아닙니까."

"야, 이놈. 연우! 많이 컸네. 형님들 옆에서 그저 듣기만 하던 놈이 요새는 형들에게 훈계도 하고. 많이 컸어…. 네가 이만큼 큰 것은 다 나 때문인 것 알지? 철수 너 욕망시 법원에서 일하고 있을 때 나 연우와 자주 만나서 이놈 많이 가르쳤다. 이놈 이렇게 큰 것은 다 내 도움이야. 내가 이놈 옆에서 얼마나 좋은 말 많이 해주고 많이 가르쳐 주었는데. 연우야, 내 덕분인 거 알지?"

"그럼요, 형님. 제가 큰 것은 다 형님 덕분이죠. 철수 형님도 마찬가지고요. 감사합니다."

"그런데 그건 맞아. 연우가 그 늙은 여우…아니, 화영을…연우가 착한 게 자신보다 나이 많다고 거부한 게 아니라 감사하게 받은 거야. 그러니까 철수야 너도 어린 여자만 추구하지 말고 늙은 여자…아니… 취하니까 나도 말이…자꾸 헛소리가 나온다. 하하하…어린 여자가 네 상상 속에서나 놀아주지, 현실에서 너와 놀아주겠냐?"

"자신의 능력보다 너무 높은 목표는 귀한 젊음만…, 시간만 낭비하게 할 뿐이죠." 연우가 말했다.

연우는 형들을 반면교사로 삼았다. 형들처럼 나이 들고 싶지 않았다. 형들처럼 될까 봐 두려워하고 있었다. 연우는 향우회를 통해 철수와 영식을 알게 된 후부터, 그들의 생각과 행동을 관찰하며 깨달음을 얻었고, 그들을 반면교사 삼아 다른 길을 선택했다.

"연우야, 이번엔 왠지 나에게 하는 말 같다." 젊은 날 부모의 돈으로 많은 사업에 뛰어들었지만 정작 성공하지 못해 돈만 날리고 이제 나이만 먹게 되어 자괴감이 큰 영식이 말했다.

"아니요. 사실 저에게 하는 말입니다. 법대 나와서 철수 형님처럼 전공을 살려 경력을 쌓은 것도 아니고, 공무원 시험도 준비했지만, 매번 낙방만 해서 방구석에 혼자 앉아 눈물을 훔치곤 했죠. 이러다 장가도 못 가고 계속 방황하는 낙오자가 되겠구나 싶더라고요. 시간이 아깝더라 이 말입니다. 그래서 그때부터 전공을 버렸지요. 닥치는 대로 아르바이트도 해보고 파견사원도 해보고 하다 보니 화영 씨도 만나고 이제 맥줏집도 개업하게 되고요. 형님, 몸도 이렇게 아프게 되어버렸는데, 위에서 그러고 살지 마시고 여기에 정착하시는 게 어때요? 우리와 가끔 이렇게 만나 회포도 풀고…운동과 취미 생활도 계속하시고… 좋잖아요. 형님 나이부터는 건강을 생각해야 해요."

"나도 연우의 말에 동감한다. 철수야 욕망시에서 언제까지 그 조그만 원룸에서 살 거야? 예전에 한 번 가봤는데 숨이 탁 막히더라고. 난 거기서 공짜로 살라고 해도 못 살겠더라. 이왕 이렇게 아프게 된 거 여기에서 정착해라." 고향에서 만족스러운 삶을 사는 연우와 영식은 철수를 설득했다.

가을이 시작되는 9월. 철수는 형의 편의점 아르바이트를 시작했고 피아노 교습 시간을 아침에서 저녁으로 바꾸었다. 피아노 학원 선생님은 추석이 있는 주간을 모두 학원 방학으로 정했다. 하지만 학원 방학이 끝나고도 다음 이틀 동안 학원에 출근하지 못했다. 아이들의 말로는 선생님이 아프다고 했다. 철수는 그녀의 건강을 염려했다. 학원 방학이 끝나고 이틀 후 학원으로 돌아온 선생님의 얼굴은 많이 부어 있었다. 비록 마스크를 쓰고 있었지만, 얼굴이 부은 것을 알 수 있었다. 그는 그녀의 건강을 또다시 염려했다. 하지만 그녀의 태도는 어느 때와 변함없이 밝고 화창했다. 아니, 예전보다 더 활기차고 더 생명력이 흘러넘쳤다. 철수는 그녀의 생명력과 아름다움에 감탄했다.

어느 날 그녀는 마스크를 벗었다. 그녀의 얼굴이 약간 달라져 있었다. 중고등학교 여자아이들은 선생님이 안면 윤곽 성형수술을 했다고 소곤거렸다. 피아노 선생님은 아이들의 소곤거림을 모른척했다. 학원비를 결제하러 온 학부모들은 달라진 그녀의 모습을 보며 가끔 질문했다.

"송 선생님, 요즘 기쁜 일이 있으신가요? 뭔가 달라 보이시네요."

"꿈이 생겨서요."

그녀는 그 외에는 아무 말도 하지 않았다.

'꿈?' 철수는 그녀가 사용한 단어에 놀랐다. 젊은 시절 가슴을 두근거리게 하고 삶의 이유가 되어 주었던 단어. '꿈'은 너무도 탐스럽고 매력적이고 갖고 싶은 것이다. '꿈'을 생각하면 가슴이 뛴다. 하지만 그것을 이루기 위해 치러야 할 대가가 너무나 크고 그 대가를 다 치른다고 해도 이룰 수 있다고 장담할 수가 없다. 철수는 인생에서 가장 아름다운 젊은 시기를 꿈과 이상을 좇으며 보냈다. 자신의 젊은 30년을 꿈과 이상에 산 제물로 바치며 열심히 살았지만 뒤돌아보니 열매가 없고 헛되었다. 남들 다 이루는 가정 하나 이루지 못했다. 사회적으로도 큰 성공을 이루지 못했다. 이제는 나이가 들어버렸다. 조카들이 부르듯이 '법원 할아버지'가 돼버렸다. 그는 한때 삶 자체에 절망했다. 완전히 속아서 살아온 느낌이었다. 한때는 삶의 이유였던 그 단어를 이제는 피하고 싶다니 아이러니였다. 하지만 그녀가 말하는 꿈이라는 단어가 무엇을 의미하는지 궁금했다.

"……송 선생님……요즘……무슨……꿈이……?"

"요즘 공부를 좀 해요. 상상도 하고…. 상상하면 하나씩 그대로 되는 것이 즐겁더라고요."

"……저는……안되던데요……."

"안되지 않아요. 돼요. 저에게는 그런 말씀 하지 마세요."

그녀는 엄격했다.

"……현실만……보고 살다 보니……. "

아니, 철수도 그녀의 나이대에는 꿈과 야망이 컸다. 판사가 되어 이루고 싶은 사회적 성공이 많았다. 하지만 사법시험에는 계속 아슬아슬하게 떨어졌다. 그때마다 자신의 존재마저 부정당한 기분이 들었다. 아르바이트해서 번 돈들을 사법시험 준비에 써서 가난에 허덕였다. 귀한 젊은 시절의 노력에 열매가 없자 그는 점점 더 꿈과 야망에 배신감을 느꼈다. 그리고 조금씩 그 단어들이 불편해지기 시작했고 세월과 함께 점점 더 현실만을 바라보게 되었다. 그에게서 직관, 꿈, 야망. 이런 단어가 사라졌고 대신 '현실'이라는 단어가 그 자리를 대체하게 되었다. 다만 자신과 다르게 그녀는 대학 졸업 후 20대 중반부터 자기만의 사업을 운영하고 있고 그 열매들을 보고 있으니 그녀가 대단해 보였다. 적어도 그녀에게는 그녀의 꿈대로 삶이 펼쳐지고 있기 때문이다.

"저는 상상을 하는데, 삶이 상상대로 되더라고요. 이 학원 개원한 것도 상상을 먼저 했거든요. 주변에서는 잘 안될 거라고 했는데 저는 주변 사람들 말 듣지 않았어요. 저의 직관과 상상을 따랐죠. 5년을 잘 운영해왔는데, 앞으로 사업도 더 확장하고 싶고…또 곧 결…"

그녀는 잠시 멈추었다. 그리고 화제를 바꾸기 위한 말을 찾았다.

"요즘 전 더 확장된 미래를 상상하고…공부도 하고 있어요."

"……무슨……공부를……하시는데요?"

"권철수님, 음악 레슨 외의 사적인 질문은 안 하셨으면 해요." 그녀는 단호하게 말했다. 그녀는 수강생이 수업 외에 사적인 질문을 하는 것을 금했고 자신도 수강생들에게 사적인 관심을 보여주지 않았다.

006

어느 멋진 날

초겨울이 시작되는 11월. 피아노 학원에 가면 철수는 늘 원장실 바로 옆 부스에서 연습했다. 언제부터인가 원장실에서 어떤 소리가 들렸다. 그것은 작고 미세한 소리였다. 강의를 빠른 배속으로 틀어놓은 소리 같았다. 가끔은 어떤 남성의 목소리가 들리기도 했다. 철수는 피아노 선생님이 미래의 꿈을 위해서 인터넷 강의를 빠른 배속으로 틀어놓고 공부한다고 생각했다. 가끔 들리는 남성의 목소리는 정상 속도일 때의 인터넷 강사의 목소리라고 생각했다. 자신도 한창 사법시험을 준비할 때 빠른 배속으로 인터넷 강의를 듣곤 했기에 알 수 있었다. 원장실에서 그 소리가 들릴 때마다 그는 피아노 선생님에게 감탄했다. 젊고 아름다운 여성분이 생각까지 올곧다고 느꼈다. 미래에 대한 야망이 있다는 것이 그녀를 더욱 빛나게 했다.

피아노 선생님은 가끔 레슨 시간을 어길 때가 있었다. 연습을 마치고 한참을 기다려도 그녀는 오지 않았다. 그럴 때마다 철수는 원장실의 문을 노크하며 선생님을 불렀다. 피아노 선생님은 원장실의 문을 두드리는 그에게 화를 내며 자신이 알아서 올 테니 문을 노크하지 말라고 엄하게 말했다. 다행히 그녀는 그 뒤로 레슨 시간을 잊지 않았다.

하지만 그와 동시에 언젠가부터 철수는 피아노 학원에서 허함을 느꼈다. 그 허함이 무엇 때문인지는 몰랐다. 피아노 선생님은 여전히 차분하게 잘 가르치기는 했지만, 예전과는 조금 달랐다. 그녀가 미래를 위해 상상하고 공부한다고 말하던 시기부터 레슨에 소홀했고 레슨 시간도 짧아졌다. 그녀의 레슨 성실성이 줄어들던 때부터 철수의 마음은 피아노에 지쳐갔다. 하지만 그녀에게 레슨을 계속 받기 위해 마음을 다잡았다. 레슨 시간이 그녀를 볼 수 있고 그녀와 대화할 수 있는 유일한 시간이었기 때문이다. 그러나 피아노 레슨을 받고 나면 그의 허한 감정은 더욱 심해졌다. 허한 감정은 그가 피아노를 배우기 전에도 수년 동안 느꼈던 친숙한 감정이었기 때문에 굳이 그녀와 연관 짓지는 않았다.

비가 오는 어느 날, 편의점 야간 아르바이트생이 일찍 출근하여 철수는 편의점 일을 예정보다 일찍 끝냈다. 그날은 온종일 비가 내렸다. 철수는 편의점 비닐우산을 하나 꺼내 쓰고 피아노 학원으로 갔다. 우산에서 빗물을 털어내고 학원 문 앞 우산 통에 자신의 비닐우산을 꽂았다. 학원생들이 꽂아놓은 알록달록한 우산들 사이에서 검은색의 긴 알렉산더 맥퀸(Alexander MacQueen) 우산이 하나 보였다. 학원에는 방과 후에 온 몇몇 학생들이 연습 중이었다.

어떤 날은 피아노 선생님에게서 진한 장미 향이 났다. 그 장미 향은 곧 강한 스모크 잔향을 남겼다. 평생 향수를 뿌려본 적이 없는 철수는 그 향을 좋아하지 않았다. 선생님에게서 나던 본래의 향긋한 향이 좋았다.

피아노 레슨을 마치고 나면 철수는 영식과 연우를 종종 만나 국밥집에서 저녁을 먹었다. 어느 날 연우에게서 피아노 선생님에게서 나던 향과 같은 향을 맡았다.

"너 향수……뿌렸냐?" 철수가 물었다.

"네. 좋지요?"

"……아니. ……싫다."

"이거 비싼 거예요."

"국밥 맛 떨어진다. 국밥집에 향수를 뿌리고 오면 어떡하냐?" 영식이 끼어들었다.

"화영 씨가 이 향을 좋아해서요."

"야, 다음에는 그 늙은 여우. 아니…화영이 향수 뿌리고 와라."

"화영 씨 향수요? 왜요?"

"넌 젊은 놈이 그것도 모르냐? 요즘 연인들은 향을 바꾸어 쓰기도 하잖아. 여자는 남자 친구의 향수를 뿌리고, 남자는 여자친구의 향수를 쓰고. 연인들이 서로의 향을 바꾸어 쓰는 게 요즘 젊은 사람들 사이에 유행인데 넌 36살밖에 안 된 놈이 그것도 모르냐!" 영식이 말했다.

"헤헤…저도 연애가 처음이라서…형님은 우리 중 나이가 제일 많으신데 유행에 대해 모르는 게 없으시…잠깐만요."

그때 연우에게 전화가 왔다. 연우의 휴대전화 너머로 화영이 앙칼지게 쏘아 붓는 목소리가 들렸다. 연우는 지금 누구와 무엇을 하고 있는 지 설명하기 시작했다. 연우의 얼굴은 심각해졌고 수화기에 대고 "미 안해."를 반복했다. 연우가 통화를 하는 사이 주문했던 순대국밥 두 개와 돼지국밥이 나왔다.

"형님들, 전 이만 가봐야겠어요. 사실 화영 씨와 만나기로 했었는데 시간은 정확히 말하지 않고 저녁 먹고 9시쯤에 보자고 했는데 화영 씨가 오해한 거 같아요. 제 것은 형님들이 드세요."

연우는 서둘러 국밥집을 빠져나갔다. 화영은 영식과 철수를 싫어했 다. 그들이 연우의 오랜 친구여서 연우와 함께 가끔 만나 밥과 차를 사기도 했지만, 영식이 고마워하지 않고 순간순간 자신에 대해서 나쁘 게 말하는 것이 언짢았다. 철수는 뇌경색을 앓고 있는 데다가 눈빛은 멍하고 말과 행동은 느리고 굼떠서 거슬렸다. 화영은 연우에게 영식과 철수에게 거리를 두라고 했지만, 연우는 그녀 몰래 그들과 어울렸다. 하지만 이번엔 잘 둘러대지 못해 들켜 버렸다. 연우는 화영이 그들을 계속 못 만나게 한다면 그녀를 위해 형들을 포기하겠다고 마음을 정 했다.

연우가 떠난 자리는 국밥집과 어울리지 않는 강하고 독한 장미 스 모크향만이 남아있었다. 독한 향수 냄새로 국밥의 맛이 제대로 느껴 지지 않았다.

"저게 연인관계냐? 상사와 부하 관계지!" 연우가 떠나고 한참 침묵하 며 국밥을 먹던 영식이 못마땅하게 말했다.

"다 저 자식 야망 때문이지. 놓치면 안 되거든." 영식은 한마디 더 덧

붙였다.

"저놈 화영이가 맥줏집 차려주고 사장님 소리 듣고 사니까 화영을 못 놓는 거야. 영혼까지 묶인 삶 사는 거지. 자유가 없잖아. 화영이 그것이…순진한 연우 잡아서 꼭 쥐고 살잖아. 일거수일투족을 통제하고…. 화영이 그 계집애 완전 동네 깡패야. 여자 깡패…."

영식은 화영의 욕을 계속했지만, 영식의 말은 철수의 귀에 들어오지 않았다. 철수의 생각은 다른 곳에 가 있었다.

'연인들끼리……향수를……바꾸어 쓴다고?'

철수는 요즘 피아노 선생님에게 나던 그 진한 남성 향수가 생각났다. 동시에 '아닐 거야.' 하고 고개를 저었다.

추운 겨울이 지나고 새로운 해가 시작되었다. 봄이 다가오고 있다. 작년 2월 철수는 그의 야망의 도시 서울 서초에서 뇌경색으로 쓰러지고 고향으로 내려와 1년을 요양하며 보냈다. 1년이 지난 2월 지금, 그는 건강이 많이 회복되었다. 3월에 복직하라는 두 번째 러브콜을 받고 철수는 마음속으로 그녀에게 할 작별 인사를 연습하고 있었다. 지난 9개월간 정말 그녀 덕분에 즐거웠다. 인생에서 처음으로 경험한 즐거움이었다. 그의 우울증도 무기력도 그녀의 음악 수업 덕분에 사라지지 않았던가. 그녀 덕분에 운동해서 체중도 많이 감량되지 않았던가. 철수는 욕망시에서 재판연구원 일을 할 수 있을 때까지 계속할 것이고 10년 후, 은퇴한 후에는 이곳 고향으로 돌아올 것이다. 피아노를 1년을 배우고 멈춘 후 10년 뒤 은퇴한 후에 다시 돌아왔다던 그 어르신처럼 그도 60세가 넘어 은퇴한 할아버지가 되어서 다시 그녀의 피아노 학원으로 돌아올 수도 있다. 그때쯤이면 그녀는 이미 누군가와 결혼한 상태이고 아이들을 키우며 그들과 씨름하는 평범한 중년의 여성이 되어있겠지. 아니면 은퇴하고 돌아온다고 해도 그때쯤이면 철수가 피아노를 배우고 싶은 마음이 사라져 영원히 그녀를 보지 못할 수도 있다. 어쩌면 고향으로 돌아오지 않고 서울에서 여생을 보낼 수도 있다.

철수는 욕망시에 있는 수원지방법원 욕망 지원으로 돌아가 상사와 동료들과 안부를 나누었다. 하지만 삭막한 사무실 안으로 들어섰을 때, 그리고 앞으로의 업무에 관해 이야기할 때 과거에 받아야 했던 커다란 스트레스가 다시 밀물처럼 그에게 밀려왔다. 가슴이 답답하고 숨이 막혔다. 경쟁과 사내 정치에 찌든 삶, 커다란 조직 생활에 맞춰주며 위축되고 분열된 자아와 낮은 자존감으로 살아야 하는 삶, 업무에 붙들린 영혼 없는 삶으로 다시 돌아가는구나… 하지만 이 스트레스는 지난 10년간 익숙한 것이기에 그것을 이기고 다시 과거처럼 일에 몰두할 수 있었다. 다시 과거의 삶으로 돌아갈 수 있었다. 하지만 피아노 선생님, 그녀를 영원히 보지 못할 생각을 하니 가슴이 답답했다.

철수는 복직을 고사했다. 계약직이기에 언젠가는 구조조정의 대상이 될 것이고 퇴직하게 된다. 그냥 좀 더 일찍 퇴직을 앞당길 뿐이다. 철수는 퇴직 절차를 밟았다. 그리고 다시 시골로 돌아가 아예 집을 사고 정착하여 그녀에게서 몇 년간 더 피아노를 배워야겠다고 다짐했다. 다시 가슴이 두근거렸다. 이 결정은 많은 것을 포기한 어리석은 결정

일 수 있지만, 그녀를 볼 수 있다는 생각에 가슴이 두근거렸다.

지난 1년간 비워두었던 원룸으로 걸어갔다. 욕망시의 법원에서 이 원룸까지는 도보로 20분 거리였지만 1년 전까지 그는 자가용을 타고 다녔다. 차 수리를 맡기는 날이면 택시를 타고 다녔다. 1년 전까지 그 가 10분 이상 걷는다는 것은 상상할 수도 없는 일이었지만 지금은 가 볍게 해내고 있다.

집주인에게 전화해 이사한다고 말했다. 세입자가 들어오는 즉시 보 증금은 그에게 돌아올 것이다. 원룸 안에 독서실 책상이 덩그러니 놓 여있고 그 책상을 사이에 두고 양쪽 벽에 커다란 두 책장이 거대한 빌 딩처럼 솟아있었다. 숨이 막혔다. 작년까지 익숙했던 것들이 이제는 숨 막히게 했다. 거대한 두 책장에는 법 관련 책들과 수험서들이 가득 꽂혀 있다. 2017년 사법시험이 폐지된 후에도 지난 6년간 차마 버리지 못했던 그의 과거의 흔적들이었다. 이제는 사라지고 없는 그의 젊음의 상징물이었다. 욕망 지원에서 재판연구원으로 근무하며 퇴근 후에도 휴일에도 저 독서실 책상에 앉아서 사법시험을 준비하던 자신의 뒷모 습이 아련히 보였다. 허리를 구부정히 하고 의자에 앉아 공부하고 있 는 그의 뒷모습이 측은했다. 그에게 다가가 그의 어깨를 두드리며 말 하고 싶었다.

'난 미래에서 온 너야. 여기까지 온 너는 대단해. 이렇게 살지 않아 도 돼. 야망을 좇으며 큰일을 하려고 힘쓰지 마. 너의 현 직업에 감사 하고 인생을 즐기며 살아. 너의 젊음은 다시 오지 않아. 너의 젊음을,

너의 열정을, 너의 에너지를 더는 낭비하지 마. 그리고 너의 사랑을 찾으렴. 젊어서 아내를 찾고 그녀와 먹고 마시며 즐거워하렴.'

그는 행정복지센터에서 폐기물 스티커를 사서 독서실 책상과 의자, 책장, 이불장 등의 가구에 붙였다. 그리고 그것들을 빌라 앞에 두었다. 조만간 폐기물 처리 담당자들이 와서 수거해갈 것이다. 책장에 빼곡히 쌓인 법 관련 책들, 판사의 꿈을 버리지 못하고 공부해왔던 고시 관련 책들과 수험서들이 모두 폐지 분리수거함으로 들어갔다. 구석구석에서 그가 한때 좋아했지만, 사법시험 준비로 나중에 즐기자고 미루고 처박아 두었던 물건들이 쏟아져 나왔다. 음악 CD들, 스타워즈 영화 CD들, 건담, 에반게리온, 아톰 등의 만화 영화 CD들, 이 만화 영화의 주인공 피규어들과 조립식 장난감들, 베어브릭, 큐브릭, 퀴베어 등 아트토이 장난감들. 한때 그의 호기심을 불러일으켰고 그에게 낭만을 선물했던 물건들이지만 그의 꿈과 야망, 그리고 힘든 현실에 밀려 구석에 처박혔다. 그의 관심이 닿지 않고 빛도 들어가지 않는 구석으로, 깊은 서랍 안으로 들어가 먼지만 쌓인 채 방치되었다. 그는 이 물건들에서 여전히 가슴을 설레게 하는 몇 가지를 선택했다. 그리고 먼지를 털어내고 자신의 여행 가방 안에 넣었다. 나머지는 커다란 쓰레기 봉투로 들어갔다.

용산역에서 ktx를 타고 고향으로 내려갔다. 모든 것을 정리하고 힘찬 발걸음으로 다시 돌아왔다. 십 년의 직장에 작별을 고하고 단순히 취미인 피아노를 선택했다. 아니 더 정확히는 피아노 선생님을 선택한 것이다. 하지만 다시 고향으로 돌아왔을 때, 고향이 그에게 낯설게 느껴졌다. 고향으로 돌아와 맨 처음 향한 곳은 피아노 학원이었다. 피아노 학원 앞 횡단보도에서 초록불을 기다리며 서 있던 철수에게 또다시 그 느낌이 찾아왔다. 이 거리가 낯설다···. 저 맞은편에 있는 피아노 학원이 낯설다. 지난 1년 가까이 거의 매일 연습하러 오고 가던 이 피아노 학원 앞의 풍경, 너무 낯설다.

'나 지금 이곳에서 뭘 하고 있는 거지?'

하지만 그는 그 느낌을 무시했다.

다음 날 아침, 철수는 지역 신문에 아파트 매도 광고가 뜬 것을 보고 그 집을 보자마자 바로 선 계약금을 넣었다. 바로 뒷날 예·적금을 해지하고 집값의 1/2을 계좌이체 시켰다. 통장에 숫자로만 찍혀있던 돈이 그에게 의미를 주는 순간이 된 것이다. 숫자를 이체시키고 대신 자신만의 넓은 공간을 얻는 거였다. 숫자만 이체시키면 되었다. 숫자만 옮기면 되었다. 그리고 그다음 날 모든 잔금을 치르고 아파트 매수의 행정적 절차를 모두 끝내버렸다. 철수는 자신의 추진력에 놀랐다. 집을 완전히 매수하고 법무사를 통해 행정절차를 끝낸 그날, 그는 피아노 선생님에게 말했다.

"송 선생님, 저 집을 샀어요. 오늘 아침에 잔금을 모두 치르고 법무사를 통해 행정절차까지 모두 끝냈지요."

그의 말의 속도는 이전처럼 굼뜨고 느리지 않았다. 빨라졌다. 자신의 이삼십 대 시절 말의 속도와 비슷해졌다.

"네? 그럼 이전 도시로 가지 않으시고 앞으로 계속 이곳에 사시는 거예요?"

"다른 도시로 이사 가지 않는 이상 그러지 않을까 싶습니다."

"얼마 들었어요?"

"많이 안 들었어요."

그는 허풍을 떨고 싶지 않아서 겸손의 의미로 말했다.

"대출 없이 사신 거예요?"

"네."

"대단하시네요. 대출 없이 집을 사신다는 게."

철수는 그녀가 자신을 '대단하다'라고 표현해준 것에 어깨가 으쓱해졌다.

007
운명의 장난

다음 날 철수는 새벽 3시에 깨었다. 다시 잠들 수 없었다. 후회가 밀려왔다. 한낱 계약직 직원에게 1년의 병가를 주고 다시 복직하라고 러브콜을 보내오는 상사가 어디 있다는 말인가! 복직하라는 러브콜을 고사시키고 퇴직해 버리다니! 그리고 여기에 집을 사 버리다니!

"내가 무슨 짓을 한 거야?"

그는 전날 아침 집을 완전히 매수해 버렸다. 전세로 살아볼까 했지만, 보증금 사기 뉴스가 종종 텔레비전에 보도되었고, 또한 그가 다니는 피아노 학원 선생님을 좋아하게 되어서 이 시골에 정착해서 그녀에게 계속 피아노를 배우고자 하는 순진한 마음으로 집을 사버렸다.

하지만 뒤늦게 안 것이 있었다. 이 아파트가 곧 엘리베이터 교체공사에 들어간다는 것이다. 어쩐지 전 주인이 서둘러 이사했다. 철수는 이 아파트를 검토하기 위해 몇 번 엘리베이터를 타고 오르내렸지만, 엘리베이터 교체공사를 곧 시작한다는 것을 전혀 알지 못했다. 아파트 잔금을 다 치르고 자신의 소유가 다 된 것을 확인하고서야 엘리베이터에 붙어있던 엘리베이터 교체공사 공고가 눈에 들어왔다.

'0일부터 1달간 엘리베이터 교체공사를 합니다.'

철수는 리모델링 업체를 이리저리 알아보았지만, 아무도 엘리베이터가 없는 곳에서 일하고 싶어 하지 않았다. 결국 리모델링을 엘리베이터가 완공된 후로 미루었다. 철수는 갑작스럽게 집을 사고 이리저리 리모델링 업체를 알아보면서 많이 피곤해졌다. 엘리베이터 교체공사로 집을 빈집으로 사십일가량 두어야 한다는 것도 모른 채 빨리 집을 사려고 서두르다니.

갑자기 눈물이 났다. 그것은 기쁨과 감동의 눈물이 아니라 허무하고 슬퍼서 흘리는 눈물이었다. 어릴 적부터 야망이 컸던 그가 군대를 다녀오고 대학을 졸업하고 24년간의 사회생활을 해서 산 집이 서울의 건물도 아니고, 서울의 아파트도 아니고, 지방의 24년 된 아파트라는 것을 알았을 때 눈물이 났다. 결과론적으로 계산해보니, 24년간의 그의 젊음, 에너지, 열정의 소산이 24년 된 이 지방 아파트였다. 이삼십대 때 그는 지금의 이 나이쯤 되면 모든 것을 완벽하게 이루어놓고, 또 대도시에서 비싼 고급 아파트에 살고 있고, 사회적 신분과 경제력도 좋고, 어리고 예쁜 피아노 치는 여자와 결혼도 해서 토끼 같은 자식들을 키우고 있을 줄 알았다. 하지만 그의 24년은 그를 전혀 생각하지 못했던 곳으로 데려다 놓았다. 그렇게 떠나고 싶었던 고향에 집을 샀다는 것을 깨달았을 때 그는 자신의 운명의 아이러니에 놀랐다.

집을 구입하고 며칠 뒤에는 일주일간 아주 거센 비가 왔다. 베란다 타일 바닥은 어느새 빗물이 들어와 축축하게 젖었다. 공인중개사를 통해 전주인과 연락이 닿았고 전주인은 별 대수롭지 않은 듯이 말했다. 철수는 비가 새는 것은 별 대수롭지 않은 일이 아니라 전주인이 책임지고 시공해줘야 하는 일이라고, 매매 계약서에도 나와 있듯이 3개월간 발생하는 집의 잔고장은 매수인 책임이 아닐 경우, 매도인이 책임지고 고쳐 주어야 하는 것이라고 확고하게 말했다. 법률상의 계약 조항을 제시하자 전주인은 뒤로 물러나 자신은 직장 일로 바쁘니 철수에게 대신 업자를 알아보라고 했다.

철수는 그때부터 타일 업자들을 알아보았다. 인터넷을 검색해서 가까운 타일 업체를 찾아가서 비가 샌다고 말을 했다.

"베란다 타일이 깨져서 비가 새는 것 같습니다. 베란다 타일을 바꾸면 해결되는 문제일까요?"

"아니요. 타일을 새로 한다고 해서 해결되는 문제가 아니에요. 그건 베란다 샤시를 시공할 때 쿠킹과 실리콘 작업을 제대로 하지 않아서 비가 새는 거예요."

"쿠킹과 실리콘요?"

철수는 요리에 사용되는 용어가 건물에도 사용되는 것에 놀랐다.

"해주십시오."

"아니요. 그거 해봤자 돈이 안 돼요. 돈이 안 돼서 사람들이 안 하려고 하죠. 샤시업자에게 물어보세요. 그쪽에서 해줄 겁니다."

철수는 인터넷에 '베란다, 샤시, 쿠킹'이라는 검색어를 입력했다. 요리 정보 외에는 아무 정보도 나오지 않았다. 철수는 여러 차례 더 검색한 후에 쿠킹이 아니라, 코킹(Caulking)임을 알게 되었고 코킹과 실리콘 작업을 해주는 업체 중 한 곳을 정하여 통화하고 날짜를 잡았다. 욕실 리모델링 업체 주인의 말과는 달리 가격이 꽤 되었다. 매도인과 통화하고 가격을 전달하는 작업도 고되었다. 엘리베이터 교체공사로 인해 코킹 작업과 외부 실리콘 작업도 한 달 뒤로 미루어졌다.

평생을 공부와 법원 일 외에는 해본 적이 없는 그에게 집 문제와 관련된 이런 실제적인 문제들은 새롭기도 했지만 적지 않은 스트레스를 주었다. 엘리베이터 공사로 모든 일이 한 달 뒤로 미루어졌지만, 철수 역시 지쳐서 집에 관한 모든 일을 잠시 중단했다.

이 도시에 집을 산 게 과연 잘한 것일까? 아파트 주변에 새 아파트 두 곳이 지금 한창 공사 중이고 1년 후에는 이 도시에서 제일 높은 주상 복합이 들어설 예정인데 그것도 모른 채 이 집을 산 것이 옳은 것인지 회의가 들었다. 사람들이 모두 새 아파트로 들어가려고 할 텐데 이 오래된 아파트를 리모델링에 들어간 비용까지 모두 손해보지 않고 되팔 수 있을까 염려가 되었다.

철수는 어느 날, 편의점에서 일하다 몇몇 고객들이 하는 말을 우연히 듣게 되었다.

"지금 이 도시 아파트 점유율이 100%가 넘고 120%잖아. 인구수보다 아파트가 더 많아."

"지금은 다들 아파트 팔잖아. 아파트값 더 떨어질 텐데 지금 사면 바보지 바보. 아파트값 정상화된다고 다들 팔아서 현금화시켜서 은행에 맡겨 놓잖아. 이자가 높아서 현금 이자만 모아도 재산이 불어난단 말이야."

고객들이 하는 이런 말들이 그의 근심을 가중했다.

3월 하순. 형의 편의점 아르바이트를 끝내고 평소처럼 바로 학원으로 향했다. 그날도 비가 내렸다. 피아노 학원 문을 열었다. 피아노 학원 입구에 있는 우산 통에 철수는 자신의 편의점 비닐우산을 꽂았다. 우산 손잡이가 은색 해골인 검은색의 긴 남성 우산 하나가 보였다. 알렉산더 맥퀸(Alexander MacQueen) 브랜드였다. 이 해골 우산을 작년 11월 비가 오던 날 본적이 있었다. 비싼 유명 브랜드 우산이어서 철수는 기억하고 있었다.

학원에는 아무도 없었다. 고요했다. 아이들이 아직 오지 않았나 보다. 곧 오겠지. 철수는 자신이 항상 연습하는 원장실 바로 옆 부스로 들어갔다. 바로 옆 원장실에서 빠른 배속의 강의 소리가 여느 때처럼 나지막이 들렸다.

'송 선생님이 강의를 듣고 있구나.'

철수는 그녀의 꾸준한 배움의 열정에 감탄했다. 마음이 따뜻해졌다. 하지만 레슨 시간이 되었는데도 피아노 선생님은 철수의 연습실로 오지 않았다. 피아노 선생님이 시간이 되면 자신이 레슨을 하러 나올 테니 원장실 문을 두드리지 말고 연습실에서 기다리고 있으라고 두어 번 화내듯이 엄히 말한 적이 있어서 철수는 계속 기다렸다. 그녀는 오지 않았다. 기다리다 지친 철수는 결국 원장실로 가서 문을 두드렸다.

똑똑똑!

아무 반응이 없었다.

"…송 선생님."

여전히 아무 반응이 없었다.

"…송 선생님."

피아노 선생님은 나오지 않았다.

'이상하다. 분명 빠른 배속으로 강의 소리가 들렸는데… 안에서 강의를 듣고 계실 텐데…'

몇 초가 흘렀다. 철수는 좀 더 크게 선생님을 불렀다. 원장실의 손잡이를 잡고 문을 열어야 할지 망설였다. 그때 원장실 문이 열렸다. 동시에 강한 장미 스모크향이 원장실에서 흘러나왔다. 하지만 기대와는 다르게 원장실에서 나온 사람은 피아노 선생님이 아니라 키가 훤칠하게 크고 잘생긴, 고급스럽게 생긴 젊은 남자였다. 철수의 눈은 동그랗게 커졌다. 할 말을 잃었다.

"…선생님은…"

"오늘 학원에 계시지 않아요."

그 젊은 남자는 조용하게 말했다.

"…아, …죄송합니다."

철수는 이 뜻밖의 상황에 무슨 말을 해야 할지 몰라 순간적으로 사과를 하고 돌아섰다. 그 젊은 남자의 모습을 본 이상 연습실에서 차분하게 연습할 수가 없었다. 알렉산더 맥퀸 해골 우산 옆의 자신의 비닐 우산을 집어 들고 학원을 나왔다.

작년 가을부터인가…나지막이 들리던…빠른 배속으로 돌아가던 강의 소리의 주인이 저 남자였구나. 그럼 그 소리는 피아노 선생님이 공부하던 소리가 아니라 저 남자가 틀어놓은 소리였다는 거야? 그리고 저 소리가 날 때마다 피아노 선생님은 원장실에서 저 남자와 함께 있었다는 것이고. 가끔 나직이 들리던 남자 목소리가 저 남자 목소리였던가? 그래서 연습하고 있으면 자신이 시간 맞추어 올 테니 원장실로 찾아와서 문을 노크하지 말라고, 나에게 그렇게 엄하게 말했던 거였구나. 피아노 선생님에게서 나던 향수 냄새가 저 남자의 향수 냄새였고, 작년 늦가을에 비가 오던 날 보았던 저 해골 우산의 주인이 저 남자라는 거였고, 그럼 그들은 그때도 사귀고 있었던 거였네. 그녀에게 남자 친구가 없는 줄 알았어. 그녀가 남자 친구와 함께 원장실에 있다는 것도 모른 채 나는 매일 가슴설레며 학원에 왔었고…. 그의 세상이 흔들렸다. 놀라서 몸이 떨렸다. 다리가 후들거렸다. 그녀의 남동생이거나 오빠일 수도 있잖아. 남사친일 수도 있잖아. 철수는 부인하고 순수하게 생각하려고 애를 썼다. 하지만 그의 직감은 그가 피아노 선생님의 남자 친구라고 말하고 있었다.

집으로 돌아오면서 철수는 익숙한 몸의 증상을 느꼈다. 작년 2월, 욕망시 자신의 원룸 앞에서 중고차를 처분하던 날, 서울 서초동에서 이와 비슷한 증상을 느끼며 쓰러진 적이 있었다. 어지러움을 이기며 천천히 집으로 걸어갔다. 그날 저녁 열이 39도까지 올라갔다.

다음 날 아침, 아픈 몸을 겨우 일으켜 세우고 병원으로 갔다. 열을 떨어뜨리는 약을 처방받았다. 며칠간 깊은 잠을 자며 앓았다. 식욕은 사라졌다. 거의 먹지를 못했다. 약만 먹었다. 며칠 뒤 열은 떨어졌지만, 목구멍의 통증은 약을 먹어도 사라지지 않았고 시간이 지날수록 더 심해졌다. 목구멍의 통증 때문에 침을 삼킬 수조차 없었다. 목소리는 변해갔다. 말할 때마다 쉿소리가 났다.

'병가가 끝났을 때 떠났어야 했는데. 퇴직하지 말았어야 했어. 집을 사기 전에 그녀의 남자 친구를 보았더라면… 아니, 그 전으로 돌아가 복직을 준비하고 있었을 때 그녀의 남자 친구를 보았더라면… 그렇다면 미련 없이 이 도시를 떠났을 텐데… 퇴직하고 돌아와 집을 구입하고 정확히 3주가 지나서야 그녀의 남자 친구를 보다니. 운명의 여신이 이렇게 장난을 치다니!'

며칠 뒤 열이 떨어지자마자 철수는 다시 학원으로 갔다. 그녀에게 묻고 싶었다. 그 젊은 남자의 존재에 대해서 말이다. 피아노 학원 출입문을 열고 들어갔다. 풍경이 여느 때처럼 청명하고 맑은 소리를 냈다.

"권철수님, 어서 오세요."

한 초등학생을 레슨해주고 있던 그녀가 들어오는 철수를 향해 밝고 환하게 웃었다. 그녀의 웃는 모습을 보자 철수의 어둡던 마음에 한 줄기 빛이 들어왔다.

"미리 알려드리지 못했네요. 저번 주 금요일에 가족 여행 떠나서 이번 주 화요일에 돌아왔어요. 금요일 날 오셨지요?"

"아!"

철수는 안도의 한숨을 내 쉬었다.

'금요일 그녀는 원장실에서 그 남자와 단둘이 있지 않았어. 그날 가

족 여행 갔다잖아. 그리고 다음 화요일에 돌아왔다잖아. 그날 그 남자
는 혼자 있었던 거야.'

"연습하고 계세요. 이 친구 레슨 끝나면 바로 레슨해 드릴게요."

"……네."

철수는 예전처럼 느리게 말하고 천천히 자신이 평소 연습하던 원장
실 옆 부스로 들어갔다. 곧 레슨을 마친 피아노 선생님이 부스로 들어
와 철수 옆에 앉았다. 그녀에게서 강한 장미 스모크향이 났다. 그녀의
작고 귀여운 하얀 손가락이 건반 위에서 나풀거리며 나비처럼 춤을 추
었다. 새 곡 치는 법을 설명하는 그녀의 잔잔하며 차분한 목소리는 여
전히 그의 가슴을 설레게 했다. 철수의 머릿속에는 많은 상념이 지나
갔다. 그는 망설이다가, 레슨이 끝나자 용기 내어 물었다.

"……송 선생님……금요일 오후에……원장실에 계셨던 남자분……."

철수의 목소리에서 고르지 못한 쇳소리가 났다. 열은 떨어졌지만,
아직 낫지 않은 목감기 때문이었다. 스스로 자신의 목소리가 괴물 목
소리 같다고 생각했다.

"아, 제 남자 친구예요."

그녀는 차분하고 가볍게 말했다. 철수의 가슴이 철렁 내려앉았다. 그
의 눈이 가늘게 떨렸다. 그는 더는 아무것도 묻지 않았다. '남자 친구'
라는 말이 칼처럼 그의 마음을 찔렀다. 그녀는 레슨을 마치고 연습하
라는 말을 남기고 떠났다. 순식간에 그의 눈에 눈물이 차올랐다. 그녀
는 쇳소리 나는 그의 달라진 목소리에 대해 왜 그런지 전혀 궁금해하
지 않았다. 그의 건강 상태에 관해 묻지 않았다. 더군다나 그녀는 철수

가 열이 39도까지 올라가 며칠간을 앓으며 죽었다가 살아났다는 것도, 몸이 조금 나아지자마자 그녀를 보기 위해 달려왔다는 것도 알 턱이 없었다. 그녀가 떠나고, 며칠간 아파서 면도하지 못한 그의 까슬까슬한 뺨에 또르르 눈물이 흘러내렸다. 눈물을 닦았다. 초등학생도, 그렇다고 십 대 청소년도 아닌 오십 먹은 아저씨가 어린 소년들이 겪을법한 순수한 짝사랑으로 눈물을 흘린다는 것이 자신도 어이가 없었다.

먼지가 되어

철수는 이제 편의점 아르바이트가 끝나면 피아노 학원으로 가지 않았다. 대신 매일 10층 자신의 아파트로 올라갔다. 24년 된 낡은 공간을 보고 있자니 식욕이 떨어졌다. 자신이 벌인 일들에 대한 후회로 거의 먹지를 못했다. 지난 1년간 끊었던 술을 다시 마셨다. 아파트 한쪽에는 어느새 철수가 매일 마신 빈 맥주 캔들이 쌓이게 되었다.

어느 날 철수는 아파트를 청소하기 시작했다. 자신의 선택에 책임을 져야 했다. 구석구석 찌든 때들을 벗겨냈다. 매일 편의점 아르바이트가 끝나면 10층까지 헉헉대며 올라갔다. 지난 1년간 식단 조절과 운동으로 살이 빠지긴 했지만, 여전히 뚱뚱한 철수는 숨을 쉴 수가 없어서 삼 층마다 벽을 잡고 멈추어 섰다. 그리고 숨을 돌렸다. 처음에는 청소업자를 부르려 했지만, 그 누구도 엘리베이터가 작동되지 않는 아파트에서 청소하기를 원치 않았다. 결국 자신이 직접 아파트를 청소했다. 엘리베이터 교체 작업이 끝나면 철거하게 될 부엌 가구와 타일, 욕실 기구 등 오래된 가구들은 제외하고 걸레로 모든 공간의 얼룩들을 지우고 닦기를 반복했다. 지난 24년간 이 공간에서 거주한 전주인들이 남긴 가난의 때를 벗겨냈다. 그에게서 땀이 비 오듯 쏟아졌다.

통장 잔액을 보았다. 퇴직 후 아르바이트는 하고 있지만 들어오는 돈은 적고 돈은 자꾸 빠져나갔다. 비용을 절감하기 위해, 또 이곳에 계속 정착하지는 않을 것이기에 필요한 부분만 리모델링을 했다. 코킹 작업, 주방, 욕실, 조명 등 부분적으로 업체에 맡겼다.

경기가 좋지 않아 부동산 거래가 없는 이 시기에 철수는 전 집주인에게는 후한 돈을 주고 그의 집을 사주었고, 각 리모델링 업자들에게 일거리를 제공해주는 은인이 되었다.

리모델링 비용을 절감하기 위해 벽지는 기존의 벽지에 자신이 직접 화이트색으로 페인트칠했다. 이 작업은 며칠간 지속되었다. 페인트가 몰딩에 묻고 페인트 방울이 바닥에 떨어졌다. 그의 얼굴, 그의 목, 그의 팔, 그의 옷 곳곳에 페인트 방울이 튀었다. 벽마다 페인트 작업을 마치고 몰딩에 묻은 페인트와 바닥 곳곳에 떨어진 페인트 자국을 걸레로 여러 번 닦으며 지웠다. 자신의 몸에 묻은 페인트도 물로 여러 번 씻어냈다.

철수는 얼굴과 팔에 떨어진 페인트 방울들을 지우며 욕실 거울로 자신의 얼굴을 가만히 쳐다보았다. 얼굴에 살이 많이 빠져 있다. 그간 마음고생과 식욕감퇴, 그리고 편의점 아르바이트가 끝난 후에 10층을 매일 오르고 내리며 청소를 했고, 아파트 리모델링 업자들과의 소통으로 애를 쓴 탓인지 살이 급격하게 빠진 것이다. 그는 거울을 보며 활짝 웃어보았다. 눈가에 주름이 잡혔다. 놀라운 변화였다. 얼굴에 살이 쪄서 아무리 찡그려도 팽팽할 뿐 주름이 잡히지 않던 얼굴이었다.

입을 다물었다. 주름이 보이지 않았다.

　피아노 학원에 가지 않은 지 한 달이 넘었다. 피아노 선생님에게는 잠시 쉬겠다고 문자만 보냈다. 운명의 장난으로 점점 살이 빠지다 못해 이제는 초췌해져 가고 안색이 어둡게 변해가는 그의 모습을 그녀에게 보여주고 싶지 않았다. 자신만의 굴로 들어간 것이다.
　철수의 친형은 철수가 한때는 심하게 뚱뚱해서 염려했는데, 이제는 살이 너무 빠지고 먹지도 못해서 염려했다.
　"철수야 너무 심하게 살을 빼는 것 아니냐?"
　"아니요. 살을 빼는 게 아니라, 알아서 빠져요."
　"퇴직해서 그런 것 같은데, 사오십 대 남자들 다 거쳐 가는 과정이지. 상심하지 마. 일에는 법원 일만 있는 것이 아니야. 대기업에 다니던 사오십 대들 퇴직하고 다른 직업으로 제2의 인생을 시작하는 사람들 많아. 다른 회사에 다시 들어가기보다는 자영업…자신만의 사업장을 운영하기도 하지. 시야를 넓게 가져."
　철수의 친형은 철수가 법원 일만이 전부라고 생각하지 않도록 권면했다.

　연우는 맥줏집 사업과 화영과의 연애로 바빠서 자연스럽게 철수와 영식과만 어울리게 되었다. 철수는 지금 이 시기가 힘들어 영식을 만날 때마다 맥줏집으로 가자고 설득했다. 알코올의 힘으로 잠시나마 그의 근심을 잊고 싶었다. 그들은 연우의 맥줏집으로 가지 않고 다른 맥줏집에서 만났다. 철수는 술집의 밝은 분위기를 즐겼다. 잠시만이라도 그의 근심에서 나올 수 있는 시간이었다. 영식은 점점 살이 빠져가는 철수가 염려스럽기는 하지만 리즈 시절의 날씬하고 잘생긴 모습을 되찾고 있는 것 같아 보기가 좋았다. 성격 또한 민첩해지고 말수도 많아져서 늘 의아해했다. 하지만 영식은 철수에게 종종 이런 말을 하며 그의 신경을 긁었다.

"너, 연우가 없어서 날 자꾸 대타로 불러내지? 나 솔직히 말은 안 했지만 너에게 자꾸 연우 대타 취급당하는 것도 싫고 너랑 이렇게 계속 만나는 것도 너에게도 나에게도 안 좋은 것 같다."

"형님, 전 형님을 연우 대타 취급한 적이 없어요. 형님은 누구의 대타가 될 수 없는 형님만의 고유한 특징과 매력이 있는 분이십니다."

"지난 1년간 연우가 너의 소울 메이트였는데 연우가 화영에게 가서 날 대신 만나는 거잖아. 연우가 없어서 마음이 허한 거고."

"형님, 자꾸 소울 메이트 이러시는데, 전 연우에게도 형님에게도 동일하게 행동했어요. 혹시 연우가 형님에게 소울 메이트였던 거 아닙니까? 연우가 화영 씨에게 가버려서 형님이 허한 것이고요."

영식은 순간 뜨끔했다.

"너 욕망시에서 일할 때, 연우와 난 거의 매일 만났지. 그러다가 연우가 화영을 알게 됐고, 연우, 화영이 그리고 나 이렇게 셋이서 종종 만났었다. 연우와 화영이가 한번은 크게 싸웠었지. 연우는 화영을 다시는 보지 않을 거라 했어. 화영도 연우를 보지 않을 거라고 했지. 그때부터 화영이가 밤마다 내게 전화했어. 때로는 새벽까지 통화했지.

그런데 웃긴 게 뭔지 알아? 화영이는 나와 통화하는 내내 연우 이야기만 했어. 나에 관해 묻지를 않는 거야. 자신도 자기가 연우 이야기만 한다는 것을 모르더라고. 그리고 항상 '연우는 왜 그럴까?'하고 끝을 맺었지. 그런데 너도 연우 얘기를 자주 하잖아."

"제가요? 오히려 형님이 더 많이 하시는 것 같은데…."

"연우가 착했지."

"물 같은 존재죠. 있는 듯 없는 듯 자리를 채워주고…어리고 재미있기도 하고."

"아니야, 지금은…. 애가 영악해져 가. 지 애인을 닮아가는 거지."

"그런데 지금 연우와 화영 씨가 어떻게 연인 사이가 된 거죠?"

"화영이가 다리를 놔달라고 하더라고. 다시 연우와 화해하고 싶다고 나에게 연우와 만날 수 있게 다리를 놔달라고 하는 거야. 뭐, 연우를 잘 달래서 다리를 놔주었지. 그러다가 서로 연인 사이로 발전한 거고."

"그러고 보면 연우가 남자로 태어나서 다행이에요. 여자로 태어났다면 여러 남자 울리고 다녔을 거예요. 보세요. 우리의 대화도 온통 연우잖아요."

"그 돼지 같은 놈을 어떤 남자가 좋아해? 얼굴 피부는 화산분화구에, 몸은 돼지처럼 살만 쪄서!"

"여자로 태어났다면 다른 외모였겠죠. 연우의 착한 성격을 말하는 거예요."

"그놈 변했어. 착하지 않아. 또 많이 컸지. …어릴 때는 형님하고 따라다니는 모습이 이뻐서 이거저거 많이 가르쳐주었는데…이제는 너무 커버려서 내가 해줄 수 있는 게 없다."

영식은 더는 말하지 않고 다시 맥주를 마셨다.

철수는 영식을 택시로 태워 보냈다. 그를 보내고 천천히 밤거리를 걸으며 집으로 돌아오는데 영식에게서 문자가 왔다.

'나 당뇨 때문에 술 끊었었는데 요즘 너랑 계속 만나면서 맥주와 고기를 먹게 되고 나에게 안 좋은 것 같아. 그리고 너를 만나면서 매일 택시 타고 오고 갔는데 집에서 돈도 벌지 않는 백수 놈이 어딜 그렇게 쏘다니냐고 성화다. 부모님 용돈 받고 사는데 택시 값이 부담된다. 앞으로는 서로를 위해 만나지 않는 게 좋겠다. 오늘 고기와 맥주 사준 것은 고맙고 앞으로 우리 연락하지 말고 지내자. 잘 지내라.'

그 문자가 철수의 마음을 아프게 했다. 돈은 문제 되지 않았다. 자신이 사주면 되는 거다. 하지만 헤어지자는 말은 철수를 외롭게 했다. 그마저 사라지면 이곳에 그를 붙잡아 두는 건 친형 가족 외에는 아무것도 없다. 그리고 이곳은 이제 그의 집이 있는 곳이다. 집 때문이라도 철수는 이 도시에 있어야 할 이유를 만들어야 했다. 그는 답신을 보냈다.

'형님, 전화해도 될까요?'

'그래.'

어둡고 극단적인 문자 내용과는 반대로 영식의 목소리는 밝고 경쾌했다.

"형님. 목소리는 밝네요. 정말 놀랐습니다. 문자 보고 형님께 무슨 일이 있는 줄 알고 걱정돼서 전화했습니다. 부모님과 또 무슨 일이 있었습니까?"

"아니, 무슨 일은…. 다 자."

"무엇하고 계셨습니까?"

"지금은 나의 자유 시간이야. 게임도 하고."

"형님, 저만 만나면 술과 고기를 먹게 된다고 하셨는데…저 지금 퇴직하고 집을 사서 힘든 시기여서 잠시 알코올에 의지했던 건 맞습니다만 이 힘든 시기가 지나가면 맥주를 더는 마시지 않을 겁니다. 그리고 오늘 전 맥주 500짜리 하나만 먹었습니다. 과거처럼 다시 술독에 빠지는 게 싫어서 절제했지요. 오늘 두세 병씩 마신 분은 형님이시고, 또 고기 먹고 싶다고 서너 번 말씀 하신 것도 형님이십니다. 건강을 위해 맥주만 조금 마시고 기분을 좋게 하자고 말했지만, 형님이 계속해서 맥주와 고기를 더 먹고 싶다고 말했고 그래서 사드린 거고요."

영식은 순간 당황했다. 철수가 언제부터 이렇게 확실하게 꼬집고 들어갔었나. 피할 곳이 없다. 이 아이가 이런 아이가 아닌데… 철수도 많이 변했구나. 이삼십 대의 확실하고 명철했던 모습으로 돌아가고 있구나. 게다가 법원에서 일하더니 하나하나 분명하게 따지는 것은 확실하구먼. 연우만 변한 게 아니었다. 다들 변하고 있다. 나만 정체되어있는 거 같다.

"아니 그건 고맙게 생각해. 그런데 택시비가…. 과거에 연우 만날 때는 같은 동네여서 택시비도, 돈도 안 들었거든. 그런데 철수 너를 만나면 자꾸 돈이 든단 말이야. 통장에 택시비, 택시비, 택시비 다 이렇게 찍혀. 어머니 카드로 택시비를 내고 있지만, 어머니가 돈도 벌지 않는 것이 택시 타고 어디를 그렇게 쏘다니냐고 잔소리하는데 거기에 일일이 대답해야 하고 정말 억압받고 자유롭지 못한 삶 힘들다.”

“형님, 그러면 이유가 돈이라고 분명하게 말씀하셔야지요. 자꾸 다른 이유를 들먹거리시면…. 형님에게 최선을 다하고 맞추어 드리는데 자꾸 다른 이유를 대시면 혼란스럽습니다. 형님에게는 택시비도 부담이 되는 상황이니 올 때마다 내가 사잖아요. 택시비까지 내가 책임져 드리기에는 좀 힘드니 아르바이트라도 하셔서 형님의 용돈은 형님이 벌어보세요.”

“난 당뇨가 와서 이제 일 못 해. 남의 밑에서 일해본 적도 없고, 이 나이에 남의 밑에서 일하고 싶지도 않아. 부모님이 내가 연금을 매달 탈 수 있도록 젊은 시절에 보험에 가입해 두셔서 그거로 살지. 얼마 되지는 않지만.”

“그러면 부모님에게 감사하고 사셔야지요. 부모님 험담만 하지 마시고.”

“내 연금 들어줄 때만 해도 감사했지. 그때는 착하셨거든. 그런데 지금은 아주 못된 노인들이 되어서 날 하인 다루듯이 취급해. 나이가 들어서 무거운 것 못 드니까 꼭 나를 불러서 들게 하고 제대로 걷지 못하니 늘 옆에서 내가 시중들어야 해. 나 요양보호사로 살고 있지. 아니 요양보호사보다 더하지. 그들은 날 아들로 생각하지 않아. 노인 시기에 필요한 하인, 일꾼으로 날 보지. 아주 악마야 악마. 이 두 사람이 죽어야 내가 자유로워지지. 두 사람이 죽으면 내가 이 아파트 물려

받고 혼자 자유롭게 살지. 부럽다. 철수야. 넌 이제 집도 있고 정말 자유롭잖아. 누가 널 억압하고 통제하냐. 취미도 많고. 피아노 치는 남자…. 운동도 열심히 하고 이제는 살도 다 빠져서 리즈 시절 권철수로 복귀도 하고.”

“형님, 부모님 원망은 그만하시는 게 좋겠어요. 부모님 입장은 생각해보지 않으셨어요? 서양은 10대 후반만 되면 대학이나 취업을 통해 부모님을 떠나지요. 한국은 오랜 교육 시기와 비싼 집값 등 한국 사회 특징 때문에 이삼십 대까지 부모와 같이 살 수 있다고 생각은 돼요. 하지만 오십이 넘어서까지 자식이 결혼도 하지 않고 취업도, 독립도 하지 않고 부모님에게 계속 붙어 있다고 생각해보세요. 답답하시죠? 부모님 마음은 애가 타실 거예요. 지구상에 모든 동물은 청소년 시기가 되면 부모를 떠나잖아요. 형님이 계속 독립하지 않고 부모님 집에서 사신다면 부모님의 잔소리는 계속 들을 수밖에 없어요.”

영식은 더는 철수와 이야기하고 싶지 않았다. 연우가 그립다. 하지만 연우는 자기 야망을 따라 6살 연상의 화영이라는 늙은 여우를 물어서 떠났다. 성격도 점점 영악해졌다. 더 어릴 때 연우는 착했고 내 상처를 싸매어 주었는데 이 자식은 훈계질이다. 이 자식은 고등학교 졸업 후 서울로 독립을 했고 생계비를 벌며 자신의 생계는 스스로 책임졌다. 나하고는 다르다. 생활력이 강하다. 이놈이 아파서 고향으로 내려와 친형 집에 1년을 얹혀살았지만, 이제는 아파트를 사서 독립해 버렸다. 외모도 변하고 성격도 변했다. 이제 철수와 연우와 엮이기 싫다. 지긋지긋하다. 다들 내게 상처를 주는구나. 이게 이놈과 마지막 통화다. 이놈도 외로워서 앞으로 내게 계속 전화하고 문자도 계속 보낼 것이다. 이놈도 의외로 스토커 같은 면이 있다. 연우도 화영이 만나기 전에는 내가 잠수만 타면 전화를 해대고 문자를 해대더니 어찌 두 놈이 똑같냐. 사회적 야망을 추구하는 놈들은 비슷한 것 같다. 연우 놈은 말로는 내가 걱정된다며 문자를 계속 보내고, 전화를 계속했지만, 사실 자신을 위한 거였다. 자신의 깊은 마음을 나 말고는 나눌 사람이 없어서였다. 정서적 교감과 대화가 가장 잘 통하는 사람이 나였기 때문이다. 내게 중독된 것이었다. 야망이 있는 놈들은 자기 마음을 지켜야 한다. 자기 마음 하나 통제 못 하고 전화와 문자를 계속 보내는 것이 내게는 스토커처럼 보인다. 철수 이놈도 비슷한 증상을 내게 보인다. 난 야망에 관심이 없다. 그냥 큰 꿈 없이 이렇게 하루하루 즐겁게 사는 것이 좋다. 차단했지만 계속 문자와 전화가 온다면 별수 없다. 또 번호를 바꾸어야지. 도대체 이게 몇 번인가. 이게 다 연우 놈 때문이다. 그놈 때문에 전화번호 바꾼 것만 해도 열 번이 넘는다.

4월과 5월. 엘리베이터도 완공되었고, 집도 리모델링이 거의 끝나갔다. 아파트는 예전의 낡은 모습에서 깔끔하고 세련된 모습으로 바뀌어 갔다. 리모델링은 한 업체에 다 맡기지 않고 각 부분의 업자들에게 따로 맡겨서 리모델링을 했다. 돈을 줄이는 방법이기도 했지만, 철수는 곧 이곳을 떠날 계획을 세우고 있었기에 리모델링에 많은 돈을 쓰고 싶지 않았다. 편의점 아르바이트를 끝내고 아파트에 도착해보니 마지막 단계인 주방 리모델링이 다 끝나 있었다.

그때 현관 벨 소리가 울렸다. 연우였다. 얼마 전에 새집의 주소를 알려주었는데 찾아온 것이다. 오랜만에 철수의 모습을 본 연우는 깜짝 놀라 소리쳤다.

"세상에! 철수 형님이 맞습니까? 살이 왜 이리 빠지셨습니까? 딴사람이 되셨네요! 몰라보겠어요!"

연우는 까만 비닐봉지에 넣어온 맥주 캔들과 안줏거리를 거실 테이블 위에 올려놓았다.

"형님, 그런데 술 끊었다고 하셨잖아요. 맥주를 가져오라고 시키시다니요?"

"내가 요양하면서 술을 끊었지만, 이 집을 사고 나서 버틸 수가 있어야지. 나 얼마 전에 완전히 퇴직했잖아. 내 주소지가 이제 이곳이라고. 내가 이 집을 산 것이 과연 옳은 선택인가에 대해 확신도 없고, 또 이 집에 들어가야 할 리모델링 비용, 세금, 이 집의 미래 수익성 등을 생각하니 골치가 아프더군. 또 청소하면서 리모델링이 안 된 우중충한 집을 매일 보다 보니 기분까지 더 우중충해지더라. 게다가 이번 여름은 장마라더니 여름이 되기 전부터 비가 자주 오잖아."

연우는 맥주 캔을 따서 철수에게 내밀었다. 철수는 맥주 캔을 받더니 맥주를 벌컥벌컥 마셨다.

"너 한창 사업으로 바쁘고 해서 그간 영식 형님과만 만났어. 매일 저녁 여기저기 맥줏집에 다녔지. 아, 미안! 영식 형이 다른 맥줏집으로 가자고 해서…."

"그간 영식 형님 만나고 계셨군요."

"응. 그런데 너 영식 형님과 무슨 일 있었어?"

"내 말에 기분이 나빠졌나 봐요."

"무슨 말을 했는데?"

"글쎄요. 저도 그게 늘 퀘스천이에요. 나이가 들수록 유리 같아지는 영식 형님 마음을 어떻게 알겠어요. 극단적인 문자를 보낸 후에 또 저를 차단했더라고요."

"네가 화영 씨와 데이트하느라 바쁘고 영식 형님께 소홀해져서 아닐까?"

"…그런데 형님…, 건강이 걱정되네요. 살도 갑자기 이렇게나 많이 빠져버리고 끊었던 술까지 다시 마시고…"

"내가 다시 술을 마시게 된 건 유감이지만 술이 없으면 지금 이 상황을 버틸 수가 없어. 너도 술집을 운영해서 알 거야. 많은 사람이 맥줏집에 와서 술과 음식을 먹으며 웃고 소통하고 즐거워하고… 술집에서 느낄 수 있는 그런 밝은 기운이 없으면 순간순간 치솟는 내 선택에 대한 부정적 생각과 기분을 처리할 수가 없더라고. 부정적 상념에 묻혀 버리지. 압사당하고 말지. 살기 위해 마시는 거야. 부정적 생각과 기분에 압사되지 않으려고."

"지금 한창 힘드실 테지만 이 시기도 곧 지나가겠죠. 저도 사업 시작하면서 잘하고 있는 건지 확신이 없고 걱정도 많았는데 그거 다 기우더라고요. 잘 되어가고 있어요. 형님도 그러겠죠."

"영식 형은 또 잠적했어. 문자도 확인 안 해서 전화해보니 번호가 바뀌었더라고. 너는 바빠서 시간을 낼 수 없다는 걸 알기에 그간 형님과 어울렸는데…, 형님이 사라져서 인생에 낙이 없다. 형님과 매일 술집에서 만나 대화하는 거로 이 시기를 버티고 있었는데 말이야."

"그 형님 자주 그래요. 잊고 지내면 언젠가 다시 연락이 올 거예요."

"어떻게 알아?"

"형님 욕망시에 있을 때 저 영식 형님과 여기서 10년을 지냈어요. 저화영 씨랑 사귀기 전에 거의 매일 만났죠. 지난 10년간 잠적하고 다시연락 오고 다시 잠적하고 또 연락 오고 반복이었습니다. 그런데, 형님이젠 술 그만 마셔요. 형님 건강 챙겨야죠."

"끊어야지. 이 시기가 지나면 끊을 거야. 하지만 지금은 좀 더 의지해야겠어. 술을 마시면 기분이 좋아지거든. 매일 밤 알코올이 없으면잠을 잘 수가 없을 정도야. 머릿속이 온통 후회와 걱정 근심이야. 생지옥을 경험하고 있지. 직장도 그만두고 서울도 아닌 이곳에 집을 사버리다니 말이야. 내가 과거 24년간 생존을 위해 자신을 너무 억압하며살아와서 생각이 너무 극단으로 치우쳤던 거 같아."

"이미 24년간 극단적으로 살아오셨어요. 그래서 육체와 정신이 견디지 못해서 아팠던 거고요."

"넌 아직 어리니까 극단적으로 살지 마라. 일과 야망에 매달려서 자신이 원하는 게 뭔지 잊어버리는 지경까지 가지 말란 말이지. 순간순간 자신을 기쁘게 하는 선택도 해주면서 마음을 돌봐주라고. 하여튼요즘 알코올이 들어가면 그때만이라도 정신적으로 편해지고 기분이좋아지거든. 걱정 근심이 사라지지."

"이곳을 떠나실 건가요?"

"아마도. 하지만 당분간은 여기에 주소지를 둘 거야. 다음 행보가 정해지면 분명해지겠지. 그래서 리모델링도 모두 다 하지 않고 필요한 부분만 했어. 다음에 이곳에 정착할 사람이 다른 부분은 하도록 말이야."

"그런데 형님. 많이 변하셨습니다."

"뭐가?"

"살이 너무 많이 빠져서 외모도 딴사람이 되셨는데, 성격도 딴 사람 같습니다. 형님의 말의 속도가 굉장히 빨라지셨습니다. 그리고 말씀도 많이 하시고."

"응?"

"작년에 요양차 귀향했을 때 형님은⋯아니, 10년 전 제가 향우회에서 형님을 처음 뵙고 그 후로 형님을 만날 때마다 느끼는 거지만 형님은 늘 말수도 없었고, 도통 속을 알 수 없는 분이셨죠. 형님의 속마음을 알려면 질문을 많이 해야 했어요. 게다가 대답을 들을 때까지는 몇 초 기다려야지 겨우 입을 떼셨고, 대답해도 늘 짧은 단답형이었죠. 형님의 마음을 알려면 여러 번 질문해야 했고⋯. 정말 질문하는 입장에서 에너지가 너무 소진되고 지쳤죠. 근데 지금 형님을 보세요. 누가 먼저 질문하지 않아도 먼저 알아서 말도 많이 하시고, 또 길게 말씀하시고 있어요. 그리고 속도도 빨라요. 영식 형님이 철수 형님 이십 대 때 지적이고 총명하고 말도 워낙 잘하고 인기 많았다고 했는데⋯그 모습이 상상이 안 됐는데⋯지금은 조금 알 것 같아요. 아마 지금 이 모습과 비슷하지 않았을까 하는 생각이 드네요."

"내가 많이 변했구나…."

"이 집도 마찬가지예요. 리모델링 된 집을 보니 산뜻하네요. 이 집이 과거에는 오래되고 우중충했다고 하셨는데 과거 모습이 상상이 안 가네요."

연우는 리모델링이 된 집을 여기저기 살폈다.

"아, 마저 뱃살을 떼어낸다고 하셨는데…지금도 여전히 뱃살을 떼고 계세요? 아주 날씬해지신 거 보니 뱃살을 엄청나게 떼어내셨겠어요. 하하하."

"아니, 지금은 알아서 살이 빠져서 떼어낼 뱃살이 없다. 집을 산후로 몇 달간 떼어내지 않았어."

"예전에 떼어낸 뱃살은 어디 있습니까?"

"이리 와 봐."

철수는 연우의 팔목을 잡고 방으로 들어갔다. 그곳에 옷장이 있다. 철수는 옷장 아래 서랍을 조심스럽게 열었다.

"이게 내가 지금까지 떼어낸 뱃살들이야. 징그러운 복부의 지방 덩어리. 이제는 하도 많이 봐서 탐스럽게도 보인다."

연우는 서랍 안을 들여다보았다. 회색 먼지들만 쌓여있고 텅 비어 있었다.

"무슨 말씀이세요? 아무것도 안 보이는데요?"

철수는 연우에게서 고개를 돌려 열린 서랍을 보았다. 그곳에는 연우의 말대로 아무것도 없었다. 이게 어떻게 된 일인가! 그 산처럼 쌓여있던 지방 덩어리들은 다 어디로 사라진 것인가. 철수는 손가락으로 서랍 안의 공간을 쓱 그었다. 그의 손에는 먼지들만 묻었다.

"형, 형이 집을 샀다고 해서 오늘 특별히 시간 내서 형 집을 방문한 거지만 앞으로 저 바빠서 형하고 못 어울려요. 저 맥줏집 운영으로 매일 바쁘고 좀 시간이 나면 화영 씨와 함께 여기저기 세미나도 다니고 사업 운영을 더 잘하려면 배워야 할 것도 많고…." 연우는 이 말을 남기고 철수의 아파트를 나왔다.

연우의 여자친구 화영은 그가 영식과 철수를 만나는 것을 금했다. 영식과 철수에게는 화영 씨의 반대 때문에 더는 만날 수 없다고 말하지 않고 그럴싸한 이유를 둘러대며 그들과 만나는 것을 피해왔다. 새로 생긴 인맥들 만나기도 바쁜데 영식과 철수가 계속 연락이 와서 안 만날 수도 없고 난처했었다. 화영 씨의 반대도 있지만, 이제는 더는 배울 것 없는 그들과 거리를 두고 싶었다. 영식 형이 잠수에서 나와 다시 연락이 오면 일 핑계를 대며 만나지 않으면 되고…, 철수형은…그는 달라졌다. 집을 사고 살도 빠져서 전혀 다른 사람 같다. 철수형은 좀 더 만나고 싶지만 화영 씨가 반대하니 정리해야 할 듯하다. 또 그는 여전히 뱃살 헛소리를 한다. 화영 씨의 조언대로 이제 형들과의 인연을 정리해야 할 것 같다. 사실, 형들이 더는 커 보이지 않는다. 이젠 형들에게 배울 것을 다 배운 것 같다.

연우가 돌아가고 철수는 다시 한번 서랍장을 살펴보았다. 얼마 전까지 존재했던, 산처럼 거대한 복부 지방 덩어리가 도대체 어디로 간 거지? 다른 사람들 눈에는 보이지 않더라도 철수의 눈에는 보였던 그 지방 덩어리…. 그때 한쪽 구석에서 뽀얀 작은 지방 덩어리가 보였다. 풍선이 바람이 빠져서 점점 조그맣게 변하는 것처럼 그 뽀얀 지방 덩어리가 미세하게 작아져 갔다.

대학을 졸업한 후, 지난 24년간 스트레스, 분노, 좌절, 열등감, 슬픔, 원한 등의 부정적 감정과 생각이 복부 비만의 형태로 그의 복부에 쌓여있었다. 매일 새로운 부정적 감정들이 생겨났고 세월과 함께 거대해져 갔다. 과거의 매일 쌓여만 가는 고생과 부정적 감정을 버리지 못하고 여태까지 붙잡고 살았다. 그것들이 사라지면 자신의 과거가 사라져 버리는 듯했고 현재의 자신도 사라져 버릴 것 같았기 때문이다. 자신을 대변해왔던 존재가 사라지는 것을 견딜 수가 없어서 그 부정적 기억을 버리지 않고 같이 살아왔다.

과거의 고생과 고통은 한을 풀지 못해 그를 떠나지 못하고 있었다. 전래동화에서 귀신들이 원한이 많아서 이승을 떠나지 못한다고 하듯이 말이다. 철수는 자신의 젊은 시절에 애도를 표하고 한스러움을 풀어주었다. 한이라는 귀신을 그들이 가야 할 곳으로 떠나보냈다.

서랍 안의 철수의 복부 지방 덩어리는 바람이 빠져가는 풍선처럼 계속 작아져 갔다. 이제는 눈에 보이지 않게 미세해졌다. 그리고 하나의 먼지가 되었다. 그리고 시야에서 영원히 사라졌다.

009

시절 인연

6월 초순. 여름이 시작되었다. 몇 주간 지속됐던 장마가 잠시 멈추었다. 철수는 자신의 아파트를 나와 걸었다. 구름 사이로 태양이 얼굴을 드러내며 여름 햇살을 선물하고 있었다. 그는 오랜만에 햇살을 느끼며 한동안 걷지 않은 학원 가는 길을 걸어보았다. 무인 사진관 앞에서 자신의 모습을 비춰보았다. 오랜만에 비추어본다. 그 거울에는 아주 낯선 남자가 서 있었다. 과거의 권철수가 아니었다. 정상 체중의 남자가 서 있었다. 뚱뚱한 배불뚝이 아저씨가 아니었다. 전과 같은 것은 희끗거리는 머리카락과 알이 두꺼운 안경뿐이었다.

더 걸어가면 은행 지점 앞에 자귀나무, 즉 소가 좋아한다는 소 쌀밥나무가 있다. 철수는 소띠이다. 그는 자귀나무를 볼 생각에 갑자기 가슴이 뛰었다. 신비롭고 아름다운 진분홍색의 꽃, 강렬하고 아름다운 향기를 뿜어내는 자귀나무꽃을 다시 볼 수 있다는 생각에 가슴이 설레었다.

철수는 자귀나무 가까이 다가갔다. 자귀나무꽃들이 조금 발화하였고 신비롭고 아름다운 꽃을 떨어뜨리고 있었다. 철수는 떨어진 자귀나무꽃을 서너 송이 주워들었다. 향기를 맡았다. 처음으로 이 꽃을 알게 된 때를 돌아보았다. 정확히 1년이 지났다. 자귀 꽃이 필 때 피아노를 배우기 시작했으니 피아노를 배운지도 1년의 시기가 지났다. 피아노 선생님이 보고 싶다.

그는 자귀나무꽃을 들고 학원으로 곧장 걸었다. 횡단보도는 즉시 빨간불에서 초록불로 바뀌었고 철수는 기다릴 필요도 없이 횡단보도를 건넜다. 횡단보도에서부터 아이들이 치는 정겨운 피아노 소리가 들렸다. 어린아이들이 하나둘 1층 피아노 학원으로 들어가는 것도 보였다.

철수는 피아노 학원 문을 열었다. 문에 매달아 놓은 풍경이 투명한 소리를 냈다. 부스마다 아이들이 단풍잎 같은 손가락으로 피아노 건반을 두드리고 있었다. 한 부스에서 아이를 가르치고 있는 원장님의 목소리가 들렸다. 철수는 자신이 늘 연습하던 원장실 옆 부스로 들어갔다. 자귀나무꽃을 피아노 위에 올려두고 피아노를 연주했다. 오랜만에 하는 연주라서 실수를 좀 했지만 괜찮았다. 한창 연습하고 있는데 피아노 선생님이 들어왔다. 그녀는 못 보던 사이에 표정과 태도에서 여유가 묻어났다.

"권철수님, 오셨어요?"

"아, 네. 그동안 좀 바빠서…."

"오늘부터 다시 시작하시는 거예요?"

"네. 그간 아파트 리모델링하느라 스트레스가 많았어요. 그래서 오지 못했고요."

그는 지난 두 달간 오지 못했던 이유를 둘러댔다. 근본 이유는 숨겼다. 그녀는 의례적인 인사말뿐이었고 언제나 그렇듯이 사적인 관심은 보이지 않았다. 두 달 사이 살이 많이 빠져서 전혀 다른 모습으로 그녀 앞에 나타났는데도 그녀는 그에게 그간 무슨 일이 있었냐고 묻지 않았다. 크게 기대하지는 않았지만, 서운함이 드는 것은 어쩔 수 없었다. 그녀와 좀 더 대화하기 위해서 철수가 더 많은 말을 하며 그녀를 붙잡아야 했다.

"그동안 리모델링 업자들을 찾아다니느라 바빴어요."

"얼마가 들었는데요?"

"비용을 절감하기 위해 한 리모델링 회사에 모두 맡기지 않았어요. 제가 발품을 팔아서 부분부분 각 업자를 찾아가서 문의하고 각각 나눠서 리모델링 했지요."

"총 얼마가 들었나요?"

그녀는 비용이 얼마가 들었냐고 두 번을 반복해서 물었다. 오로지 관심은 돈에 있었다.

"그렇게 많이 들지는 않았어요. 스트레스를 받아서 살이 많이 빠졌습니다. 저 살이 많이 빠진 것 같지 않나요?"

철수는 그녀와 더 대화하기 위해 계속 질문을 이어갔다. 그녀는 자신에 대한 사적인 질문은 원하지 않았기에 철수 본인과 관련된 질문을 하며 그녀를 붙잡아야 했다.

"핼쑥해지셨어요."

"이리저리 업자들을 찾아가서 리모델링 비를 협상하고 깎아달라고 하고…이런 과정들이 기운 빠지게 하더라고요. 또 계산기 두들기고 있는 내 모습도 싫고요."

"네…."

그녀는 무언가를 그에게 말하고 싶어 하는 것 같았지만 말하지 않고 부스를 나갔다. 철수는 계속 피아노를 연습했다. 잠시 뒤 그녀가 다시 부스로 돌아왔다. 그녀는 철수에게 무언가를 말하고 싶어 했다. 철수는 아마도 학원비이겠거니 생각하고 그녀의 어려움을 덜어주기 위해 먼저 운을 띄었다.

"송 선생님, 제가 두 달 전에 등록했지만…등록을 하고도 며칠만 나왔고 그 뒤로 계속 레슨을 받지 못했기 때문에 기간을 더 연장해주었으면 해요."

"그런데, 권철수님, 레슨은 받지 못해도 레슨 받지 않은 날에 몇 번 나오셔서 연습하고 가셨잖아요."

사실 그것은 그녀를 일부러 피한 것이었다. 그녀의 남자 친구를 보았던 날, 그녀가 자신의 남자 친구와 함께 거의 매일 원장실에 같이 있었다는 것을 알고부터는 그녀를 볼 자신이 없었다. 그녀를 피하고 싶었다. 하지만 피아노를 그만둘 수는 없었기에 그녀가 없는 시간에 나와 잠시 어르신 수강생들과 연습하고 간 적이 있었다.

"권철수님, 연장은 해드리지만 다 쉬시고 오셔서 연장해 달라고 하지 마시고 다음부터는 언제 쉬시겠다고 미리 알려주세요."

아픈 것을 어떻게 예측해서 미리 말할 수 있다는 말인가. 그리고 열이 39도까지 올라갔었고 죽었다가 살아난 것은 오로지 그녀 때문이 아닌가. 그녀의 남자 친구가 원장실에서 나오는 걸 보았던 날…; 지난 몇 달간 원장실에서 들렸던 빠른 배속의 강의 소리가 원장님이 공부하는 소리가 아니라 원장님과 그녀의 남자 친구가 같이 있을 때마다 나던 소리였다는 것, 그녀가 남자 친구와 매일 원장실에 있었다는 것도 모른 채 그녀를 짝사랑하며 원장실 바로 옆 실에서 매일 아무것도 모른 채 피아노를 쳤던 자신…. 그녀에게 계속 레슨을 받기 위해 법원 직장을 퇴사해버리고 이곳에 집을 사버렸던 것, 집을 리모델링 하면서 들어간 고생과 비용….

비록 상대방이 알지 못하는 짝사랑이기에 모든 책임은 자신에게 있었지만, 지난 1년 가까이 그녀에게 피아노를 배웠는데 그에게 '정(情)'조차 가지고 있지 않은 그녀가 실망스럽고 서운했다. 그동안 그녀 때문에 벌인 자신의 실수로 마음고생이 심해 다른 사람으로 보일 정도로 살이 빠져서 나타났는데…, 자신을 짓누르는 근심을 결국 뚫고 나왔는데…. 오직 그녀를 보기 위해 모험을 감행하고 자신을 무너뜨리려고 달려드는 부정적인 감정들을 무찌르고 이 피아노 학원으로 왔는데…. 모든 역경을 뚫고 피와 땀을 흘린 남루한 용사의 모습으로 오직 그녀만을 보기 위해 달려왔는데…그녀는 그에게 사적인 관심은커녕 정(情)조차도 없었다. 그녀의 관심은 오직 수강료, 지금 등록할지 말지였다.

그녀의 레슨이 머릿속에 들어오지 않았다. 그녀의 얼굴을 처다볼 수도 없었다. 예전처럼 동경과 온전한 즐거움으로 그녀를 바라볼 수가 없었다. 아무 걱정 없이 피아노를 순순히 배웠던 그때로 돌아갈 수가 없었다. 그녀는 짧은 레슨을 마치고 "연습하세요."라는 사무적인 말만

남기고 부스를 나갔다. 철수는 연습을 좀 더 지속했지만, 내적인 동기가 생기지 않았다. 마음이 지쳐서 더는 연습할 수가 없었다.

철수는 피아노 덮개를 덮고 일어섰다. 피아노 위에 올려두었던 자귀꽃을 집어서 부스의 불을 끄고 부스 밖으로 나왔다. 학원 안은 열정을 불태우는 아이들의 연습 소리가 가득했다. 원장실의 문은 굳게 닫혀 있다. 피아노 선생님은 원장실에 있다. 그녀의 남자 친구와 함께…. 철수는 학원 문을 열고 밖으로 나왔다.

그녀는 작년 몇 개월 혹은 1년간 요양의 시기에 음악과 소통으로 철수의 건강 회복에 도움을 주었던 시절 인연이었을지도 모른다. 그저 몇 개월에서 최대 1년짜리 인연이었을지도 모른다. 작년 5개월의 병가가 끝났을 때 그는 이곳을 떠났어야 했을지도 모른다. 그것도 아니라면, 올해 초 1년의 병가가 끝났을 때 이곳을 떠났어야 했을지도 모른다. 순전한 짝사랑으로 몇 개월의 인연을 지금까지 이끌어 온 자신을 또다시 책망했다.

돌아가는 밤거리는 저녁 8시가 넘었지만, 편의점 아르바이트 후 피아노 연습을 마치고 나오던 지난 1년간의 가을, 겨울, 그리고 봄의 8시와는 달랐다. 어둑하지 않고 밝았다. 자귀나무가 있는 방향과 다른 방향으로 걸었다. 집으로 향했다. 가는 길에 어두움이 조금씩 내리고 있었다. 그는 자귀나무꽃을 코에 가져다 대었다. 이제 꽃은 생기를 조금 잃었지만, 향기는 아직도 가득하다.

010

협주곡

6월 중순. 영식은 다시 수면으로 올라왔다. 잠수함처럼 수면을 오르락내리락하고 잠수와 컴백을 반복하는 그. 혼자만의 굴속에서 오래 있자니 답답했다. 이제는 친구들을 만나 놀고 싶었다. 연우 놈은 사업하면서 화영이와 노느라 바쁠 테니 철수에게 먼저 문자를 쳤다. 연우는 내가 잠수와 컴백을 반복하는 거에 익숙해져 있지만, 철수는 처음 겪는 거라서 당황했을 것이다. 하지만 괜찮다. 철수는 착하다. 연우처럼 나를 다시 환영해 줄 것이다.

영식의 연락을 받은 철수는 기뻐했다. 영식의 생각대로 철수는 영식이 갑자기 잠적한 것에 대해 왈가불가 판단하지 않고 현재와 앞으로의 일에 대해서만 말했다.

'형님, 오늘 예술회관에서 음악회가 있습니다. 같이 가시겠습니까?'

욕망시에 거주할 때 서울 예술의 전당 소식을 받아보며 공연을 관람했던 철수는 고향에 와서도 고향 예술회관의 소식을 받아보고 있었다. 영식에게 문자로 금요일 7시 오케스트라 연주 공연 포스터를 보냈다.

'철수야, 연우도 불러라.'

'네.'

'연우야, 음악회 있다. 나와라.'

철수는 연우에게도 문자를 보냈다. 곧 답문이 왔다.

'좋죠.'

그들은 6시 30분에 예술회관에서 만나기로 했다. 한동안 영식은 잠적하였었고, 연우는 자신의 사업으로 바쁘고, 화영과 데이트 중이어서 몇 달간 셋이서 만난 적이 없었다. 그래서 영식과 철수는 이 기회를 통해 다시 세 명이 뭉칠 수 있게 되었다고 기대했다.

영식과 철수가 먼저 도착하여 예술회관 앞에서 연우를 기다리며 서 있었다.

"역시 음악이야. 음악이 우리를 묶는다니까. 연우는 오보에, 철수 너는 피아노, 난 바이올린."

"화영 씨도 오는데 좀 늦게 도착한다고 연우가 말하네요."

"연우 그놈도 화영이 만나면서 좀 허함을 느낄 거야. 화영이가 돈은 잘 벌지만, 그 애가 음악에는 젬병이거든. 그래서 우리를 알고는 음악에 관심 가지려고 스스로 노력을 하더라고. 오랜만에 우리 셋이 아니 넷이 다시 모이게 되네."

곧 연우가 좋지 않은 표정으로 예술회관 안으로 걸어 들어왔다. 막들어오려던 찰나 바람이 불었다. 바람이 한껏 멋을 낸 연우의 앞머리를 훑고 지나가며 그의 크고 넓은 이마를 드러내었다.

'연우의 이마가 저렇게 넓었었나?'

연우의 큰 야망만큼이나 이마가 참으로 넓어 철수와 영식은 순간 당황했다. 철수도 이마가 크고 넓지만, 연우의 이마도 그의 이마에 못지 않았다. 연우의 앞머리가 그의 넓은 이마를 숨기고 있었다. 연우가 자신의 큰 야망을 숨기고 있듯이.

"형님들, 화영 씨는 7시에 도착해요. 그런데 영식 형님, 일단 오늘은 화영 씨를 피하는 게 좋겠어요. 화영 씨가 지금 화가 단단히 났거든 요. 화영 씨가 그간 나와 형님을 만날 때 형님 경제적 사정을 생각해서 술값 내고, 밥값 내고, 커피값 내고 했던 건데, 형님은 그걸 '생색낸다'라고 표현하셨더라고요. 한두 번도 아니고 만날 때마다 화영 씨 돈으로 사줬는데…형님이 그렇게 공짜로 드셔놓고 '감사하다'라는 말 대신 뒤에서는 다른 사람들한테 '생색낸다'라고 표현하셔서 지금 매우 언짢아해요. 그리고 화영 씨에게 돈 빌리셨어요?"

"아니, 내가 빌린 게 아니고 화영이가 은행 계좌로 보내온 거야. 내가 아쉬운 소리 좀 했는데 화영이가 그냥 쓰라고 통장으로 돈을 보내오잖아."

"그게 다 화영 씨가 마음이 넓고 안타까운 사람들 돕고자 하는 마인드가 있어서입니다. 또 형님이 내 절친이었기도 해서 화영 씨가 아무 대가도 바라지 않았던 거고요. 그렇게 화영 씨에게 도움을 받고 뒤에서는 '생색낸다'라고 말하고 다녀서 화영 씨로서는 배신감이 컸을 거예요. 화영 씨가 요즘 형님에게 실망하고 또 단단히 화가 난 상태인데 당분간 형님은 화영 씨를 만나지 않는 게 좋을 것 같아요."

"아니, 너도 알다시피 화영이는 돈 쓰는 걸 즐기잖아. 마음이 넓고 돕는 것을 좋아해서가 아니지. 자신이 돈을 쓰고 싶으면 그냥 쓰면 될 것을 그 대가로 자신이 꼭 추앙받으려고 하잖아. 추앙해주는 것도 한 두 번이지 그거 얼마나 힘든지 알아? 나 화영이 추앙 많이 해줬다. 이젠 하기 싫어. 넌 지금 그 여자에게 홀딱 빠져서 추앙하는 걸 밥 먹듯이 하고 있지만 우리는 화영이 애인도 아니고 팬도 아니잖아. 추앙해주는 것도 한두 번이지…지친다고."

"그런데, 연우야, 늘 바쁘다고 하더니 오늘은 어쩐 일로 이렇게 우리의 부름에 응답했어?" 조용히 듣고 있던 철수가 물었다.

"사실, 그간 화영 씨가 어느 라인에 설 거냐고 정하라고 해서…. 내가 화영 씨더러 좀 늦게 나오라고 한 것은 영식 형님 아무것도 모르고 화영 씨 마주치게 되면 당황하실 것도 같고. 화영 씨가 벼르고 있어서 상황이 참 난처해질 것 같아서요. 일단 영식 형님은 피하는 게 좋겠어요."

"뭐? 화영이 그년이 어느 라인에 설 거냐고 널 다그쳤다는 거지?" 잠시 잠잠하던 영식이 화를 냈다.

"형님도 알다시피 제가 요즘 시작한 사업으로 바쁘기도 하고…. 앞으로 몇 달간 더 형님을 만날 수가 없게 됐어요." 연우는 예술회관 입구와 철수와 영식을 번갈아 보며 말했다.

"앗! 저기 화영 씨가 와요."

예술회관 입구를 초조하게 바라보며 말하던 연우가 다급하게 소리쳤다. 철수와 영식은 연우가 바라보는 방향을 쳐다보았다. 저 멀리서 사람들 사이에 긴 생머리를 늘어뜨리고 하늘거리는 원피스를 입은 사십 대 초반의 여자가 보였다. 이때 영식은 사채업자를 피하듯 어딘가로 부리나케 사라졌다. 그 모습은 마치 두려운 누군가를 피해 도망가는 남자 같았다. 그때 연우가 도망치는 영식의 뒷모습을 향해 다시 소리쳤다.

"형님, 당분간 연락하지 말자고요."

그리고 그의 앞에 서 있는 철수에게 말했다.

"형님. 저 화영 씨에게 가볼게요. 일 때문에 바빠서 앞으로 당분간 형님과도 못 만날 것 같아요."

이 말을 남기고 연우 또한 사람들 사이로 사라졌다. 철수는 그곳에 혼자 남겨졌다. 두 남자가 화영의 등장과 함께 사라진 것이다. 수많은 사람 가운데 그들의 모습은 보이지 않았다. 영식도. 연우도, 화영도⋯. 얼마나 지났을까. 홀로 그곳에 서 있던 철수는 영식에게 전화를 걸었다.

"형님, 어디에 계십니까?"

"근처 마트에 숨어있다. 화영이 갔냐?"

"모르겠습니다. 형님도 사라졌고, 연우도 화영 씨도 지금 어디에 있는지 모르겠습니다. 다시 오셔서 같이 연주 공연 보시죠."

영식은 택시를 타고 예술회관으로 돌아왔고 그들은 대강당의 지정 좌석에 앉았다. 그들의 눈은 오케스트라의 공연을 바라보고 있었지만 그들의 정신은 이 음악회를 떠나 많은 상념 사이를 서성이고 있었다.

음악회가 끝나고 그들은 철수의 아파트 앞에 즐비한 맥줏집 중 한 곳으로 들어갔다. 이번에는 철수가 원한 것이 아니었다. 영식이 가자고 했다. 영식은 자신과 10년을 동고동락하며 많은 것을 공유하며 살아온 연우가 자신에게 작별을 고한 것에 큰 실망과 배신감을 느꼈다. 동네 깡패 같은 그녀가 연우에게 어느 라인에 설 거냐고 다그치며 영식에게 선을 긋고 정리하라고 했다는 말을 들었을 때 치를 떨었다. 자신이 갑자기 잠적하고 다시 전화해도 늘 반갑게 맞아주던 연우가, 착한 것 빼면 시체였던 연우가 그 늙은 여우를 만나 자신에게 점점 소원해지더니…, 연락할 때마다 일 핑계를 대고 거리를 두더니…, 이제는 당분간 연락하지 말라고 통보까지 하고 갔을 때 영식은 연우에게 큰 배신감을 느꼈다. 홍화영처럼 영악해지는 연우가 아쉬웠다. 하지만 어쩔 수 없다. 연우는 아직 젊고 결혼을 해야 한다. 자신 같은 시커먼 형들이나 만나고 다니기에는 아까운 면이 있기는 하다. 연우를 위해서도 잘 되었다고 생각하지만, 그 배신감은 이루 말할 수가 없었다. 영식은 말없이 맥주만 마셔댔다.

"철수야, 한 잔 더 시켜주라."

영식은 철수가 다시 주문한 생맥주를 또다시 벌컥벌컥 마셔댔다. 나이는 제일 많은데 동생들에게 항상 얻어먹고 다녀 스스로가 비참하고 동생들에게 미안하기는 하지만 괜찮다. 철수는 좋은 동생이다. 정이 많고 마음이 착한 동생이다. 영식은 한동안 맥주잔만 비우다가 드디어 입을 열었다.

"철수야, 오늘이 마지막이다."

"잠수 깨고 나온 지 하루 만에 또 잠적하신다고요?"

"너를 위해서도 나를 위해서도 더는 안 만나는 게 좋겠다."

"연우도 떠나버리고 형님도 또 떠나시면 전 이곳에 집도 사버렸는데 혼자서 외로워서 어떻게 삽니까."

"내가 촉이 좀 좋은데, 너 이제 곧 결혼할 것 같다. 하나님이 너 결혼시키려고 집을 사게 한 거 같다."

"오십 평생을 독신으로 살아왔는데 젊었을 때도 없던 일이 늙어서 생길까요?"

"넌 다이아몬드야. 다이아몬드가 뭐냐! 지하 150~200㎞의 지각층에서 순수한 탄소가 극도의 고열과 압력을 받아 형성된 거잖아. 나 20대의 권철수를 지금도 기억한다. 대학 시절 그 20대의 순수한 탄소 덩어리 권철수가 대학을 졸업하고 세상에서 얼마나 억압받고 상처받고 살았냐! 꿈과 야망도 컸던 젊은 권철수가 이상과 현실 사이에서 얼마나 아파하고 방황했었니! 지난 24년간 너 공부 얼마나 많이 했니! 꿈과 야망을 향해 달리면서도 돈도 차곡차곡 모아서 집도 샀잖아. 난 아버지 집에서 기둥뿌리 몇 개는 뽑아갔는데 넌 혼자 자력으로 살았잖아. 지금은 살도 다 빠지고, 리즈 시절 권철수로 다시 돌아왔어. 너 요새 완전히 딴 사람 됐다고."

"고마워요. 앞으로 이곳에서 친구들도 많이 사귀고 과거와는 다르게 살아야지요."

"너 아까부터 외롭다고 친구를 더 많이 사귀어야겠다고 나한테 줄곧 말하는데…나 서운한 게 있어. 난 너 친구 아니냐? 무시하는 거니? 그저 술 먹을 때 만나고 고기 먹을 때 만나는 술친구, 고기 친구일 뿐인 거냐?"

"아니요, 형님. 오해하셨습니다. 두세 번 만나고 나서는 그만 만나는 게 좋겠다고 먼저 선을 긋고 이별 통보를 하시는 분은 늘 형님이셨습니다. 형님은 만날 때마다 이별 통보를 하시지요. 그리고 갑자기 핸드폰 번호를 바꾸어 버려서 우리를 당황하게 하고 몇 달이 지나서 또 형님이 먼저 연락해 오시고 잠시 우리와 즐겁게 지내시다가 또 연락을 두절하고 핸드폰 번호를 바꾸고 잠적하시고. 형님에게 안정감이 느껴지지 않는다는 겁니다. 형님이 자꾸 잠적하니 제가 외로워서 새 친구들을 사귀고 싶다고 한 것이지 형님의 존재를 무시해서 그런 건 절대 아닙니다. 오늘도 저 만나시면서 계속 오늘이 마지막이라고 하시잖아요."

"하루살이 인생이라서 그래. 내일 일을 모르거든…. 하나님도 내일 일을 자랑하지 말라고 하잖아. 우리가 돈과 먹을 것을 창고에 쌓아놓고 평생 먹을 것 있다고 안심할 때 하나님이 오늘 밤 네 생명을 거둬가면 어떡할래? 라고 퀘스천을 던지잖아."

"형님, 아까부터 하나님 얘기하시는데 교회 다니십니까?"

"저번에 잠수타면서 다니게 됐다. 의지할 데가 없더라고. 난 탕자의 인생이었지. 허랑방탕하게 내 젊음과 내 아버지의 재산을 낭비해 버리고 돌아온 탕자 말이야."

"형님만 탕자이겠습니까? 우리 모두 다 어떤 면에서는 탕자이지요."

"네가 왜? 넌 도덕적으로 깨끗하게 살았고 사회적으로도 근면하게 살았잖아."

"아무리 도덕적으로 살고 근면하게 살아도 열매가 없고 후회만 있다면 인생을 허비한 것이니 탕자이지 않을까요? 중요한 것이 무엇인지 알지 못한 채 그저 열심히만 살았죠. 어느새 보니 나이 들어버리고…
청춘은 사라지고…뒤돌아보니 저도 중요하지 않은 것에 젊음과 돈, 건
강을 허비해 버린 탕자처럼 느껴집니다."

"우리는 다 하루살이 인생이야. 내일 일을 알 수 없어. 연우 그놈도
봐봐. 나 연우랑 10년 친구다. 서울대 법대 향우회 모임에서 연우를
처음 보게 된 후로 연우와 나는 단짝 친구였어. 소울 메이트 였지. 형
아우 하면서 거의 매일 만나고 모든 걸 허심탄회하게 이야기하고 살았
는데 오늘 하루 만에 이별 통보하고 더는 자기에게 연락하지 말라 하
고 떠나버리잖아. 나 어제저녁 잠수 깨고 나와서 연우에게 전화했었
지. 어제만 해도 서로 전화 통화했던 사이였는데 걔가 오늘 와서 이별
통보를 할 줄 누가 알았겠냐? 뭐, 화영이 그 여우가 시킨 거겠지만. 그
놈 많이 컸어. 너무 커버려서 내가 해줄 것이 더는 없다. 그놈이 우리
를 버리고 가버렸지. 뭐, 사실, 우정이 뭐가 중요하냐? 나이가 찼으니
사랑이 중요하지. 사랑 찾아간 것이지… 아니, 사랑 속에 감춰진 지
야망을 따라간 거지. …사실 나도 그러고 싶지 않아…. …잠적하고 싶
지 않다고. 내가 나이만 너희들보다 형이지…돈이 없잖아. 노부모 밑
에서 용돈 받고 사는 내가 무슨 돈이 있겠어. 얻어먹는 것도 한두 번
이지. 미안해서 그랬어."

영식은 잠시 말을 멈추었다. 철수는 비어 있는 영식의 잔을 채워주
었다.

"형님, 시절 인연이라는 게 있는 거 같아요. 연우는 우리와 십년지기
친구였지만…; 이제 우리를 떠나는 걸 보니 배움이 다 끝났나 봐요.

연우는 이제 우리가 아니라 화영 씨가 필요한 거죠."

"시절 인연⋯?"

"우리에게 또 다른 인연이 올 거예요. 서로 배움을 주고받고 성장하기 위해서 말이죠."

"연우는 날 이용하고 떠났어. 너도 날 이용하고 떠날 거냐?"

"형님, 이용이라니요? 서로에게 배우는 거지요. 서로 성장하는 거고요. 형님이 떠나지 않으면, 떠날 일은 없습니다."

"너도 이제 집을 샀으니 어서 마누라 구해. 장가가. 나는 독신으로 살 거야. 잠깐, 그러고 보니 너 집도 사놓고 살도 빼고 마누라들일 준비를 다 하고 있었구먼. 지금 네 친형 편의점 사업 도와주고 있잖아. 너도 친형에게서 잘 배워서 조만간 네 사업처 하나 마련해 독립할 것이고. 너 퇴직하면서 법 관련 일은 더는 하고 싶지 않다고 했지만, 사업하는데 너의 법 지식은 유용하게 쓰일 거야. 좋겠다. 성공하겠네. 여자 생기는 건 시간문제이구먼. 부럽다⋯."

"형님, 오늘은 저에게 좋은 말씀만 하시네요. 고맙습니다."

영식은 이제 술이 거나하게 취했다.

"넌 이 지방에 집을 샀다고 아쉬워하지만, 이 집은 너의 인생의 성적표야. 네가 인생을 헛살지 않고 성실히 살아왔다는 성적표 말이야."

"그렇게 말씀해 주시니 감사합니다."

"넌 열매가 많아. 너의 법 지식, 이 집, 네가 연주하는 피아노 실력⋯ 피아노 치는 남자는 여자들에게 인기 있단다. 그리고 외모도 너의 리즈 시절로 돌아왔고⋯."

인생의 열매가 많다는 말에 철수는 눈물이 핑 돌았다.

"형님!" 잠시 말을 멈추었던 영식이 철수를 향해 말했다.

"갑자기 형님이라니요? 취하셨네요."

"존경스러워서."

순간 철수의 마음이 따뜻해졌다. 고통과 고생으로 배불렀던 자신의 지난 삶이 치유되고 보상받은 느낌이었다.

그날 밤 영식은 택시를 타고 집으로 돌아가기 전에 철수에게 다시 "형님"이라고 불렀다. 그리고 집으로 돌아와 문자 하나를 남겼다.

'이제 서로 연락하지 말자.'

홍화영. 연우보다 6살 연상인 그녀는 긴 원피스를 즐겨 입고 긴 생머리를 풀고 다니며 나약한 여자의 이미지를 풍기지만, 그녀의 성격은 달랐다. 끊고 맺음이 분명하지 않고, 어떻게 헤어졌든지 상대에게서 연락이 오면 늘 만나주는 연우와는 달리 단호하고 강단이 있었다. 자신에 대해 포장하기를 잘했고 돈을 쓰는 것을 즐겼고 추앙받는 것을 즐겼다. 영식의 말대로 여자이지만 골목대장 같고 카리스마가 있었다. 연우는 화영이 화려한 언변으로 자신을 멋지게 포장하는 모습이 좋았다. 그녀는 늘 많은 사업가를 만나느라 바빴다. 연우는 늘 운전하며 그녀의 매니저를 자청해 그녀를 따라다녔다. 그녀를 따라다니며 경험하는 일들은 그에게 신세계였다. 그녀로 인해 넓어지는 인맥에 설레었다. 매주 다양한 모임에 참석했고, 새로운 인맥들과 캠핑 가고 여행을 갔다. 형님들과는 기껏해야 고깃집과 술집, 분식집, 편의점과 국밥집을 떠도는데 그녀와는 화려하고 비싼 레스토랑과 와인바에 갔다. 또 그곳에서 부유한 새로운 인맥들을 만났다. 영식과 철수와 어울릴 때 와는 확연히 다른 신세계였다. 그의 또래나 어린 여자들도 줄 수 없는 세계였다. 연우는 그녀를 놓칠 수가 없었다. 그녀가 나이가 많은 것도 괜찮았다. 어차피 그는 또래나 연하의 여자들에게는 인기가 없었다. 그는 외모 꾸미기에 서툴고 살까지 쪄서 자신의 나이로 보이지 않고 열 살 이상 더 많아 보였기에 외모에 달관하고 살았다. 또한 늘 중년의 형들과 어울리고 다니기에 사람들은 그를 삼십 대로 보지 않고 중년 의 형들과 또래로 생각했다.

화영이 연우에게 물었다. 누구 라인에 서겠냐고. 자신을 선택할 것 인지 아니면 형들을 선택할 것인지 확실히 하라고 했다. 그녀를 놓칠 수는 없었다. 그녀는 그에게 기회였다. 두 형들과 지난 10년간 어울리 면서 그들을 반면교사 삼아 그들이 후회하는 것들을 새겨들었고 그들 이 선택한 인생과 다르게 살아왔다. 그리고 지금은 화영을 통해 알게 된 새로운 사람들과만 만나기에도 시간이 부족했다. 화영이 싫어하는 두 형들을 계속 만나며 그녀의 화를 돋우어 그녀를 놓치면 안 되었다. 전에는 화영의 눈을 피해 형들을 만나곤 했지만, 이제는 확실하게 선 을 그어야 했다.

011

피아노 치는 남자와
자귀나무꽃

7월 하순. 7월 내내 내리던 비가 잠시 멈추고 해가 구름 사이로 얼굴을 내밀었다. 철수는 편의점 아르바이트를 마치고 자귀나무가 있는 곳으로 향했다. 여름 동안 지속된 장마로 공기는 축축하고 습도는 높았다.

한동안 이곳에 오지 않았었다. 매년 여름 6월부터 8월까지 세 달간 개화하며 향기롭고 강렬한 향기를 터뜨리는 신비로운 여름 나무. 작년에는 더위의 열기 속에 이곳만 지나면 자귀나무꽃향이 가득했는데 올해는 향기가 없다. 몇 달간 지속된 장마로 자귀나무꽃들이 아름다움과 향을 뿜어내지도 못하고 빗줄기에 떨어져 어디론가 쓸려갔기 때문이다. 자귀나무는 꽃이 거의 사라지고 푸른 잎사귀로 무성했다. 길바닥에는 오래전에 떨어진 꽃 몇 송이가 하얗게 퇴색되어 말라가고 있었다. 철수는 아직 싱싱한 자귀나무꽃 몇 송이를 주웠다. 빗물에 축 늘어져 있었다. 코끝으로 가져갔다. 향기롭다. 자귀나무가 있는 곳에서 피아노 학원이 있는 방향을 바라보았다. 작년 이맘때의 추억이 떠오른다.

작년 2월, 쉼 없이 달려오던 그의 삶이 자신을 위해 달려주던 자가용이 멈춘 것처럼 한순간에 멈춰버렸다. 육체적으로는 뇌경색 진단을 받았고 정신적으로는 우울증과 무기력, 공허함, 인생무상 등 삶의 회한에 빠져 이 도시를 요양차 방문했다.

6월의 첫날 아침, 우연히 발견한 피아노 학원, 그리고 피아노 선생님을 처음 만났을 때 그녀의 모습. 그는 그 만남이 자신을 어디로 데려갈 것인지 그때는 알 수 없었다. 무더운 여름, 피아노 선생님을 볼 생각에 마음 설레며 걸었던 이 길. 언젠가부터 이 길을 걸을 때마다 은은하고 신비한 향기가 났다. 늘 그 향기가 어디서 나는지 궁금했다. 유난히도 향기가 강하던 7월 중순 어느 날, 드디어 발걸음을 멈추고 뒤돌아보았다. 이 향기가 어디서 나는 것일까. 향기를 따라가다 발견한 자귀나무. 조금 더 걸으면 곧 피아노 선생님을 볼 수 있다는 설렘에 신비스럽고 강한 자귀나무꽃 향까지 더해져 가슴이 터질듯하고 현기증이 나서 쓰러질 것 같았다. 그때 얼마나 행복했던가! 얼마나 설레었던가! 학원 가는 길이 얼마나 향기로웠던가! 꿈꾸는 것 같았다. 결국, 자귀나무꽃향이 가장 강렬하던 그때, 8월부터 복직하라는 콜링을 고사했다. 그리고 일 년이 지났고 철수는 아예 퇴직하고 다시 이 자귀나무 아래에 서 있다.

작년처럼 이 향기를 마음껏 맡으며 설렘과 낭만 속에서 이 길을 다시 걷고 싶지만 더는 그럴 수 없다. 인간의 삶은 어떤 면에서 영식 형의 말대로 하루살이 인생일지도 모른다. 내일 일을 알 수 없다. 예측했던 미래가 한순간에 어긋나기도 한다. 그는 자귀나무꽃을 코끝으로 가져갔다. 1년 전의 그때처럼 자귀나무 아래에서 향기를 마셨다. 올해는 장마로 자귀 꽃이 많이 져서 향기가 약했지만, 작년 이맘때의 향기, 설렘, 두근거림…그때의 감정은 지금도 여전하다.

1년 전의 그와 1년이 지난 지금의 그는 달라져 있다. 체중은 많이 감소하여 정상 체중이 되었고 뇌경색은 치료가 되었다. 정서적으로 힘들게 했던 우울증과 무기력도 많이 사라졌다.

그때 모르는 번호로 장문의 문자가 왔다. 영식이었다.

'철수야, 잘 지내? 여전히 집 때문에 술 마시면서 힘들어하는 건 아니지? 네가 첫 주택을 마련한 곳이 너의 꿈의 도시였던 서울은 아니지만 그런 꿈이 있었기에 이 지방에라도 집을 마련하게 됐다고 생각해. 그린 후에 보니 호랑이가 아니라 고양이였다고 너무 실망하지 말고. 혹시 아니? 이 경험이 발판이 되어 네가 건물을 사서 건물주가 될 수도 있는 거고, 땅을 살 수도 있는 거고. 이 집이 어쩌면 너의 첫 시작이 될 수도 있어. 미래는 모르는 거니까 너무 부정적으로 생각하지 마. 그리고 나, 집 앞 마트에서 계산원 아르바이트 시작했어. 나도 변해야겠더라고. 처음으로 남 밑에서 일해보는 거지만 재미있어. 이제 너희들에게 얻어만 먹지 않고 형답게 살 수 있게 됐다. 화영이가 빌려준 돈도 절반은 갚았지. 화영이 계좌로 이체시켰어. 다음 월급 타면 나머지도 계좌이체 시켜야지.'

철수는 기쁜 마음으로 바로 영식에게 전화했다.

"형님, 저녁으로 같이 국밥 먹을까요?"

"좋지."

영식은 바로 택시를 타고 나왔다. 철수는 자귀나무 아래에서 주운 자귀 꽃 몇 송이를 왼손가락으로 집고 나타났다. 그 꽃을 처음 본 영식이 물었다.

"그거 뭐야?"

"꽃이에요."

"꽃 같지 않은 꽃이네."

"사랑 같지 않은 사랑, 짝사랑도 사랑이지요."

"뭐라고?"

"길에서 주웠어요."

"꽃이 아무리 이뻐도 줍고 그러지 마. 꽃가루 알레르기 증상이 일어날 수 있어."

"네."

그렇게 말하고는 철수는 다시 한번 꽃을 코에 가까이 대고 향기를 맡았다. 여전히 향기롭다. 식당에서 국밥을 먹고 있는데 영식의 전화가 울렸다. 영식이 스피커를 켜고 받아서 수화기 너머로 연우의 목소리가 들렸다. 통화를 끝마치자 철수가 물었다.

"연우와도 다시 연락하는 거예요?"

"응. 너에게 문자 보냈을 때 연우에게도 같이 보냈어."

"같이 저녁 먹자고 부르지 그랬어요?"

"선약이 있대."

"누구와요?"

"화영이."

"화영 씨가 옆에 있는데도 형에게 전화했다는 것은 화영 씨가 형에게 화가 좀 풀렸다는 의미일 것예요."

"화영이가 빌려준 돈 절반을 갚았거든. 우리 밥 먹고 어디 갈까?"

"우리 집으로 갈까요?"

"좋지. 연우 놈이 있었으면 독한 향수 냄새로 국밥 맛이 안 났을 텐데 그놈이 없으니 국밥이 맛있다, 야. 국밥집은 향수가 안 어울려. 하하하. 그놈은 여자들이 좋아하는 고급 레스토랑에서 화영이와 향수 뿜어내며 스파게티 먹으라고 해. 하하하."

철수와 영식은 오랜만에 호탕하게 서로를 바라보며 웃었다. 입에서 먹었던 밥알들이 튀어나왔다. 그 모습이 웃겨서 그들은 또 웃었다. 식사를 마치고 철수는 식당 테이블 위에 올려놓았던 자귀 꽃을 조심스럽게 집어 들고는 식당을 나왔다.

"그 꽃 이제 시들었지?"

"아직 괜찮아요."

"이리 줘봐."

철수는 자귀나무꽃을 영식에게 건네주었다. 영식은 꽃향기를 맡았다.

"이거, 향기가 좋네. 아직 향기가 살아있어."

철수는 영식에게서 꽃을 받아 다시 왼손가락으로 집고 길을 걸었다. 그때 누군가의 손이 꽃을 집고 있던 그의 손등을 스치며 치고 빠르게 지나갔다. 그 반동으로 철수는 꽃을 떨어뜨렸다.

"어!"

철수는 당황했다. 길바닥 위에 떨어져 흩어진 자귀나무꽃들을 보고 있자니 마음이 아려왔다. 불안해졌다. 그는 반사적으로 한쪽 무릎을 세우고 앉아서 떨어진 꽃들을 한 송이씩 조심스럽게 주웠다. 지나가면서 철수의 손등을 자신의 손등으로 친 여성이 자신이 실수한 것을 알고 바로 뒤돌아보았다. 그녀는 길바닥에 떨어진 꽃들을 하나씩 조심스럽게 집어 들고 있는 철수를 미안한 표정으로 바라보았다. 철수에게 미안하다고 말하고 싶었지만, 철수는 당황하여 꽃을 줍는 데만 정신이 팔려있어 대신 철수 옆에 서 있는 영식에게 연신 어깨와 허리를 굽히며 미안하다고 말했다.

"야, 야, 이제 시들었으니 버려라. 버려!"

옆에 있던 영식이 철수에게 소리치면서도 그녀에게 너그럽고 환하게 미소를 지으며 연신 "괜찮습니다."라고 말했다. 그제야 그녀는 뒤돌아서서 그녀가 가던 길을 갔다. 꽃을 다 주운 철수도 일어났다. 철수와 영식은 다시 걷기 시작했다. 몇 보 더 앞에서 걷고 있는 그녀의 뒷모습을 보며 영식이 말했다.

"저 여자가 미안하다고 했어. 네가 꽃을 줍는데 정신이 팔려있어서 대신 나에게 사과하더라."

"그렇군요."

앞에서 빠른 걸음으로 자기 길을 걸어가고 있던 그녀는 이제 철수와 영식의 시야에서 사라졌다. 철수와 영식은 천천히 걸었다. 저녁이 되니 더위는 사라지고 날씨는 선선하고 좋았다.

"여름 장마가 이제 거의 다 끝났다고 하더라."

"일기예보 보니 앞으로는 자주 맑은 날을 볼 수 있을 거라고 하더군요."

　날씨 이야기를 하며 걷는데 앞에서 철수의 손등을 스치며 치고 지나
간 여성이 한 카페 앞에서 그녀의 친구와 이야기하며 서 있었다. 영식
과 철수는 천천히 계속 걸었고 그녀들에게 점차 가까워져 갔다. 그녀
들과의 거리가 점차 좁혀지자 영식이 갑자기 호들갑을 떨기 시작했다.

　"야, 이거 역사가 이루어지는 순간 아니냐? 소설이 한 편 만들어지
는 순간이야. 남자가 우연히 자신의 꽃을 박살 낸 여자와 사랑에 빠지
다! 캬~!!"

　영식의 호들갑이 당혹스럽고 시끄러웠지만, '남자의 꽃을 박살 내다'
라는 표현이 웃겨서 철수는 웃음을 터트렸다. 그때 카페 앞에 서 있던
그 여성이 철수 앞으로 다가왔다. 철수와 영식은 걸음을 멈추었다.

　"아까는 죄송했어요. 소중한 꽃인 것 같은데 조심히 간수 하셔야겠
어요."

　"아닙니다. 저의 실수였습니다. 꽃을 앞에 두고 걸었어야 했는데
요…."

　"숙녀분들, 죄송하시면 커피 한 잔 사세요. 여기 바로 카페가 있네
요." 옆에서 그들의 모습을 보고 있던 영식이 끼어들었다. 영식은 그
두 여성이 마음에 들었다. 둘 중 한 명이라도, 아니 철수의 손등을 스
치고 간 여성은 철수와 그리고 그 여성의 친구는 자신과 잘 되었으면
좋겠다는 생각이 스쳤다. 이 기회를 놓치고 싶지 않아 적극적으로 말
을 걸었다.

　"아니, 제가 사겠습니다. 죄송하시면 커피 한 잔씩들 마시고 가세

요." 영식은 적극적으로 그녀들에게 다가가 활짝 미소를 지어 보이며 그의 손을 카페 쪽으로 펼쳤다. 그녀들은 웃으면서 순순히 카페로 앞서 들어갔고 철수와 영식도 경쾌하게 뒤따라 들어갔다.

작가의 말

　작년 겨울 12월 어느 날, 학교 기말고사 출제와 시험 관련 일들로 정신없이 바쁜 나날을 보낸 후 한숨 돌리기 위해 학교 도서관에 갔습니다. 책장에 꽂힌 부피가 큰 책들 사이로 아주 작고 얇은 책 하나가 눈에 띄었습니다. 그 책은 단편소설이었고 영어 번역과 같이 출간된 책이었습니다. 또한 어느 도의 문화재단에 선정되어 지원받아 출간한 소설이었습니다. 전 그 당시 한 친구에게 전남문화재단 소설 분야에 도전해보라는 격려를 받았었는데, 이 작은 책과의 우연한 만남으로 저도 국가문화예술지원시스템에 선정되면 한영 소설을 창작해서 출간해야겠다는 생각을 마음에 품었습니다. 그리고 선정되었습니다.

　책 쓰기에 집중하기 위해 집필실을 마련하고 마음을 정하여 아침에 일어나면 집필실과 카페로 가서 매일 6시간에서 10시간을 집중하며 창작과 번역에 몰두했습니다. 올해 2023년은 전업 작가의 길을 걸어보았습니다. 집중에 방해되지 않고 책상에 오래 앉아 글을 쓰기 위해 하루 글쓰기와 번역이 끝나고 나서야 비로소 저녁에 첫 끼를 먹고 휴식 시간을 가졌습니다. 참으로 힘든 나날이었습니다. 이제는 꿈처럼 지나간 날들이지만 이렇게 노력의 결실을 보게 되어 뿌듯하고 기쁘게 생각합니다. 그리고 하나님께 감사드립니다. 모든 것을 보고 계시는 신의 눈에는 그런 나의 수고로운 날들이 어쩌면 빛나 보이지 않았을까 하는 생각도 듭니다. 많이 읽어주시고 감동을 나눠주시기를 바랍니다.

그리고 하늘나라에 있는 나의 사랑하는 토끼 사랑이와 행복이, 그들의 자손들, 또 지금까지 나를 거쳐 간 과거의 모든 동물 친구들 - 병아리들, 닭들, 새들, 햄스터들, 고양이들, 강아지들, 개들, 토끼들, 등 - 에게 미안함과 사랑을 담아 보냅니다. 그들의 영혼에 하나님의 축복이 가득하기를…. 그리고 어딘가에 살아있는 사랑이와 행복이의 자손들에게 하나님의 사랑과 돌봄이 가득하기를….

2023년 11월 가을
정민주

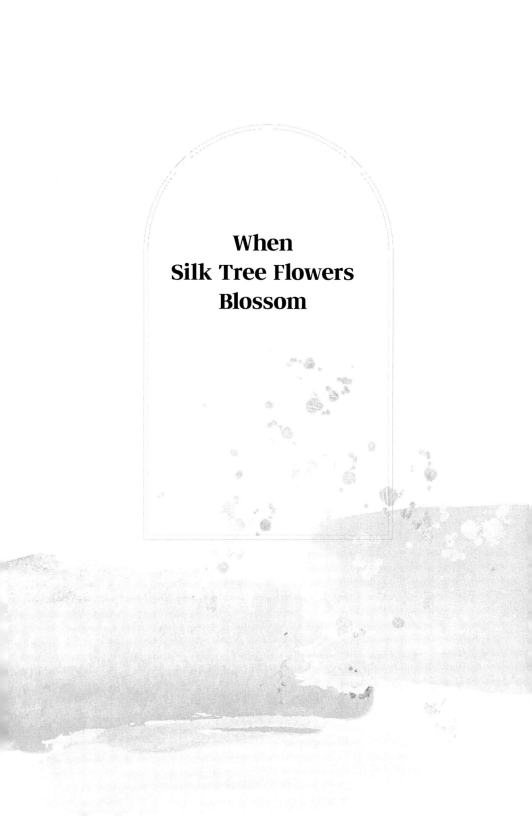

When
Silk Tree Flowers
Blossom

001

A Stalled Car

One Saturday morning in February, Cheol-su Kwon placed his laptop and the work-related documents he had examined until late at night the previous day, on the passenger seat of his used car and then he sat in the driver's seat. Ipchun[5] had passed, but it was still as cold as the middle of winter, and he blew his cold hands with warm air from his mouth and started the engine. The engine didn't start. There had been times like this. After two or three attempts, it started and ran well, so he tried to do so again that day too. However, after several more attempts, he still couldn't get the car running. The used car that had been running for him for the past decade now completely got to stop.

He didn't know at that time that his life, which he barely managed to lead, would also stop for a while like his car. He phoned a used car dealer. Then he crammed into his bag review reports and draft verdicts of already finished cases which were piled up on the back seat of his car, along with documents of ongoing

---

[5] The onset of spring according to the lunar calendar but still cold.

cases. Law-related books that had been placed on the back seat for years, and for months were also put in the bag. He carried a laptop and his heavy bag on both shoulders and went to his studio and spilled them on the floor.

"What a mess!"

Looking at the documents, books, and a laptop spilled on the floor of his studio, he just blurted that word out. After selecting only the review report and draft ruling documents of the ongoing case, he put them in his bag. He left the studio with his bag and laptop carried on his shoulders. Soon the used car trader arrived and Cheol-su went through the process of selling his car. He completed the process of transferring his car ownership in the vehicle registration department of city hall in Desire city, Gyeonggi Province, where he had lived.

He went to the nearest station by taxi to take the subway. Cheol-su, who didn't like to walk even though it was a 10-minute walk, drove his own car or took a taxi for a short distance. He took the subway to Seoul Nat'l Univ. of Education Station, where the Seoul Central District Court was located. There were no seats on the subway. He put down his bags on the subway floor and sighed and once again uttered "What a mess!" Starting at some point Cheol-su had always thought his life was a mess. It was a pity that his used car, which had been running well for 10 years, stopped today. It was also regrettable that he spent all his precious morning on that Saturday in the processes of finding a used car dealer and selling his car.

Cheol-su, who was working as a judicial researcher at Desire branch of Suwon District Court in Desire city, drove to Seoul in his car once or twice a month on weekends. Among others, visiting Seocho-gu, where the Supreme Court, the Seoul Central District Court, and the Seoul Arts Center were located, had been his habit for a few years. When he visited Seocho-gu, he did his work at cafes near the Supreme Court or the Seoul Central District Court. He also regularly received news from the Seoul Arts Center and came to see interesting art performances. But today, he sold his own car, so he transferred subway lines and arrived at Seoul Nat'l Univ. of Education station. He stood on the subway for over an hour with a fat body weighing over 120kg[6] and was extremely exhausted from having to walk with his bags on his both shoulders. Although Ipchun came, the wind chill temperature was still low as if it were in the middle of winter. He was sweating even in this cold.

As soon as he got out of Seoul Nat'l. Univ of Education station, he breathed in the surrounding air. Whenever Cheol-su visited

---

[6]   about 265lb

this place, his job stress accumulated during the week was relieved and he felt spirited and alive. He felt a little emotional healing and pride when he came to Seoul, the city of his dreams and ambitions, and Seocho-gu, a wealthy neighborhood where Korea's two representative courts and the Seoul Arts Center were located. And he vowed to become a Seoul citizen and live in this high class neighborhood one day.

The area around the cafe he often visited was a place where shopping malls, restaurants, and cafes were concentrated. Although there was a traffic light at a crosswalk, there was a risk of accidents on weekends because too many people and vehicles came and went. Part-timers were hired there on week-ends to reduce the risk of traffic accidents. They organized the flow of vehicles and people with LED signal traffic wands so that vehicles and people could pass smoothly without colliding with each other. They had been replaced a lot. But for the past four seasons, Cheol-su saw a skinny male part-timer every time he visited here, thinking the man was probably the longest working part-timer. In summer, he worked, perspiring in a wide-brimmed hat under the hot sun. On rainy days he worked in a raincoat in the rain. Now in the cold winter, he was organizing traffic, wearing a thick blue parka and a navy fur hat. The young man looked as expressionless as usual that day too. He stopped the people with a LED traffic baton so that vehicles could pass by. When a lot of people gathered at the traffic light, he stopped vehicles by giving signals with his traffic baton. Then he went to the center of the crosswalk, stretched out his baton to the side, blew a whistle loudly and signaled people to pass.

Cheol-su came here without a car that day, so the area around Seoul Nat'l Univ. of Education station was unfamiliar. He would often get lost. Each time this happened, he returned to this crosswalk to start all over again. The crosswalk served as a benchmark for his direction.

After crossing the crosswalk, he entered his favorite cafe. Soft piano music was playing gently in the background. Young women glanced at Cheol-su, who was immersed in something alone, sweating even in the middle of winter. It seemed unique to them that he was typing something while studying hard alone in a noisy cafe with the sound of chatter. Well, it wasn't anything special. It was not just first or second time. It happened often, so he ignored their gazes and continued to focus, but it was uncomfortable to continue sitting down on that day. His body was incredibly tired and he broke out in a cold sweat. Eventually, he couldn't concentrate on his work any more and left the cafe.

He stopped at the crowded crosswalk. The traffic light changed from red to green. The skinny young man holding the LED traffic baton stretched it to his side and blew the whistle. The crowd began to stampede. Cheol-su also walked in the crowd, but he gradually lost his strength. He couldn't walk properly. He barely slipped by. The skinny young man noticed him, who crossed this crosswalk several times in the afternoon of that day. He was annoyed by this fat middle-aged man, who was still walking slowly even after a long time after pedestrians had passed by and the light had turned red. The cars that stopped at the crosswalk began to honk. Until this fat middle-aged man arrived at the sidewalk, the thin young man gave him a disapproving look and spat out a word.

"What a nut job!"

The young man blew his whistle loudly, and soon the cars began to speed and run frightfully. Cheol-su thought he might look like a nut job, so he ignored what the young man said and kept walking. But rather than that, it would be more accurate to say that he had a pain in his stomach and became more and more dizzy and couldn't pay attention to what the young man said. His ears kept ringing.

He entered a building with a ENT[7] clinic right in front of him. He managed to arrive there, but the door was closed as Saturday's office hours were over. He felt increasingly nauseous. His head was spinning and his arms went numb. A cold sweat broke out all over his body. He couldn't stand or walk, so he collapsed and kept vomiting. There was still a nonstop ringing 'beep' sound in his ears. He felt like his chest was tightening and something seemed to weigh him down. The most intolerable thing was that the inside of his head was spinning. The world before him was spinning and pain became unbearable. The building manager saw him and called an ambulance. Emergency workers who arrived soon laid him on a stretcher and took him to the ambulance.

"Sir, can I take out your wallet from your bag and check your ID card? Or can you tell me yourself?" said one of the emergency workers kindly but urgently. Cheol-su couldn't even answer. His whole body was numb and he broke into a cold sweat. The vomiting got worse and his head kept spinning. He then lost his consciousness.

---

7 ear-nose-throat

002

Forever Alone

Cheol-su had been working as a contract judicial researcher at Desire branch of Suwon District Court in Desire city for 10 years. He reviewed records, worked on review reports, and prepared draft judgments to help judges. While assisting judges, he admired judges' timeously efficient judgments. He was also in awe of judges who produced verdicts strong enough for the court to be convinced and accept the outcome of trials. Even though he gave a sigh of grief at his unfulfilled dream of being a judge, at the same time, there was another feeling in him that not just anyone could be a judge.

Born in a local city, he retook a year at cram school in Seoul after graduating from high school. He was accepted to the law department of Seoul university. In his 20s, he earned to cover his own tuition and living expenses through working part-time.

Even after completing military service and college courses, he spent his early 30s working part-time jobs. After that, he started studying for the bar exam to become a judge, his life-long dream and ambition, with money he earned. He went to Nory-angjin[8] and spent the first two years as a full-time test-taker and only focused on the bar exam. The amount of money he spent every month was huge; tuition fees for academies, fees for dog-seosil[9], gosiwon[10] housing costs, food expenses, and expenses for textbooks, etc. He passed the first exam in the first year. The following year, he passed the second test, but suffered a setback in the third. It was a test that he had been preparing for two[11] full years as a full time examinee, investing all his earn-

---

8 This area is located in Seoul. Some of college and civil service exam takers stay here to prepare state exams. It is surrounded with numerous academies, private reading rooms which are called dogseosil, student restaurants, and small-narrow residential facilities which are called goshiwon. Many go-getters spent huge money and their young years here for their dreams.

9 It is a private reading room designed for quiet study. Inside, there are many carrel desks having partitions on the front and both sides, which block one's view to make them concentrate only on studying. Lights are not turned on or only weak lights are turned on. Each seat user is allowed to turn on the installed light on their designated desk.

10 It is a room around 3 to 7m² that is rent out monthly to test takers so that they can study and sleep. Depending on whether it has a window, the rental fee differs by tens of thousands of won. It furnishes a small bed, a small desk, a small refrigerator, and a small chest of drawers. It mainly targets those preparing for various national exams, but low-income workers also reside in due to comparatively low rental fee.

11 The traditional bar exam was a 2 full year process. If you passed the 1st exam, you were allowed to take the 2nd exam in the following year, and if you passed the 2nd exam, you were allowed to take the 3rd exam in the same year.

ings. But when he failed the third round, he felt empty. However, it was common at that time to study for bar exam for a basic few to 10 years, so he soon settled himself down to study again. When all the money he earned ran out, he worked part-time again and spent another four more years preparing for the bar exam, but failed to pass. He couldn't let go of studying for the exam because he thought he could pass if he did a little more. It was like a drug.

Being economically distressed, he lowered his sights and turned to the general court civil service exam. After studying for two more years, he was hired as a contract judicial researcher at the age of 40 at Desire branch of Suwon District Court in Desire city. Even after being hired, he could not give up his dream of becoming a judge, so he continued to study for the bar exam until 2017, taking online classes with monthly salary. He spent his time after work and holidays studying until his mid-40s.

He never dreamed of dating like other young people. He didn't have breadth of mind to date. His focus was only on work and study. He didn't want to distract himself with doing such things like dating, marriage, sports, and hobbies, so he put off them till the day of his success, which was to pass the bar exam and become a judge. Due to this, poverty followed him throughout his youth. In addition, bitter roots grew up in his mind. The unfulfilled dream of being a judge, his other delayed wishes, poverty, competition, and countless failures and hardships had turned into frustration and despair over the years and piled up in his mind. Disappointment about his life and anger about the world grew up in his mind, but he didn't realize it.

After the bar exam was abolished in 2017, success for him now went down from being a judge to being re-signed at the end of every two or three years of his contract term. To keep his contract job, he worked his best and tried to win favor of his current presiding judge and colleagues without showing his feelings and thoughts. Starting at some point, he lost his true self and was living like a man whose anger had been castrated. He didn't get angry for the most part. He only worked silently and calmly, so there were times when he even thought he had forgotten how to speak. When eating in a cafeteria, he sweated like a pig due to hyperhidrosis, so he always carried a towel and wiped his sweats while eating. The court officials avoided eating right in front of him. It was because watching him eating made them lose their appetites and unpleasant. When eating with them, he went to the far end where his colleagues could see him less and ate, wiping his sweats with a towel.

This life of a contract worker was a future that he had never even thought of until the age of 40, when he had invested everything he had in studying at Noryangjin. It seemed to him that his current life was an inferior life, which was very different from his high ideal.

Externally he was a competent judicial researcher who diligently worked and quietly solved problems raised by incompetent employees, but on the inside he was angry with himself for only living like this. He lived without expressing his various emotions and stresses that had accumulated in him over the years, but suppressed them in his heart.

His title of a worker in court, although he was a contract worker, occasionally brought opportunities for a blind date from a dating agency he joined. However, women were quite embarrassed to see a fat man weighing more than 120kg with thick glasses on and raggedly breathing. The thick lenses for his bad eyesight made his eyes look smaller than the actual eyes. His eyes seen through the glasses were unfocused and blank. It was because, for decades, his eyes had been failing from reviewing numerous articles and working with computers in court and studying the bar exams and public service exams. But women in the matchmaking market didn't know that. It was even misunderstood as his eyes looked like those of people who took drugs. In addition, the profile picture he posted in the dating agency was taken before he gained too much weight, so women who only saw the picture were surprised at his real appearance.

He was quite slow to speak, to act, to laugh, to react. When the women asked a question, he slowly opened his lips after about three seconds and answered with a very short answer, and remained silent again. The women were frustrated with him. Moreover, when they ate food together, he continued to sweat and wiped the sweats running down his scalp, face and neck with a towel or restaurant napkins. No matter how much he wiped, his face and the back of his neck continued to spout perspiration as if he were a fountain, and his upper body clothes were damp. Looking at it, they felt like throwing up the food they were eating, but the women couldn't do it out of courtesy. The women swallowed the food so that it could not come out of their mouths and pushed it into their throats, and after that, they no longer ate. No woman could think that he was once an intelligent, smooth-tongued, and charming young man, who was handsome enough to be dubbed a 'Leonardo DiCaprio' and to captivate girls' hearts at once.

He was always dumped by women after a blind date. It rarely led to 2nd or 3rd dates with them. In addition, his contract job was undesirable for women who wanted a man with a stable job. Even his unmarried female colleagues in court did not consider him more than just a colleague. He felt skeptical of meeting women as he continued to spend money without leading to follow-up dates and for one reason or another. It would have been more than 10 million won if he had saved up the money he paid for food and teas on dates. Eventually, he rejected even meeting women.

Even though he poured out money on dates, it only ended with 1st or 2nd meeting. However, Cheol-su was not disappointed. Although he was forever alone and lived a life of female deficiency, his ideal type existed. The more he failed to date a woman, the more he became obsessed with success and devoted himself to studying for the bar exam, saving minutes after work. It seemed like everything would work out well if he passed the bar exam. He also became more obsessed with his ideal type. His ideal type was a woman playing the piano well, young and pretty, with fair skin, with long straight hair and thin and long fingers. He devoted himself to his goal, dreaming and hoping that he would succeed one day, date and marry a woman of his ideal type, have sons and daughters, and live happily. He insisted on a young and pretty woman even though he got older. It was due to a kind of compensation psychology for spending his youth struggling without enjoying it.

After he fainted in Seocho-dong, Seoul, He was diagnosed at the hospital that he could not work for the time being due to cerebral infarction. He was a contract worker in court and worked hard for 10 years without ever taking any sick leave or absences. His performance and contribution were great, so he was allowed five-month paid sick leave. He packed his luggage to go down to his hometown. He thought that it would be better to go down to his hometown to take care of his health than to stay in his studio apartment in the multi complex house he lived in.

On both walls of his studio apartment in the multi complex house, two large brown bookshelves stood to the height of the ceiling and covered the walls. The bookshelves were packed with books, textbooks for exams and test papers related to law. The towering bookshelves in the narrow studio apartment reminded one of huge buildings in the city center. So his studio was frustrating and stuffy. However, such a frustration was familiar to him, who once studied for the bar exam at Nory-angjin for a long time. There was a brown study carrel desk[12] at the wall with a window. It was a desk purchased in 2012, when he was hired as a judicial researcher by Desire branch of Suwon District Court in Desire city, Gyeonggi province. And he had sat there until 2017. It had already been five years since he had stopped sitting there with the abolition[13] of the bar exam on December 31, 2017. Now he didn't need that carrel desk, the law books, textbooks for exams and test papers, yet he couldn't throw them away. If they disappeared, he would feel like his youth would disappear together. They were things that represented his youth.

The abolition of the bar exam seemed to uproot a mental pillar that gave him support during difficult times. Hadn't he put off all his love and happiness, looking for passing the exam? Hadn't he sacrificed time, energy, and money of his youth on the altar of the bar exam? Weren't all his thirties and evenings after work, weekends, and holidays in his forties, sacrificed as a

---

12 It is a wooden desk with high partitions blocking the front and sides of one's view, so that you can concentrate solely on studying.

13 Korea's traditional bar exam disappeared into history after the last test in 2017, and the training of legal professionals has been left to graduate school of law since then.

living sacrifice? Life was in vain. It occurred to him that he had been deceived by his foolish beliefs and ambitions.

From 2018, to become a judge, hopefuls entered law schools to complete a three-year course and take a new bar exam, but he didn't want to gamble on quitting his job to enter a law school as there was no night course. He didn't want to go back to the drawing board and repeat the process because he had already had enough of a similar process.

The hunger for success which made him work and study for up to 20 hours a day, drinking a lot of coffee every day for the caffeine energy, disappeared. He didn't know for sure whether it was a change caused by disappearance of the goal or the aging, but he was always sorry that the enthusiasm and passion that had supported him disappeared. It was hard to forgive himself for getting older without success. He hated his environment, which drove him to waste most of his precious youth and health in pursuit of futile things. He lamented that he wasted his youth foolishly, deceived by society's standardized view of success and his wrong beliefs. As a contract worker, fear of the future also intensified.

Whenever his acquaintances asked him to drink, he went out without refusing it to deal with such emotions as emptiness, void, and loneliness that had never been felt in the past due to busy daily life. He thanked his acquaintances for calling him, who had no sense of humor, spoke little, sweated like a pig when eating, and wiped his sweats off with a towel repeatedly. The atmosphere of people gathering in the pubs, drinking moderately, laughing and chatting took away feelings of loneliness and emptiness and gave him pleasure instead. Now drinking with his acquaintances was his only pleasure. It was a way to escape for a while from his harsh reality and frustrating thoughts, which weighed him down. It also gave a power that pushed him to go to work the following day, jump into the daily life of competition and office politics and be loyal. On days when he had no appointments, he sat blankly on the floor of his studio and stared at a newly-purchased TV. Such days continued.

He suffered from abdominal obesity due to his long sedentary life and lack of exercise from the time he was preparing for the bar exam. The lumps of fat piling up in his abdomen made him look like a pregnant man. It was hard to walk because he was fat. He just wanted to sit down all the time. He was out of breath after walking even a short distance. Due to his busy daily routines and heavy body, he didn't want to exercise at all. He was sitting all the time and drove even short distances.

Starting at some point, when he came into his studio drunk after work, he imagined that he tore off some of the belly fat from his body and always folded it finely and put it into the drawer of the blanket chest. The belly fat was a proof of his past life. A life of studying at the carrel desk toward the goal, putting off the privilege and joy of youth. A life of studying until past midnight without rest even after work, with law books all over the floor and the dining table. A life of sitting, focusing, and working hard at his desk at work. A life that had always been tailored to presiding judges and colleagues without show-ing his thoughts and feelings. A life of solving problems that other colleagues couldn't solve. A life of dealing with rude peo-ple kindly, controlling his temper and keeping his cool. Ironical-ly, to him, his belly fat was the embodiment of his struggles and efforts.

003

Leonardo DiCaprio Becomes an
Old Man

He packed things to take to his brother's house in his hometown to recuperate. In one corner of the studio, there were two
small plastic chests of drawers storing things. They sharply con-
trasted in size and area with the two heavy bookshelves and the
carrel desk, which were occupying three walls of the studio, but
they were the only furniture that brightened the dark and stuffy
studio with pastel yellow and sky blue colors. He opened the
drawers one by one. There was a mix of objects that once
expressed his emotions and wishes. The objects had been also
left unattended without his care, like his youth. Photos and CDs
that had been stuck for a long time were also seen between the
chests of drawers and the walls, and between the two chests of
drawers. He took out photos and CDs from a corner, which was
filled with dust of time and without light. It was a picture of him
when he was in his 20s. Cheol-su Kwon, a young, handsome,

immaculate man who was called 'the Leonardo DiCaprio of Seoul university', was smiling brightly with his mouth open showing his white teeth. The CD was a collection of classical piano pieces. On the cover of the CD, the date and place of purchase were written with a brief note. He remembered buying the CD.

His first fascination with piano music came when he was 31 years old, 19 years ago, when he worked hard to earn money by doing two or three part-time jobs. On that day, as usual, he finished his job and took the subway. He was lucky to get a seat on the subway that day. It was about an hour to gosiwon where he resided, so he was able to give his tired body rest during that time. He fell asleep slowly.

Cheol-su heard music from somewhere. He seemed to be dreaming. It felt like his crumpled brain was slowly unraveling. His brain had become moist. A fragrant wind swept through his brain. Each brain cell seemed to come alive and dance. He slowly woke up from his deep sleep and opened his eyes. The music was from a CD player played by a vendor selling piano music CDs to subway riders. Cheol-su bought a CD for 10,000 won[14]. It was because the piano music not only revived his tired brain, also serendipitously woke him up in time for his station.

After that day, whenever he finished his part-time job, he used to listen to piano music on the subway or at gohiwon with his earphones plugged into a portable CD player. However, he once again got caught up in his busy routine and soon returned to his life without music. The piano CD album and its player, along with other objects, were left for a long time out of Cheol-su's reach and without any light.

Cheol-su packed the CD album and its player in his bag and went down to his older brother's house, where he planned to spend five months recovering from his stroke. Cheol-su's brother hugged him. It was heartbreaking to see that his younger brother, who was once lively and active, lost his true self and became a different person over time, and now returned sick.

"Resting for a while will be rather a blessing in disguise. Even though your heart and body often have signaled to you that they are hurt, you have ignored it, and it has gotten much worse. From now on, don't ignore what your body and mind are telling you. You will recover." He comforted Cheol-su with warm

---

14 The national currency of South Korea.

words. In order to help Cheol-su recover, his sister-in-law focused on his meals, preparing healthy foods such as vegetables and fruits.

He had a nephew and a niece, who were fraternal twins in their junior year of high school. They called him 'the court grandpa,' because Cheol-su looked 10 years older than their father, though he was younger. Instead of the young and handsome uncle in the old family photos, an old man who was full of gray hair and had a big belly appeared during annual holidays, saying he was their uncle. The uncle became fatter and older each year they saw him. They couldn't believe that the young and immaculate man with a slim figure in the old family photos was the same person as their uncle. The handsome, star-like uncle existed only in family pictures.

However, Cheol-su had some nice things the twins liked. Cheol-su bought hundreds of thousands of won worth of sashimi every time he visited his brother's house. The day Cheol-su came was a day when the twins could eat a variety of sashimi, as much as they wanted. In addition, Cheol-su was happy when he was drunk, so he gave each twin tens of thousands of won each time he saw them. Sometimes, he gave them hundreds of thousands won. The twins waited for their uncle to drink beer, expecting him to give them money. If they saw an empty glass, they filled it up quickly. Cheol-su thought the twins were cute even though they stuck to him for sashimi and money. This time, even though he couldn't drink due to his health issues, he still provided each twin with a suitable monetary gift.

During his stay at his brother's house he continued to wake up early in the morning, as was his habit at work. But he just opened his eyes and couldn't do anything. Pointlessness and lethargy weighed heavily upon him. It was really hard to get up under that intense pressure. He questioned himself, "What have I lived for so far?" He felt that he had used up his precious youth and health on things, which were useless and meaningless.

The twins transferred Cheol-su's piano music from his CD to an MP3 so that their uncle, Cheol-su, could listen to it while taking a walk. He spent every day walking around the local park with the MP3 in his pocket and earphones in his ears. On one such morning, Cheol-su received a text message from his bank requesting that he renew his savings accounts. He returned home and withdrew his bankbooks from his suitcase that had remained packed for weeks since coming with him to his brother's house. He checked his savings accounts one by one. Each had a list of numbers representing his contributions, which he saved up while working as a judicial researcher for the past decade. The numbers in his bankbooks had each gradually increased, but these larger numbers did not transform his life. They were just numbers in little books. There was nothing he could do with these numbers. No, he didn't know what he wanted to do… No, there was one thing he wanted to do. It was to buy an apartment in Seoul. From the time he was young he had always looked for an opportunity to go to Seoul. He had always wanted to have the word 'Seoul Special City' on his resident registration card. When he realized that he couldn't buy a home in Seoul no matter how hard he tried, he began losing interest in buying or doing things which could give him joys of daily life. Returning to the present, Cheol-su went to a bank with his expired bankbooks and ID card. He renewed his savings accounts.

Cheol-su went straight to the meeting place after doing some bank job. He was supposed to meet Young-sik Oh, two years senior, and Yeon-woo Lee, 14 years junior, in law department at Seoul university. Yeon-woo was a hometown junior whom he met first 10 years ago at Seoul university's law department home-town alumni. He met them every time he visited his hometown, but the last time he met them was two years ago. The meeting place was Yeon-woo's recently launched beer bar.

Yeon-woo Lee. He was 14 years younger than Cheol-su. Unlike the name, which sounded soft and neutral, he was tall, looked rough, and had a beard. Not as much as Cheol-su, but he was also fat, and he was called a 'Sanjuck'[15] by women. He was not as popular with women as Cheol-su. His personality was similar to that of older Cheol-su. He did not show his thoughts and feelings but only listened. However, the motivation to listen without showing his real thoughts and feelings was different from that of Cheol-su. While Cheol-su is suppressing himself without revealing himself in order to survive in an organization, Yeon-woo was due to his ambition. When listening to older bros who lived longer than himself, he could gain and realize many things. He didn't say anything such as right or wrong about their thoughts and actions. He was just listening. He thought they could be a good reference for his success. Listening to their life history, he learned from their mistakes, thought differently from

---

15 A kind of bandit based in the mountains in Korea long time ago. They were very hairy and vicious. Today, people often use this word informally to refer to hairy, tough, and unattractive guys just for fun.

them, and made different choices.

Yeon-woo, who was standing at the counter of his beer bar, smiled broadly at the incoming Cheol-su. Young-sik, who arrived in advance, was sitting at a table. He waved toward Cheol-su, who was entering his pub.

"Long time no see, bro. How many years has it been?" Yeon-woo greeted Cheol-su with a friendly handshake.

"······I think······it's been two or······three years."

"Right. You've been here hometown on Chuseok[16] two years ago."

Yeon-woo was inwardly jealous of Cheol-su because among the three he was the only one who was working in the field related to the major 'law' without letting go of it. However, whenever he saw Cheol-su gaining weight and his eyes getting blank every year, he thought it was rather fortunate that he didn' t work in law field. Rather, he thought his life would be better than that of Cheol-su, even though he made money regardless of his major by doing various part-time jobs such as serving at a pub, grilling meat at a meat restaurant, working part-time at a convenience store, and working a delivery driver. Whenever He saw Cheol-su, who had a similar body type and personality, he

16 Korean Thanksgiving Day

didn't think he could guarantee that he would not change like Cheol-su if he worked on law. Yeon-woo was satisfied with his life because he was earning as much as Cheol-su while working part-time, and expanding ties by attending various local gatherings. Now that he had a girlfriend to spend his whole life with and he opened a pub and started his own business, he didn't feel jealous of others anymore. Unlike Cheol-su, he had solidified his position in communities with low entry barriers without wasting energy and time by insisting on highly competitive jobs and Seoul and the area around it, which required a lot of money and efforts.

"Congratulations, Yeon-woo. You're finally starting a business. There are many customers here. Your business is booming." Young-sik said when Yeon-woo and Cheol-su came to the table which he was at.

Young-sik Oh. He was Cheol-su's two-year senior at law department in Seoul university and his hometown friend. He also studied with Cheol-su at Noryangjin for two years as a full-time test-taker to become a judge or prosecutor after graduating from college. When he unpassed the test for two years in a row, he quit it because he did not want to spoil his youth in studying and he thought civil service life was not suitable for him.

Thanks to the financial support from his father, a former dentist, he was able to enjoy his life without having a job when he was young. He wanted to succeed in business, so he took money several times from his father for his business funds. Thanks to his bright and bubbly personality, his business once ran a successful path, but starting at some point his business did not go its way. Eventually, his father stopped providing him with financial support. When the support was cut off, he sold his foreign cars one by one and barely survived. When his money ran out, he returned to his parents in his hometown after 40. However, his parents were older and tired, and they got sick a lot because of the old age. It was unclear how much inheritance would be left for Young-sik as his parents were using their property for their hospital expenses and medical care. Without gaining recognition from his parents, Young-sik often complained to Yeon-woo and Cheol-su about his situation in which he was tied to his old parents to take care of their health and run errands for them. He enjoyed his youth by driving foreign cars to date various women and playing various sports, but he was now over 50 and could not walk long due to diabetes. He sold all his foreign cars, so he took a taxi every time he moved. Taking a bus had not yet been allowed by his pride.

"……Bro, you……early arrived……, didn't you?" said Cheol-su, sitting next to Young-sik.

"Taxi is the fastest option."

"Young-sik, I'm glad you get back to me. I'm always worried something might happen to you whenever you ghost me." said Yeon-woo.

"Why worry? I'm doing fine, so don't worry. I was just curious about Cheol-su's recent situation, so I called him and he said he came hometown. So I came out to see him."

"Yes. It's all thanks to Cheol-su. His coming made you contact me again."

"……Ghosting you……?"

"Young-sik sometimes ghosted me. We lose contact. Young-sik, did I hurt your feelings? Don't go into hiding. Don't even change your phone number."

"I'm sorry. I won't get off the grid. I promise."

"Anyway Cheol-su, you got fatter. You look like a pregnant man. You've become extremely fat."

Yeon-woo poured beer into the glasses of Young-sik and Cheol-su, pointing Cheol-su's belly fat with his chin.

"……Oh……, for a few days, the belly fat……I didn't tear it off……."

"The same goes for you, Sanjuck. Don't think you're an exception because you're less fat than Cheol-su. You guys don't have any muscles and only have bulging tummies. That's abdominal fat, which sends bad inflammatory signals. They're what make the brain cells bad and causes the aging of the nerves. Work out. You need to move to burn the fat. If you don't, you'll die early. Your brains are going to get messed up. You sleep irregularly, you drink and smoke, you eat food having no nutritious value, so hundreds of thousands of brain cells are dying and don't regenerate. If your brains don't enough nutrients and waste builds up, your brains will die. Your belly fats prove it. A lot of your brain cells are already dead. When you are older, it leads to dementia."

They listened quietly, accepting all the words of Young-sik, who did not drink nor smoke. Young-sik, now 52 years old, the oldest of the three, was the only one who didn't smoke. In the past, he enjoyed drinking, but after he had got diabetes, he sometimes had a beer or two but drank no more. Young-sik studied medical general knowledge by himself to protect his health. Also, He needed common sense about health because he was taking care of his old parents. From the day he met Yeon-woo at the hometown alumni for law department of Seoul university, he hung out with Yeon-woo in his hometown. Concerned about the health of fat Yeon-woo, who had volcanic crater-like facial skin, he told him common senses about health and nagged him to take care of his health.

"By the way, Cheol-su, do you tear off the belly fat?"

"······If I tore some of it off······I feel comfortable······. It makes it easier to breathe······."

"Cheol-su sometimes talks nonsense."said Young-sik, who was patiently listening to Cheol-su's slow words.

Soon, a part-timer brought a cooked whole chicken and fish-cake soup as side dishes. The part-timer put on plastic gloves and carefully tore off the flesh of the whole chicken in front of them. Cheol-su stared at the chicken. He thought that the milky-white chicken flesh that the part-timer ripped off and piled up resembled his belly fat that was separated and piled up in the drawer. When the part-timer tore off all the flesh, Cheol-su began to gobble them up. Beads of sweat formed all over his body. Yeon-woo asked the part-timer to bring a towel. Young-sik drank beer.

"Cheol-su, don't you drink beer?" asked Yeon-woo.

"······My doctor······gave me a······stern warning. I have to stop drinking······. Ever since I passed out in Seocho, Seoul······I quit drinking……."

"But why are you sweating so much while eating?" Yeon-woo received a towel from the part-timer and held it out to Cheol-su.

"That's……since I became overweight……I have sweated every time I eat."

"By the way, Yeon-woo, the part-timer is really good-looking. Do you pick up part-timers based on their appearance?" said Young-sik.

"That's right. I don't pick anyone. Since the main customer base is in their 20s and 30s who are sensitive to appearance, I select handsome and sincere candidates."

"Yeon-woo, you have a good means of business. That's right, if the part-timers are handsome and pretty, customers will come again to see them. That's how you get regular customers. Cheol-su was also beautiful in his 20s. He was called 'the Riardo DiCaprio of Seoul University'. To see Cheol-su, girls deliberately took the liberal arts course that Cheol-su took. There were also dozens of female students who joined the club because of Cheol-su. There were three boxes of love letters that Cheol-su received at that time. Can you believe it? Three big boxes! The letters and postcards that the girls wrote neatly. The beauty of your part-timers can't catch up with that of Cheol-su in his prime." said Young-sik, tapping Cheol-su on the back, who was eating chicken.

"What did you do with all the love letters? Are you keeping them? If you show me, I'll believe that you were once the Leonardo DiCaprio." said Yeon-woo to Cheol-su.

"Cheol-su, what did you do with the love letters? Do you still have them?" asked Young-sik.

"······I threw them away."

"Why?" Young-sik was wide-eyed in surprise.

"······Whenever life is hard······from time to time······I used to see them, but it kept me stuck in the past······. I thought······it could get in the way of······my success and my future."

"When did you throw them away?" said Young-sik.

"······As soon as I graduated from college······."

"Cheol-su. Hahaha! You were joking, right? There's no way to prove it. Hahaha!" Yeon-woo burst out laughing.

"Tsk tsk···. That's so like you." Young-sik clicked his tongue and shook his head.

"I'm sure there are pictures of our college days. I'll have to look back on my past albums." added Young-sik.

"By the way, Cheol-su. Did you have some kind of gastrectomy? What do you mean by 'tear off the belly fat'?" asked Yeon-woo.

"He sometimes talks nonsense. His character has changed a lot. The agile and intelligent appearance and personality of the past Cheol-su Kwon was gone. Instead, absent-minded, reticent, slow, and sometimes talking nonsense like this." said Young-sik on behalf of the silent Cheol-su. Cheol-su smiled slightly at Young-sik's words. Since no one believed it anyway, it only hurt him to say more.

004

When Silk Tree Flowers Blossom

On the morning of the first day of June, the beginning of summer, Cheol-su took a walk listening to piano music on his MP3 as usual. On that day he walked on a road he had never taken before. While walking down the road, he ran into a piano academy. Since he was young, he had had a dream of marrying a woman who could play the piano, but he never got the opportunity to connect with a woman who could play an instrument, let alone play the piano. Now he wanted to play the piano himself. Cheol-su entered the piano academy.

In the morning two retired seniors were practicing, and in the afternoon kindergartners and elementary school students flooded into the piano academy. In the evening a small number of middle school students and a couple of high school students who wanted to major in piano in the university were attending.

Having lived in a world where only adults existed, these small creatures seemed unfamiliar to him. Their chatter and vitality energized him.

The piano academy teacher, Hye-eun Song, was a 31-year-old sweet and kind woman. Her face was as shiny as a celebrity's face and her skin was fair. So were her hands, her arms, and her neck. Her skin was untanned. Long straight hair added calmness to her. When you think of a woman playing the piano, the first thing that comes to mind is her long fingers. But her hands were small and stubby. Her fair nails were clipped out of sight. Small, stubby fingers moved busily on the piano keys.

'She plays the piano with such small hands.' thought Cheol-su.

Her fingers broke his stereotype. Although they weren't his ideal, they looked rather cute. In particular, her thumbs were really small and stubby.

She always smelled fragrant when she sat next to him while teaching. She looked like a goddess in his eyes. The ideal woman he dreamed of his whole life was sitting right next to him and teaching him how to play the piano kindly. Even the strong provincial accent, which sounded crude and irritating when others spoke it, did not bother him at all when it was spoken by her. Her accent sounded rather cute.

The woman he had dreamed of for a long time and Cheol-su, who had been dreaming of and waiting for her, met each other at age of 31 and 50 respectively. And they were now sitting side by side on the same piano chair. Instead of just looking at the ideal type like celebrities on television, he was sitting right next to her on the same chair in the real world and talking with her. This was a miracle!

The piano teacher's lessons were saving him little by little every day. Without this music class, he would have continued to live in lethargy and despondency. He had been rejected by countless women and knew that he was unpopular with women, so he tried to feel no more than a student-teacher relationship for her. Besides, she was 19 years younger than he was, so he couldn't even think of having deeper feelings for her.

It was the first time in his 50 years of life in which he had never talked with young and beautiful women, to converse with such an ideal woman. A young and beautiful woman was talking to him every day! It could only be said that a miracle happened.

It was also healing for him to be able to communicate as an equal without any oppression or stress, away from the form of communication, where orders were delivered and he should report back within the upper and lower hierarchies at work. For Cheol-su, this moment of each day was such a precious time, which he didn't want to be taken away by anyone.

He hoped these moments would last forever. She was young, beautiful, and charming, and would soon meet and marry a good young man. He thought it would be hard to date someone in the future because he had been forever alone all his 50 years of life and now he was old, fat, and unattractive. So he thought he would be satisfied and grateful if he could live like this, talking with her while getting her kind piano lessons for the rest of his life.

A few weeks after he started practicing piano, he suddenly discovered an unmanned self-photo studio[17] on his way to the piano academy. One wall of the photo studio was made up of a large and wide full-length mirror. He had come and gone this way many times before, but he passed by without knowing the existence of the mirror because he lived so indifferently to his

---

[17] It has several photo booths and unmanned cameras inside. One wall of the entrance usually has a large full-length mirror to attract customers. There is no photographer. The main customer base is young people. People take pictures by themselves in a fun and unique way after paying.

appearance. He looked at himself in the mirror. There stood a fat old man, or 'the court grandpa' as his twin nephew and niece said.

'·····Who's·····that monster·····?'

It was truly shocking to see his full body for the first time in decades. How did I become such a fat monster? Why am I so old? What the hell has happened to me over the years? Where did the fresh and beautiful youth of my 20s and 30s go? He could no longer keep watching himself in the mirror. He wanted to deny it. He was afraid.

Cheol-su headed to the piano academy. There was a bank on the way. In front of the bank, there was a crosswalk. Right across that crosswalk was the piano academy. Starting at some point, every time he passed by that bank, he could smell some fragrance. The fragrance was nice, but he couldn't tell where it was coming from.

As always, his piano teacher welcomed Cheol-su with a bright smile and praised Cheol-su for his consistency and sincerity. In the morning, two elderly people, who retired and learned how to the play piano as a hobby, practiced in each booth. After practice, the elderly students would sit on the sofa and chat, and

Cheol-su would join them and listen to their conversation.

"10 years ago when I was still working, I learned how to play the piano for a year after work. Of course, I learned it from another teacher then. But I quit. 10 years has passed and I started again after retirement. It's been a year since I started practicing again, but I forgot everything I learned 10 years ago. I'm starting over from the basics. I shouldn't have quit then, I should have continued. Hey, mister, don't quit. And keep practicing." They said to Cheol-su, who was listening in silence.

"······Yes."

10 years···. There were now 10 years left before Cheol-su would retire after reinstatement if he was not subject to layoffs due to restructuring and hold on to the contract position for that decade.

Mid-July. His five months of sick leave was coming to an end, but he was hesitant to return to the court in city Desire. His daily lessons from his piano teacher were precious to him and he didn't want to give up this time. He wanted to continue. It was the greatest joy of his day to be able to talk face to face with his ideal, young and beautiful piano teacher, Miss Song, via their lesson time. He could go back to the city Desire and learn how to play it from another piano teacher there, but they were not Miss Song. There are many young and beautiful female teachers in the world, but they are not her. She was like the rose in the home planet of the title character in the fairy tale 'The Little Prince'. It was like there were countless beautiful roses in the world, but just as the single rose on the little prince's planet was special to him, Miss Song was special to Cheol-su. He wanted to delay their impending separation as much as possible. Back in the city Desire, he would be engrossed in work, and she would be forgotten by him with time. He didn't want to forget her.

Now going to the piano academy at a fixed time every morning had become a routine like going to work. When he was in city Desire, he used to take his own car or taxi even to nearby places, but after disposing of his car, he came down to his hometown and walked to the piano academy. He always stopped in front of the unmanned self-photo studio on his way to the academy. He stopped in front of the full-length mirror at the photo studio and groomed himself like a cat. Walking a little further, there was a bank. Passing in front of the bank, there was a crosswalk. Crossing the crosswalk, there was the piano academy. Whenever he passed by that bank, he could smell some delicate scents and his heart was pounding with excitement that he could see his piano teacher soon.

One day, the scent became more intense with the heat of the summer sun. When Cheol-su passed by the bank on the way to the academy, he couldn't ignore the intense scent, so he looked back. Where on earth did this smell come from? He examined where the scent came from. On the sidewalk he hurriedly passed, pretty tassels with mysterious colors fell in fan shapes everywhere. They were flowers. They didn't look like flowers, but they were definitely flowers. Flowers in a different shape from typical flower shapes! The gradation from white at the bottom to pink or purple at the top added a sense of mystery to the flowers. He looked up to find out where these flowers had fallen. It was one of the trees planted in front of the bank. It was a tree with sweet and strong scents. It was a mysterious tree with deep fragrance, with flowers forming gradation from white to deep pink in green and dense branches. He never thought this mysterious tree was planted here on the way to the academy. He always passed this road on the way to the academy, but he never noticed the existence of this tree.

'······What's······the name of······this tree?'

Cheol-su stopped and looked at the mysterious tree for a

while. He picked up some of the fan-shaped flowers that fell on the sidewalk. Then, holding them close to his nose, he walked to the academy while smelling the scent.

From then on, on the way to the piano academy every morning, he picked up a handful of the fan-shaped flowers that had fallen from the tree, and made a small bouquet. He always put them on top of the piano, and practiced the piano.

An elderly parking manager of the road parking lot, who watched Cheol-su picking up deep pink flowers on the sidewalk every morning, talked something to Cheol-su. Cheol-su asked him just in case.

"······Sir, do you know······what the name······of this tree is?"

"Oh, the cattle-rice[18]-tree! Cattle eat its leaves really well. They love its leaves."

"······I see, Thanks."

'Cattle-rice-tree······. Cattle love it······. I was born in the year of the ox[19]······.'

---

18 It is another informal name of silk tree in Korea. The staple food of Koreans is rice. The word 'cattle-rice' here is used metaphorically to mean that cows enjoy leaves of silk tree like Koreans enjoy rice as their staple food by personifying cows.

19 The Korean zodiac consists of 12 animal signs. Rat, Ox, Tiger, Rabbit, Dragon, Snake, Horse, Sheep, Monkey, Chicken, Dog, and Pig. It is repeated every twelve years. Each animal has its own trait, which is shared by people born in its year. People born in ox years are believed to be honest and hardworking.

"Its another name is a silk tree. It's a tree that symbolizes the perfect conjugal harmony. That's why it's also called Haphwan[20] tree, Married Couple tree, and Love tree."

"……I see. Thanks"

"It's in full bloom right now. It blooms in summer, June to August."said the parking manager again.

Cheol-su smiled. He finally got to know the name of this mysterious tree. Its name is as mysterious as its mysterious fragrance and form. The meaning of its name is also mysterious. His heart fluttered again. He smelled the scent of the silk tree flowers. His heart was pounding. The thought of seeing Miss Song soon after a little more walk mingled with the strong fragrance of the silk tree flowers, which stirred his heart and mystified his mind.

Before August began, Cheol-su postponed his reinstatement for an additional six months at the risk of being fired. His health had not recovered yet, but the bigger reason was that he didn't want to leave his piano teacher. Fortunately, Desire city branch of Suwon District Court delayed his reinstatement for an additional six months. Although on unpaid sick leave, he was able to

---

20 合歡. It has two meaning: one is that people get together and rejoice, and the other is that a man and a woman sleep together and have fun.

return to work six months later, so he did not lose his job.

He met his ideal girl that he had hoped for his whole life. He could talk to her every day through their lesson time. Her presence put him in heaven. Even though it was a secret crush on her, which was an unrequited feeling of love for her, his heart was always pounding and his mind was more at ease because of her. The futility and loneliness gradually disappeared. He came to know that there was no need to go anywhere else because heaven was here.

He wanted to be young. For the first time since his early 30s, he had a desire to smarten himself up. He quit smoking, which he had done for nearly 20 years. He went to a hair salon and had his shaggy hair cut, and his gray hair dyed black. He bought new clothes. He polished his shoes. It had become a new habit to look at himself in the full-length mirror of the unmanned self-photo studio on the way to the piano academy every day. He unknowingly fixed his hair and adjusted his clothes in front of the mirror like a cat grooming themself.

He registered at the gym and exercised every day. He began to take care of his body, which he had neglected for decades. He wanted to look attractive to his piano teacher. He wanted to remove the bulging abdominal fat which made him look like a pregnant man and build a cool six-pack in his abdominal muscles. With the help of a personal trainer, he worked on his abs and did his upper and lower body exercises, using various exercise equipment in the gym. He weighted himself on the scale before and after exercise every day and found that he was losing weight little by little. He also paid attention to his diet. He changed from an instant food, alcohol and meat-based diet to a protein, vegetable and fruit-based diet.

However, he could not easily lose his protruding belly fat due to internal fat. He had no choice but to tear off some of the belly fat that had built up day after day before going to bed. He opened the chest of drawers. The belly fat that had been previously removed formed a big mass and was finely folded like thick winter clothes. Cheol-su removed some of his belly fat and dropped it on the existing fat in the drawer. The fat chunks stuck together and were now united. Cheol-su carefully closed the drawer.

Young-sik and Yeon-woo were puzzled when they saw Cheol-su, who was getting more energetic and brighter day by day and losing weight little by little. They was amazed that the piano and exercise he started changed him to this extent. Every time they met, Young-sik and Yeon-woo discussed the effects of art, sports activities, hobbies, and adequate relaxation on humans. But only Cheol-su knew the truth. It wasn't simply because of expressing himself through music, or freeing himself from mental oppression through hobbies, or losing weight little by little through exercise, or taking sick leave to give his body and mind a good rest. They were only secondary reasons. It was the power of love that changed Cheol-su. Unrequited Love! Love that didn't look like love! Although it was an unrequited love, the feeling of love was renewing him.

005

Dreams and Ambitions

Cheol-su, Yeon-woo, and Young-sik often met at Yeon-woo's pub. Cheol-su did not drink alcohol and replaced it with other drinks. Yeon-woo's pub was always crowded with young customers. Young-sik enjoyed being in Yeon-woo's pub. It cheered him up to watch young people in their 20s and 30s, away from his daily routine of taking care of his aged parents. He also forbade alcohol due to diabetes, but whenever he came here, he felt beer was tasty, so he drank it happily.

"Alcohol could be a good medicine if you drink it pleasantly. Cheol-su, I heard you recently extended your sick leave." said Young-sik.

"……Yes. It's been extended……by early……next year……."

"Come to think of it, you must have worked really hard. Who gives a mere contract employee one-year sick leave?" said Yeon-woo.

"Good for you. You keep saying nonsense like tearing off your belly fat and your removed milky-white belly fat gets bigger like a mountain⋯. You need to get some rest." said Young-sik.

"By the way, Cheol-su. My belly fat is⋯ I'm also fat, so I have been annoyed with my visceral fat accumulation, too. Let me hear about your belly fat."

"⋯⋯Starting at some point⋯⋯when I just eat, fat accumulates⋯⋯in my abdomen⋯⋯due to a long sedentary life and⋯⋯ work stress. ⋯⋯It was difficult⋯⋯to work with this body⋯⋯ because I felt⋯⋯uncomfortable. I tore off⋯⋯some of the belly fat⋯⋯before going to bed⋯⋯. But to no avail⋯⋯. Every day, visceral fat⋯⋯builds up. After eating or drinking⋯⋯in the evening, my stomach was⋯⋯bulging like a mountain⋯⋯. That's why⋯⋯I tore off some of the belly fat⋯⋯every evening."

"Then what did you do with the belly fat you tore off?" asked Yeon-woo.

"⋯⋯In city Desire⋯⋯I put it⋯⋯in the drawer of⋯⋯the blanket chest⋯⋯ in my studio. After I came here⋯⋯countryside[21]⋯⋯my brother's house⋯⋯ I put it⋯⋯in a chest of drawers."

"If you tear it off almost every day, would it be huge?" said

---

21 Some people living in Seoul and Gyeonggi Province call local cities countryside.

Yeon-woo.

"······If the drawers······can't hold it······, it will spill out······onto the floor······and pile up."

"Cheol-su, don't you think about throwing it away?" asked Young-sik.

"······At first······, I hated my belly fat······, but on the other hand, I felt sorry······for myself, thinking that······I had worked······so hard to live. I was pitiful. I couldn't······throw it away······because it's like proof······of my youth in which······I've lived through life's ordeal."

"Cheol-su, you've worked too much. Your sick leave has been extended, so don't think about work and rest well. Cheol-su was blinded by his ambition in his youth, so he thought of his social status as his identity, which led him to this point. Tsk tsk···. That's too bad···. He turned into an ugly monster···. Sometimes he even talks nonsense···."said Young-sik, who was patiently listening to Cheol-su's slow words.

"Young-sik, you can easily say that because you have reliable supporters like your rich parents and a legacy to inherit from them. But Cheol-su and I are different. We have to make a living and come up with measures for our old age. There is no time for young people to rest, who were born with a plastic spoon in their mouths like Cheol-su and me."said Yeon-woo, who was listening quietly.

"⋯⋯Starting next month, ⋯⋯I will work part-time⋯⋯at my brother's convenience store⋯⋯in the mornings⋯⋯and afternoons⋯⋯to help him out. I'm sick⋯⋯and now taking a break from the court-job for a while, but⋯⋯ when I'm fully recovered, I'll start⋯⋯again⋯⋯for the succ⋯⋯."

Yeon-woo intervened even before Cheol-su finished talking.

"Cheol-su. You don't feel successful because you haven't dated, or enjoyed anything in your entire life. That's why you feel only a sense of deficiency, saying 'a little more, a little more.' Enjoy your life. Date women. I recently started dating. When I lowered my standard, I found my girl. I looked like a Sanjuck, but wanted pretty and young girls. That's why I used to be forever alone. She's six years older than I am. But she's a good woman."

"Yeah, she's a good girl. She supported you financially to open a pub. But don't give me a love lecture. I don't intend to get married." Young-sik, who had a lot of resistance to marriage, blocked Yeon-woo.

"This is not to you. I'm saying this to Cheol-su. Make sure to lower the level of your goals so that you can achieve them more easily. It wasn't easy to give up the bar exam because you often passed the second round, but you did well to give it up and have a job in Desire city court as a contract employee. You have to set a goal that low. If the bar exam had not been abolished in 2017, you would have been stuck in dogseosil and studied after work and on holidays. Then, your mind and spirit would have become more exhausted, and your personality would have become darker because you didn't spend time for joy of life. You would be forever ruined. However, Because you lowered your standard and chose to work even though it was a contract position, you could save money, go on a blind date occasionally, and live like a human being."

"Hey, man. Yeon-woo! You've grown a lot. The guy who used to listen to the older gives us some advice these days. You've grown a lot⋯. You know it's all because of me that you've grown this much, right? Cheol-su, when you were working in Desire city court, I met with Yeon-woo often and taught him a lot. It's all thanks to my help. I told him a lot of good things and taught him a lot. Yeon-woo, you know it's all thanks to me, right?"

"Sure, bro. It's all thanks to you that I grew up to this level. The same goes for Cheol-su. Thank you."

"Anyway, lowering standard is right. Yeon-woo didn't⋯ the old sneaky fox⋯ No, I mean⋯ Yeon-woo didn't refuse to be nice to

Hwa-young although she was older than him, but he accepted her thankfully. So Cheol-su, don't just pursue young women, but old women⋯ no, nonsense, sorry⋯ I'm drunk. Hahaha. A young women will hang out with you only in your imagination. Do you think they do in real life?"

"A goal that is too high than one's ability only wastes precious youth and time."said Yeon-woo.

Yeon-woo learned lessons from their mistakes. He didn't want to grow old like his two old friends. He was afraid of being like them. After getting to know them via the hometown alumni, Yeon-woo became enlightened by observing their thoughts and actions, and chose a different path using them as a reference.

"Yeon-woo, it seems like you are talking that to me this time." said Young-sik, who had a sense of shame because he jumped into many businesses in his youth with his parents' money, but didn't succeed. He only lost money, and now he got old.

"No. Actually that's to me. After graduating from college, I didn't build my career by using my major like Cheol-su, and I prepared for civil service exams, but failed. I used to sit alone in the corner of my room and wipe away tears. I thought if I kept this way, I'd be a wandering loser without getting married. It's a waste of time. So I have abandoned my major since then. While doing part-time jobs and working as a dispatched employee, I met Hwa-young and now I opened my own pub, this beer bar. Cheol-su, you became sick, so why don't you settle down here instead of living there? We can sometimes meet like this and catch up on old times. You can continue your workout and hobbies……. It sounds nice, doesn't it? From your age, you have to care your health."

"I agree with Yeon-woo. Cheol-su, how long are you going to live in that small studio apartment in city Desire? I've been there once and it was suffocating. I couldn't live any single day there even if it was free of charge. Since you are sick like this, settle down here." Yeon-woo and Young-sik, who lived a satisfactory life in their hometown, persuaded Cheol-su to settle down there too.

In September, when autumn begins. Cheol-su started part-time job at his bother's convenience store and rescheduled his piano lessons from morning to evening. His piano academy teacher, Miss Song, told that the week of Chuseok was all academy vacation. However, even after the academy vacation ended, she didn't come to work to the academy for the following two days. According to the children, she was sick. Cheol-su was concerned about her health. Two days after the academy vacation ended, she returned to the academy and her face was swollen. Even though she was wearing a mask, he could see that her face was swollen. He was again concerned about her health. However, her demeanor was as bright and pleasant as usual. No, she was more lively and overflowing with vitality than before. Cheol-su admired her vitality and beauty.

One day she took off her mask. Her face had changed a little. Middle and high school girls whispered by themselves that she had had a facial contouring surgery. She ignored their whispers. Parents who came to pay tuition fees for their children sometimes gave her a question about her change.

"Miss Song, do you have any good news these days? You look a little different."

"I have a dream these days."she said but nothing else.

'A dream?' Cheol-su was surprised to hear that word from her. It was a word that made Cheol-su's heart pound and became the reason for his life when he was young. 'Dream' is so coveted, attractive, and desirable. It makes your heart beat when you think of it. But the price you have to pay to make it come true is too costly and even if you pay the full price, you can't guarantee you can achieve it. He spent the most beautiful and youthful period of his life pursuing his dreams and ideals. He lived hard, offering his young 30 years as a living sacrifice to his dreams and ideals. But when he looked back, it was fruitless and in vain. He didn't make a family that everyone else did. He did not achieve much social success either. He got older now. As his twin nephew and niece called him, he became 'the court grandfather'. He once despaired of life itself. It felt like he was completely deceived. It was ironic that he now wanted to avoid that word, which was once a reason for his life. However, he wondered what she meant by the word 'dream'.

"······Miss Song······, these days······do you have any······ dreams······ ?"

"I am studying these days. And I do Imagine. It is fun to see dreams come true one by one as I imagined."

"······For me······, it didn't go······as I imagined."

"Yes, it goes as expected. Don't talk negatively like that to me."
She was strict.

"······Only into reality······I settle······."

No, Cheol-su also had big dreams and ambitions when he was at her age. There were many social successes he wanted to achieve as a judge. However, he continued to fail by a hair's breath in the bar exam. At that time, he felt that even his own existence was denied. The money earned from part-time jobs was spent on preparing for the bar exams and he struggled in poverty. When the efforts of his precious youth were fruitless, he gradually started to feel betrayed by his dreams and ambitions. And little by little, the words began to become uncomfortable, and over the years, he became more and more realistic. Words like intuition, dreams, and ambitions had disappeared from him, and a word 'reality' replaced them. Unlike himself, however, she had been running her own business since her mid-20s after graduating from college and she had been bearing fruits. She looked great to him. At least for her, life was unfolding as she imagined.

"I do imagine, and life works out as I imagined. I imagined launching this academy first. People around me said it wouldn't work out, but I didn't listen to them. I followed my intuition and imagination. I've been running well for last five years, and I want to expand my business in near future⋯ also, soon get marr⋯."

She stopped for a moment. She tried to find words to change the subject.

"These days, I imagine future expansion⋯ I'm also studying."

"⋯⋯What⋯⋯do you⋯⋯study?"

"Mr.Kwon, I don't want you to ask me any further personal questions other than music." She spoke firmly. She strictly prohibited students from giving her personal questions unrelated to music lesson. She also didn't have any special interests in them.

006

One Fine Day

In November, when early winter began. Cheol-su always practiced the piano in the booth right next to the director's office in
the piano academy. Starting at some point, he heard something
from the director's office. It was a small subtle sound. It sounded
like an online lecture played back at fast speed. Sometimes a
man's voice was heard, too. Cheol-su thought that Miss Song
was learning from online lectures at fast speeds for her future
dreams. He thought the male voice he heard sometimes was the
voice of an Internet lecturer on normal speed. He could tell it
because he used to take online lectures with increased video
playback speed for enhanced learning when he was preparing
for the bar exam. Whenever he heard that sound in the director'
s office, he admired Miss Song. He thought that the beautiful
young woman had correct thought. Her ambition for future also
made her shine more.

Miss Song sometimes broke the lesson schedule. She didn't appear even after a long wait after time for lesson. Whenever that happened, Cheol-su knocked on the door of the director's office and called for her. She got angry at him for knocking on the door of the director's office and sternly told him not to knock because she would come on her own. Fortunately, she did't forget the lesson time after that.

At the same time, however, Cheol-su felt empty at the piano academy starting at some point. He didn't know what the emptiness was about. She still taught calmly and well, but her teaching was a little different than before. From the time she said she imagined and studied for future, he felt something neglected in her lessons and the lesson time was shortened. From the time her sincerity in lessons diminished, his mind grew tired of playing the piano. However, he made up his mind to continue taking lessons from her, because the lesson time was the only time he could see her and talk to her. However, after taking piano lessons, his empty feelings intensified. The empty feeling was a familiar feeling that he had felt for many years even before he learned how to play the piano, so he did not bother to relate it to her.

One rainy day, a night part-timer at the convenience store

came to work early, so Cheol-su finished his work earlier than scheduled. It rained all day long that day. He took out a vinyl umbrella from the product shelves in the store and went to the piano academy. He shook rainwater off his vinyl umbrella and put it in an umbrella container in front of the academy door. A long black Alexander MacQueen brand umbrella was seen among the colorful umbrellas put up by the academy students. At the academy, Some students, who came after school, were practicing.

Other days, Miss Song, his piano teacher, smelled like highly scented roses. The rose scent soon left a strong smoky lingering aroma. Cheol-su, who had never worn cologne in his life, did not like the scent. He liked her original fragrant scent.

After piano lessons, Cheol-su often met Young-sik and Yeon-woo to have dinner at a gugbabjib[22]. One day, Cheol-su smelled the same scent as Miss Song's from Yeon-woo.

"⋯⋯Did you⋯⋯put on⋯⋯cologne?" Cheol-su asked.

"Yeah, doesn't it smell good?"

"⋯⋯No. ⋯⋯I don't like it."

---

[22] A diner serving rice in hot soup, where the main customer base is males rather than females. Among male customers, middle-aged and older men are more.

"This is expensive."

"The smell makes the taste of gugbab bad. How can you wear cologne at a gugbabjib?" Young-sik interrupted.

"Hwa-young likes this fragrance."

"Hey, next time, that old fox, no···, Hwa-young, put on her perfume."

"Hwa-young's perfume? Why?"

"You young bastard, don't you know that? These days, lovers exchange scents. The woman wears her boyfriend's perfume, and the man wears his girlfriend's perfume. It's a trend among young people these days for lovers to swap each other's scents. You're only 36 years old but don't know that!"said Young-sik.

"Lol···, because I'm in love for the first time···. You are the oldest of us, but you know the latest trend··· wait."

Then Yeon-woo got a phone call. Over Yeon-woo's cell phone, they heard Hwa-young's sharp retort. Yeon-woo began to explain with whom he was and what he was doing now. Yeon-woo's face became serious and he repeated "I'm sorry." into the receiver. While Yeon-woo was talking on the phone, the two bowls of sundaegukbap[23] and a dwaejigukbap[24] they ordered

---

[23] It is a hot rice soup with sundae, which is made by steaming pig's intestines stuffed with various ingredients.

[24] It is a hot rice soup with boiled pork slices.

came out.

"Bros, I just need to go. Actually, I was supposed to meet with Hwa-young, but I didn't say the exact time. I said we'd meet around 9 p.m. after dinner, but I think Hwa-young misunderstood. Please eat mine."

Yeon-woo hurried out of the gugbabjib. Hwa-young didn't like Young-sik and Cheol-su. She used to meet them with Yeon-woo and treated them to dinners and teas because they were Yeon-woo's old friends. She, however, was irritated by Young-sik, because he didn't show thanks to her but said against her often. In addition, Cheol-su suffering from a stroke annoyed her with his blank eyes and slow, sluggish speech and actions. Hwa-young told Yeon-woo to keep his distance from them, but Yeon-woo hung out with them without her noticing. But this time, he was caught because he couldn't cook up a good reason. Yeon-woo made up his mind that he would give up his old friends for Hwa-young's sake if she kept opposing them.

Only the strong scent of smoky rose, which did not go well with a gugbabjib, remained at the seat where Yeon-woo left. The tastes of the gugbabs were not felt properly due to Yeon-woo's strong cologne.

"Is that a romantic relationship? No, it's a boss-subordinate relationship!"

After Yeon-woo left, Yeong-sik, who had been having the gugbab in silence for a while, spoke disapprovingly.

"It's all because of that fellow's ambition. He doesn't want to miss out on her." Young-sik added.

"That bastard, he can't let go of Hwa-yeong, because she opened a pub for him and he hears 'boss' from part-timers and others. He is living a life where his soul is tied down with her. No freedom. Hwa-young, she got him on lock, controlling every move. ···Naive Yeon-woo is so whipped. That girl, Hwa-young, is a complete street bully, a female bully···."

Young-sik continued to swear at Hwa-young, but Young-sik's words did not catch Cheol-su's ears. The thoughts of Cheol-su was elsewhere.

'Lovers·····swap·····perfumes?'

Cheol-su remembered the strong masculine scent that Miss Song wore these days. At the same time, he shook his head, saying "I don't think so."

The cold winter passed and a new year began. Spring was approaching. In February last year, Cheol-su fainted due to a stroke in Seocho, Seoul, the city of his ambition, and returned to his hometown and spent a year recuperating. A year later, now in February, he was much better off. After receiving a second call to return to work in March, Cheol-su was practicing his farewell to Miss Song in his mind. He really enjoyed the last nine months thanks to her. It was the first pleasure he experienced in his life. His depression and lethargy disappeared thanks to her music lessons. Didn't he lose a lot of weight by exercising because of her? When going back to work, he would continue working as a judicial researcher in city Desire. He would probably return to this city, his hometown, in 10 years, after retirement. Like the old man, who said he had learned how to play the piano for a year and then quit, and re-learned it 10 years later, after retiring, Cheol-su could return to her piano academy after becoming a retired old man at the age of 60. By then she would be an ordinary middle-aged woman who already married and struggled with her children. Or even if he returned after retirement, Cheol-su may lose his desire to learn how to play the piano by then and never see her again. Maybe he would spend the rest of his life in Seoul without returning to his hometown.

Cheol-su went back to Desire branch of Suwon District Court in Desire city and shared his regards with his superiors and colleagues. However, when he entered the bleak office and talked about his future work, the great stress he had suffered in the past washed over him again like a tide. His chest felt tight and he was short of breath. Back to a life saturated with competition and office politics. A life where he has to please superiors and colleagues in the large organization and live with a shrunken, divided ego and a low self-esteem. A soulless life caught up in work⋯. However, such stresses had been familiar to him for the past 10 years, so he was able to overcome it and immerse himself in his work again like in the past. He was able to go back to the past life. But, his piano teacher, Miss Song⋯, the thought of not seeing her forever made his heart ache.

He declined to be reinstated. Since he was a contract worker, he would be subject to layoffs due to restructuring someday and would retire. It was just earlier retirement. Cheol-su went through retirement procedures. He decided to go back to the rural area[25], buy a home, settle down there, and learn how to play the piano from her for a few more years. Again his heart pounded. This decision might be a silly one that made him give up a lot of things, but the thought of seeing her again thrilled him.

---

25 Some people living in Seoul and Gyeonggi Province call local cities rural areas.

He walked to his studio in the multi complex house that had been vacant for the past one year. It was a 20-minute walk from Desire branch of Suwon District Court to his studio, but until a year ago, he had been driving his own car. On days when he had his car repaired, he took a taxi. A year ago, walking for more than 10 minutes was unimaginable, but now he could do it lightly.

He called his landlord and said he was moving. As soon as a tenant moved in, the security deposit would return to him. The heavy carrel desk was placed in the studio. Two large bookshelves rose like a huge building at both walls with the carrel desk in between. He was suffocated. Things that had been familiar until last year were now suffocating. Two huge bookshelves were filled with law-related books and textbooks of exams. These were traces of his past, so he could not abandon them for the past six years even after the bar exam was abolished in 2017. It was a symbol of his disappeared youth. He could dimly see his appearance from behind sitting at the desk and studying for the bar exam. Cheol-su of the past was focusing on study with his tired body at the carrel desk even after work and on holidays. The back of him, bent over and studying in the chair, was pitiful. He wanted to approach him and pat him on the shoulder and say.

'I'm you from future. You're amazing to have come this far. You don't have to live like this. Don't try to do big things by chasing your ambitions. Appreciate your current job and enjoy your life. Your youth never comes again. Don't waste any more of your youth, your passion, and your energy. And find your love. Find your wife while young and eat, drink, and be merry with her.'

He bought waste stickers[26] from administrative welfare center and attached them to furniture such as the carrel desk, the chair, the bookshelves, and the blanket chest and so on. And he put them in front of the multi complex house where he resided. Sooner or later, waste disposal officials would come and pick them up. The law-related books, the textbooks and exam papers, which were piled up on the bookshelves, all went into waste paper separation bins. They were the things he had been studying without giving up his dream of becoming a judge. From every corner, the things that he once liked spilled out. They were put off to enjoy later in preparation for the bar exam.

---

26 If you want to throw some furniture away in Korea, you should buy waste stickers from administrative welfare center, attach them on the things you remove, and move them to a designated place.

Music albums, Star Wars movie CDs, cartoon movie CDs such as Gundam, Evangelion, and Atom, figures of the main characters of these cartoon movies, as well as prefabricated toys, and art toys such as Bearbrick, Kubrick, and Quebec. They were the things that once aroused his curiosity and gave him romance, but were pushed into a corner by his dreams, ambitions and harsh reality. They were pushed into a corner and a deep drawer, where his attention did not reach and no light entered, and left covered with dust. He selected a few of these items that still thrilled his heart. Then he shook off the dust and put them in his suitcase. The rest went into a large garbage bag.

He took ktx train at Yongsan Station and went down to his hometown. He organized everything and came back with a vigorous step. He said goodbye to his ten-year-old job and simply chose the piano, his hobby. No, more precisely, he chose his piano teacher. But when he again returned to his hometown, he felt strange here. After returning to his hometown, the first place he went to was the piano academy. That feeling came again to Cheol-su, who was standing waiting for a green light at the crosswalk, which was connected to the piano academy. He felt this street was unfamiliar. The piano academy across from the crosswalk was unfamiliar. The scenery in front of this piano academy that he had seen almost every day for nearly a year on the way to practice and on the way back, It's so unfamiliar.

'What am I doing here?' he asked himself, but he ignored it.

The next morning, Cheol-su saw an ad for the sale of an apartment[27] in a local newspaper and immediately paid the down payment as soon as he saw the apartment. The very following day, he canceled savings accounts at the bank and transferred 1/2 of the apartment price to the account of its owner. It was the moment when the money, which was only represented in numbers in his bank accounts, gave him a meaning. It was a simple job of transferring the numbers to the owner's bank account and getting a large space of his own in return. All he had to do was to transfer the numbers into another account. It was just to move the represented numbers. And the following day, he paid all the balance and completed all the administrative procedures for the purchase of the apartment. Cheol-su was surprised by his strong momentum. On the day when he bought the home and completed administrative procedures through a

27 The most preferred type of housing in Korea is apartments, to the extent that Korea is called an apartment republic.

judicial scrivener, he told his piano teacher, "Miss Song, I bought a home. I paid all the balance this morning and completed all the administrative procedures through a judicial scrivener."

His speaking was not as sluggish and slow as before. It got faster. It became similar to the speed of his speaking in his twenties and thirties.

"What? Then, you're not going back to the previous city and you're going to live here forever?"

"I think it would be unless I move to another city."

"How much did it cost?"

"Not much."

He spoke out of humility because he didn't want to brag.

"Did you buy without a loan?"

"Yes."

"You are amazing! It's great to buy a home without a loan."

Cheol-su was flattered to be described as 'amazing and great' by her.

007

Mischief of Destiny

The following day, Cheol-su woke up at 3 a.m. He couldn't fall asleep again. Regret flooded in. Where on earth is the boss who gives a year of sick leave to a mere contract employee and calls back to return to work! How dare I refused the reinstatement and retired? And I bought an apartment here!

"What have I done?"

He had completely bought the apartment the morning before. He thought of living in Jeonse[28], but news of housing deposit fraud was often reported on television, and he liked his piano teacher, so he bought a home with a naive thought of wanting to settle down in this countryside and continue learning how to play the piano from her.

---

28 It is a type of lease or deposit common in the South Korean real estate market. Instead of paying monthly rent, a renter will make a lump-sum deposit on a rental space, at anywhere from 50% to 80% of the market value, which is then returned at the end of the lease term. The owners make profit from reinvesting the jeonse deposit, instead of receiving the monthly rent. It is also possible to combine a lower jeonse with a small monthly rent.(referenced from wikipedia)

But there was one thing he found out later. This apartment was going to go into elevator replacement work soon. Somehow, the previous owner moved out in a hurry. Cheol-su took the elevator up and down several times to review the apartment, but had no idea that the elevator replacement work was about to begin. It was only after paying off the balance of the apartment and confirming his ownership of it that he noticed a notice of elevator replacement work attached to the elevator.

'Elevator replacement work will be carried out

for one month from day 0th.'

Cheol-su looked around for remodeling companies, but no one wanted to work in an elevator-free place. In the end, remodeling was postponed until after the elevator was completed. Cheol-su became tired due to buying a home suddenly and negotiating with remodeling companies. It was so silly of me to rush to buy a home without knowing that I would have to leave it empty for about 40 days due to elevator replacement work.

Tears burst into his eyes. They were not tears of joy or being impressed, but tears of futility and sorrow. He, who was ambitious from childhood, shed tears when he learned that the home he purchased after his 24 years of social life after serving in the military and graduating from college, was not a building in Seoul, nor an apartment in Seoul, but a 24-year-old apartment in the province.

Calculated as a result, this 24-year-old provincial apartment was the product of his 24 years of youth, energy and passion. When he was in his twenties and thirties, he used to think that by this age, he would have achieved everything perfectly, lived in an expensive luxury apartment in a big city, had a good social status and economic power, married a young and pretty woman playing the piano, and raised cute children. But his 24 years have taken him to a place he never thought of before. When he realized that he had bought a home in his hometown where he longed to leave so much, he was struck by the irony of his fate.

A few days after buying the home, it rained very hard for a week. The tiled-floor of its balcony was dampened with rain. He contacted the former owner with the help of the real estate agent, and the owner spoke as if it was not a big deal. Cheol-su firmly insisted that rain leaking was not a small thing but a responsibility of the former owner, and that as stated in the sales contract, if the buyer was not responsible for any remaining breakdowns of the apartment that could occur for three months, the seller was responsible for repairing them. When the legal contract clause was presented, the former owner stepped back and asked Cheol-su to find a technician instead, as he was busy with his work.

From then on, Cheol-su searched the Internet and went to a nearby bathroom remodeling store and told that his balcony was leaking.

"It seems that the balcony tiles are cracked and the rain is leaking. Is it a problem that can be solved by changing the balcony tiles?"

"No. It's not solved with new tiles. That's because the cooking and silicone work wasn't done properly when installing the balcony sash, so rain leaked."

"Cooking and silicon?"

Cheol-su was surprised that a term used for cooking is also used for a building.

"Please do it."

"No, it's not worth money. Technicians don't want to do it because it is not lucrative. Ask sash dealers. They'll do it for you."

Cheol-su entered the search term 'balcony, Sash and Cooking' on the Internet. There was no information other than cooking information. After searching several more times, he found out that it was not cooking, but caulking. He called one of the technicians who could do the caulking and silicone work, and set a date. Contrary to what the owner of the bathroom remodeling store said, the price was quite high. It was also difficult to tell the price to the former landlord. Caulking work and external silicon work were also delayed by a month due to elevator replacement work.

To him who had never done anything other than study and court work in his life, these practical problems related to a home were new, but also quite stressful. The elevator replacement work put all the work back a month. Cheol-su was also tired and stopped all apartment-related work for a while.

Was it a good thing that I bought a home in this city? Two new big apartment complexes near my apartment are currently under construction and the tallest residential complex in this city will be built in a year. Everyone is going to move into new apartments. Could I sell this old apartment back without losing any money for remodeling? He worried.

One day, Cheol-su overheard some customers talking each other in the convenient store, where he worked.

"Right now, the occupancy rate of apartments in this city is over 100% and becomes 120%. There are more apartments than its population in this city."

"Now everyone is selling apartments. The price of apartments will plunge further. If you buy one now, you're stupid. They say that housing prices are likely to moderate and be normalized. Everyone sells theirs for cash and put the money in the bank. The interest rate is high, so even if you collect only cash interest, your property will increase." These words from customers added anxieties to Cheol-su.

Late March. After finishing part-time job at his brother's convenience store, he headed straight to the piano academy as usual. Spring rain drizzled down on that day, too. He pulled the door open. Into the umbrella container at the entrance of the piano academy, he put his plastic umbrella taken from the convenient store. He could see a long black male umbrella with a silver skull on the handle. It was the Alexander MacQueen brand. He saw this skull umbrella before on a rainy day in November last year. He remembered it because it was an expensive, famous brand umbrella.

There was no one in the academy. It was quiet. He thought

children didn't come yet. They would come soon. Cheol-su went into the booth right next to the director's office, where he always practiced. From the director's office, the sound of a lecture played back at fast speeds was heard, as always, in a low voice.

'Miss Song is listening to the lecture.'

Cheol-su admired her steady passion for learning. His heart warmed up. However, even though it was time for their lesson, Miss Song did not come to Cheol-su's practice room. Cheol-su kept waiting because Miss Song had told him sternly a couple of times to wait in the practice room without knocking on the director's door because she would come out for a lesson when it was time. She didn't come. Cheol-su, tired of waiting, finally went to the director's office and knocked on the door.

Knock! knock!

There was no response.

"… Miss Song."

There was still no response.

"… Miss Song."

Miss Song didn't come out.

'It's weird. I could hear the sound of a lecture with increased speed…. I'm sure she is listening to a lecture inside….'

A few seconds passed. Cheol-su called her a little louder. He hesitated whether to hold the handle of the director's office door and open it. Just then the director's office door was opened. At the same time, a strong rose smoky scent flowed out of the director's office. Contrary to his expectation, however, it was not Miss Song who came out of the director's office, but a tall, handsome, elegant young man. Cheol-su was wide-eyed with surprise. He was at a loss for words.

"··· Miss Song···"

"She's not here today."

The young man said in a low voice.

"···Ah, ···I'm sorry."

Cheol-su, not knowing what to say about this unexpected situation, apologized momentarily and turned around. He couldn't practice calmly in the practice room any more after seeing that young man. He left the academy after picking up his plastic umbrella next to the Alexander MacQueen skull umbrella.

That man must have been the owner of the sound of the lecture that was played quietly at fast speed probably from last fall···. So the sound wasn't the one Miss Song was studying for, but the one that the man played back. And every time that sound came out, Miss Song was with that man in the director's office. Was a man's low voice, which I sometimes heard and thought as a lecturer's voice, the voice of that man? That's why she told me strictly not to come to the director's office and knock on the door, but to stay in, saying she would come on time if I keep practicing. The smell of Miss Song was that man's cologne scent. He was the owner of that skull umbrella I saw on a rainy day in the autumn last year, which means they were dating then, too. I thought she didn't have a boyfriend. Not knowing that she was in the director's office with that guy, I came to this academy every day with excitement, with my heart fluttering⋯. His world was shaken. His body trembled in surprise. His legs were shaking. He may be her younger brother or older brother. He may be just her guy friend. Cheol-su tried to think it pure. But his intuition was saying he was Miss Song's boyfriend.

On the way home, Cheol-su felt the familiar body symptoms. In February of last year, on the day he was disposing of his car in front of his studio apartment in city Desire, he collapsed with similar symptoms like this in Seocho-dong, Seoul. He walked home slowly overcoming the dizziness. The fever rose to 39 degrees that evening.

The following morning, he barely got up and went to see a doctor. He was prescribed medicine to make his fever go down.

He fell into a deep sleep for several days. Appetite was gone. He barely ate. He only took medicine. The fever went down several days later, but pain in his throat didn't go away even after taking medicine and got worse as time went on. He couldn't even swallow his saliva because of his sore throat. His voice was gone. Every time he tried to speak, he wheezed and squeaked. His voice sounded more like heavy sound of iron machines operating in a factory.

'I should have left here when the sick leave was over. I shouldn't have retired. If I had seen her boyfriend before I bought the apartment···, no, if I had seen her boyfriend while I was preparing to go back to work···, if so, I would have left this city without any regrets···. I saw her boyfriend exactly three weeks after I came back from retirement and bought a home! How could the goddess of fate play such a joke on me?'

Several days later, as soon as his fever went down, Cheol-su went back to the academy. About that young man he wanted to ask her. He pulled the door of the academy open and entered. The wind-bell sounded as clear and pure as ever.

"Please come on in, Mr. Kwon."

Miss Song, who was giving a lesson to an elementary school

student, smiled brightly at Cheol-su coming in. When Cheol-su saw her smile, a ray of light came into his dark heart.

"I didn't tell you in advance. I went on a family trip last Friday and came back this Tuesday. You came on Friday, right?"

"Ah!"

Cheol-su breathed a sigh of relief.

'On Friday she was not alone with that man in the director's office. She said she went on a family trip on that day. And she was back the following Tuesday. He was alone on that day.'

"Please Practice. I'll give you a lesson right after this boy's lesson."

"……Yes."

Cheol-su spoke slowly as before and slowly entered the booth next to the director's office, where he usually practiced. Soon after the lesson, Miss Song came into the booth and sat next to Cheol-su. She smelled of strong rose smoky fragrance. Her cute fair little fingers fluttered on the piano keys and danced like butterflies. Her gentle and calm voice, which explained how to play a new song, still made his heart flutter. Many thoughts passed through Cheol-su's head. He hesitated, but when the lesson was over, he summoned up the courage to ask.

"……Miss Song……on Friday afternoon……the man……who

was in the director's office⋯⋯"

An uneven squeaky sound came out from Cheol-su's voice. His fever had gone down, but it was due to his sore throat that hadn't been cured yet. He thought his voice sounded like that of a monster.

"Oh, he's my boyfriend."

She said calmly and lightly. Cheol-su's heart sank. His eyes trembled faintly. He didn't ask anything more. The word 'my boyfriend' stabbed him in the heart. She left after the lesson, telling him to practice. In an instant, tears welled up in his eyes. She never wondered what the reason for his changed, squeaky voice was. She didn't ask about his health. Furthermore, she had no way of knowing that Cheol-su almost died with a fever of 39 degrees for several days and then came back to see her as soon as he got better. She left. Tears streamed down his stubbly cheeks, which he had not been able to shave for several days due to sickness. He wiped away his tears. It was ridiculous even to himself that a 50-year-old man, who was neither an elementary school boy nor a teenager, shed tears out of a pure unrequited love that young boys would experience.

008

Turning to Dust

Cheol-su did not go to the piano academy after finishing his part-time job at the convenience store. Instead, he went up to his apartment on the 10th floor every day. Looking at the 24-year-old space made him lose his appetite. He could hardly eat because he regretted what he had done. He started drinking again, which he quit for the last one year. At one side of the apartment, empty beer cans that Cheol-su drank every day were piled up.

One day, he started cleaning his apartment. He had to take responsibility for his choice. He removed dirty stains from every nook and cranny. After daily part-time work, he gasped up to the 10th floor. Although he had lost weight due to diet control and exercise for the last one year, he was still fat, and couldn't breathe while he climbed up, so he stopped to hold on to the wall on every third floor. And he took a breath. At first, he tried to leave the cleaning to a cleaner, but no one wanted to work in an elevator-free apartment. In the end, he cleaned his apartment himself. He repeatedly wiped away stains which were stuck to all spaces with rags, except for old furniture such as kitchen furniture, kitchen tiles, and bathroom fixtures that would be taken away and demolished. He removed dirt and stains of poverty left by former owners who had lived there for the past 24 years. He sweated like a pig.

He checked his bank account balance. Although he had a part-time job, income was small and money kept flowing out. In order to reduce costs, and since he would not continue to settle here, he remodeled only necessary parts. Caulking work, kitchen, bathroom, lighting, and more were partially entrusted to each renovation store.

In the period when there was no real estate transaction due to the economy recession, Cheol-su became a benefactor by giving generous money to the former landlord to buy his home and providing work to each renovation store.

To save remodeling costs, Cheol-su painted the existing wallpaper white instead of replacing it with a new one. This work lasted several days. Paint stuck to the molding and dripped onto the floor. Paint drips splattered all over his face, his neck, his arms, and his clothes. After painting each wall, he wiped off the paint stains on the molding and on the floor several times with rags. The paint on his body was also washed off several times with water.

Cheol-su looked quietly at his face through the bathroom mirror, erasing the paint drips on his face and arms. He lost a lot of weight on his face. Having suffered from heartache due to retirement and his piano teacher's boy friend, loss of appetite, the part-time job, climbing up and down the 10th floor every day to clean, and communication and negotiations with renovation stores, he lost weight rapidly. He looked in the mirror and tried grinning from ear to ear. He had wrinkles around his eyes. It was a remarkable change. His face used to be tight and plump with no wrinkles no matter how much he frowned it. He now shut his mouth. There were no wrinkles in sight.

It had been over a month since he didn't attend the piano academy. He just sent Miss Song a text message saying that he would take a break. He didn't want to show her that he was becoming haggard and his complexion was turning dark by a twist of fate. He went into his own cave.

Cheol-su's brother was worried that Cheol-su was once overweight, but now he lost too much weight and could not eat.

"Cheol-su, you are losing too much weight."

"No. I don't lose weight any more, but my body lose weight on its own."

"I think it's because you retired, but it's a process that all men in their 40s and 50s go through. There are many people in their 40s and 50s who start a second life with a different job after retiring from major companies. Self-employed rather than re-entering another company⋯, you can even run your own business. Widen your perspective."

Cheol-su's older brother encouraged him not to think that the court work was his everything.

Yeon-woo was busy with his pub business and dating Hwa-yeong, so Cheol-su and Young-sik naturally got along just the two of them. Cheol-su persuaded Young-sik to go to a bar whenever they met because he was having a hard time now. He wanted to forget his worries for a moment with the power of alcohol. They met at another bar instead of going to Yeon-woo's pub. Cheol-su enjoyed the bright atmosphere of bars. It was a time to get out of his worries even for a moment. Although

Young-sik was concerned about Cheol-su, who was gradually losing weight, it was nice to see him regaining his slim and handsome appearance in his heyday. His personality also changed. He became nimble and talkative, so Young-sik was always puzzled at his change. However, Young-sik often said this to Cheol-su and scratched his nerves.

"You keep calling me because you need a substitute for Yeon-woo, right? I haven't said it honestly, but I don't like being treated as a substitute for Yeon-woo, and it seems that it's not good for you and me to keep meeting up like this."

"Bro, I have never treated you as a substitute for Yeon-woo. You are a person with your own unique characteristics and charms, who cannot be a replacement for anyone."

"Yeon-woo was your soul-mate for the past year, but Yeon-woo went to Hwa-young and you meet me instead. Your heart is empty because Yeon-woo isn't here."

"Bro, you keep saying soul-mate, but I acted the same towards Yeon-woo and you. Yeon-woo was your soul-mate, right? Yeon-woo went to Hwa-young, so you felt empty."

Young-sik was startled for a moment.

"When you were working in city Desire, Yeon-woo and I met almost every day. Then Yeon-woo got to know Hwa-young, and three of us often hung out. Yeon-woo and Hwa-young once had an argument. Yeon-woo said he would never see Hwa-young again. Hwa-young said she wouldn't see Yeon-woo either. From then on, Hwa-young called me every night. Sometimes we talked on the phone until dawn. But you know what's funny? Hwa-young talked only about Yeon-woo the whole time she talked to me on the phone. She didn't know that she only talked about Yeon-woo. And she always ended up with 'Why is Yeon-woo like that?'. And You talk about Yeon-woo often, too."

"Did I? I think you do it more often⋯."

"Yeon-woo was nice."

"He is like water. He fills our hearts, keeping his emotion inside. And he is young and fun."

"No, not now⋯. That fellow is getting sneaky. He's becoming like his girl friend."

"By the way, how did Yeon-woo and Hwa-young become lovers?"

"Hwa-young asked me to bridge the gap between the two. She wanted to make up with Yeon-woo, so she asked me to bridge their differences so that she could meet up him again. Well, I soothed Yeon-woo and let them contact each other again. Then they developed into lovers."

"Come to think of it, it's a relief that Yeon-woo was born as a man. If he had been born as a woman, he would have seduced many men. Look. Our conversation is all Yeon-woo, too."

"What kind of guy likes that pig? His facial skin is like volcanic craters, and he is fat like a pig!"

"If he had been born as a girl, he would have looked different. I'm talking about his nice personality."

"He is not nice any more. He's changed. He's also grown a lot. ···When he was younger, he all the time followed me around. He was such a friendly guy, and I liked it. I taught him a lot···. Now that he's grown much, there's nothing I can do for him."

Young-sik drank beer again without saying any more.

Cheol-su sent Young-sik back home in a taxi. After leaving him, Cheol-su was slowly walking down the night street to return to his apartment when he got a text message from Young-sik.

'I stopped drinking because of diabetes, but these days, I keep meeting you and end up drinking beer and eating meat. It's not good for me. And to meet you, I take a taxi all the time. My parents plague me, saying that such a deadbeat roams about here and there. I live within the money which my parents supply, so the taxi fare is burdensome. It's better not to meet for each other from now on. Thanks for buying me meat and beer today, and let's stay out of touch from now on. Take care.'

The text broke Cheol-su's heart. Money was not a problem. He could buy for Young-sik. However, the word 'stay out of touch' made Cheol-su lonely. If Young-sik disappeared, there was nothing to hold him here other than his brother's family. And this city was where his apartment was now. Even for his apartment, Cheol-su had to make a reason to stay in this city. He sent a reply.

'Bro, can I call you?'

'Okay.'

Contrary to the dark and extreme text content, Young-sik's voice was bright and cheerful.

"Bro, your voice is bright. I was really surprised. I just saw your text message and I thought something was going on to you and I was worried and called you. Something happened between you and your parents?"

"No, nothing happened···. All sleep."

"What were you doing?"

"Now is my free time. I play games."

"Bro, you said you would drink alcohol and eat meat whenever you meet me. It's true that I relied on alcohol for a while because I retired and bought an apartment here and have a hard time now. But I won't drink beer anymore when this hard time is over. And today, I drank only a pint of beer. I didn't want to get drunk again like in the past, so I restrained myself. It was you who drank two or three bottles today, and it was you who said three or four times that you wanted to eat meat. I told you to drink only a little beer for health and feel good, but you kept saying that you wanted to drink more and eat meat, so I treated you to more."

Young-sik was momentarily taken aback. Since when has Cheol-su been taking things up? There is no escape. He wasn't such a fellow. He has also changed a lot. He's going back to the decisive and lucid character of his 20s and 30s. Besides, he is verifying happenings one by one, like court work. Yeon-woo wasn't the only one who changed. Everyone is changing. I think I'm the only one who is stagnant.

"No, I appreciate that. But the taxi fare⋯. When I met Yeon-woo in the past, we were in the same neighborhood, so it didn't cost a taxi fare or money. But when I meet you, Cheol-su, it keeps costing me money. Taxi fare, taxi fare, taxi fare⋯ are all listed on my mom's bank account. I'm paying for a taxi with my mother's credit card, but my mother nags me, saying that an unemployed dead beat wanders off. I have to answer her persistent financial questions. I'm living an oppressed and non-free life, which is really stressful."

"Bro, then you should say clearly that the reason is money. If you keep mentioning other reasons···, I'm doing my best for you, but I'm confused if you keep giving me other reasons. Taxi fare is also burdensome for you, so I treat you to all every time you meet me. It's a bit difficult for me to take responsibility for your taxi fare, so you can earn your pocket money by doing a part-time job."

"I can't work anymore because I have diabetes. I've never worked for anyone and I don't want to work for anyone at this age. My parents bought annuity insurance for me when I was young so that I could receive an annuity every month, so I live on that now, even though not much."

"Then you should thank your parents. Don't just gossip about them."

"I was grateful even when they bought me annuity insurance. They were nice back then. But now they are very mean old people and treat me like their servant. They can't lift heavy things because they are old, so they call me to lift them, and since they can't walk properly, I always have to wait on them by their side. I live as a caregiver. No, worse than a caregiver. They don't see me as their son. They see me as a servant, a worker needed in their old age. Very evil devils. Only when these two die will I be free. If they both die, I will inherit their apartment and live freely alone. Good for you, Cheol-su. You have a home now and you're really free. Who oppresses and controls you? You have a lot of hobbies. A man playing the piano···. You exercised hard, and now you lost all the weight, so you're back to Cheol-su Kwon in your heyday."

"Bro, you'd better stop blaming your parents. Haven't you thought about your parents' position? In the West, when you reach your late teens, you leave your parents through college or employment. In Korea, because of the characteristics of Korean society, such as a long period of education and expensive housing prices, I think that you can live with your parents until your twenties or thirties. But think of your child as not getting married, not getting a job, not getting independent, and staying with you until he is over 50. Frustrating, isn't it? Your parents will be so frustrated. All animals on Earth leave their parents in adolescence. If you continue to live at your parents' home without being independent, you will have no choice but to keep hearing your parents' nagging."

Young-sik no longer wanted to talk with Cheol-su. I miss Yeon-woo. However, he followed his ambition and left me after picking up the old fox, Hwa-young, who is six years older. His personality has become more and more sneaky. Yeon-woo was nice when he was younger and bound up my wounds. But Cheol-su is a disciplinary man. He left for Seoul and set himself up on his legs right after graduating from high school, and took responsibility for his own livelihood while earning a living. Unlike me, He has strong ability to maintain his livelihood. He came down here because he was sick and lived in his brother's house for a year, but now he bought an apartment and became independent. His appearance and character have changed. Now I don't want to get involved with Cheol-su and Yeon-woo. I'm sick of them. Everyone's hurting me. This is my last talking with this guy. This guy is lonely too, so he'll keep calling and texting me from now on. This guy also has some stalking behaviors to my surprise. Before Yeon-woo and Hwa-yeong became lovers, Yeon-woo used to call and text me every time I ghosted him. But how could they be so similar? Those who pursue social ambition seem to be similar. Yeon-woo said he was worried about me and kept texting and calling me, but in fact it was for himself. It was because he had no one to share his deep feelings with but me. It was because we were internally connected and on the same wavelength. He was addicted to me. Those who are ambitious must guard their hearts above all else. It seems like a stalker to me to keep texting and calling without control of their own mind. Cheol-su, this guy, also shows similar behaviors to me. I'm not interested in ambitions. It's good to just live a daily life happily like this without big dreams. I blocked him, but I can't help it if he keeps sending texts and calling. I have to change my number again. How many times has this been. This is all because of Yeon-woo. I've changed my phone number more than 10 times just because of him.

April and May. The elevator replacement was completed, and the remodeling of the apartment was almost finished. The apartment changed from a run-down look to a neat and stylish look. Rather than entrusting all of the remodeling to one company, the remodeling was entrusted to each vendor of each part separately. It was a way to cut down on expenses, and he didn't want to spend a lot of money on remodeling because he was planning to leave soon. When he arrived at the apartment after finishing his part-time job, the kitchen remodeling, which was the last step, had been completed.

Then the doorbell rang. It was Yeon-woo. Cheol-su told him the address of his apartment a while ago, and he visited Cheol-su. Yeon-woo, who saw Cheol-su for the first time in a while, shouted in surprise.

"Holy cow! Are you Cheol-su? You lost so much weight. You've become a different person! I don't recognize you!"

Yeon-woo put beer cans and side dishes, which he had brought in a black plastic bag, on a table in the living room.

"Bro, you said you quit drinking. What's wrong with you to ask me to bring you beer?"

"I stopped drinking while recuperating, but I couldn't be able to hold out after buying this apartment. I retired completely a while ago. My address is now here. I'm not sure whether it was a right choice to buy this home, and it's troublesome to think about the remodeling costs, taxes, the future profitability of this home, and more. Also, as I saw gloomy spaces that had not been remodeled while cleaning every day, I felt even more gloomy. Besides, I heard that this summer is a rainy season, but it rains often even before summer."

Yeon-woo opened a can of beer and held it out to Cheol-su. Cheol-su received and gulped it down.

"You're busy with business, so I've only met Young-sik. We used to go to beer houses here and there every evening. Oh, sorry! Young-sik asked me to go to another beer place…."

"You've been meeting Young-sik."

"Yeah. By the way, did something happen between you and Young-sik?"

"I guess my words made him feel bad."

"What did you say?"

"Well, it's always a question for me. How can I know the heart of Young-sik, whose heart gets more fragile like glass as he gets older? He blocked me again after sending an extreme text message."

"Isn't it because you're busy dating Hwa-young and neglect Young-sik?"

"… By the way, bro…. I'm worried about your health. You lost so much weight all of sudden and started drinking alcohol again…."

"I'm sorry I'm drinking again, but I can't get through my current situation without alcohol. You know this because you run a pub. Many people come to beer houses to laugh, communicate, and have fun while drinking and eating…. Without this kind of bright energy, I can't handle the negative thoughts and feelings about my choices that are soaring moment by moment. I'm buried in negative thoughts. Crushed to death. I drink it to live, not to be overwhelmed by negative thoughts and feelings."

"You must be having a hard time right now, but this time will pass soon. When I started my business, I wasn't sure if I was doing well, and I had a lot of worries, but all of that was overturned. It's going well. You will be like that too."

"Young-sik disappeared again. He didn't check my text message, so I called him and his number was unavailable. I've been hanging out with him because I know you're too busy to make time···. There is no joy in life because Young-sik is gone. I was enduring this period by meeting him up and talking to him every day at a bar."

"He often does that. If you forget about it, you will be contacted again someday."

"How do you know that?"

"I spent 10 years here with Young-sik when you was in city Desire. Before I started dating Hwa-young, we met almost every day. For the past 10 years, he disappeared and contacted me, disappeared again, and contacted me again and again. By the way, bro, stop drinking now. You have to take care of your health."

"I'll quit drinking. I'll quit it after this hard period passes by. But now I have to rely on it a little more. Drinking makes me feel better. I can't sleep without alcohol every night. My head is full of regrets and worries. I am experiencing the living hell. I quit my job and buy a home here, not in Seoul. I think I've been so suppressed for survival over the past 24 years that my thoughts have been shaped too extreme."

"You've already lived an extreme life for the past 24 years. That's why you were sick. Your body and mind couldn't stand such a life."

"You're still young, so don't go to extreme. Don't get to the point where you're obsessed with work and ambition and forget what you want. Take care of your mind, making choices that make you happy every moment. Anyway, when I drink alcohol, I feel at ease mentally and feel better. Worries are gone."

"Are you leaving here?"

"Perhaps. But I'll keep my address here for the time being. It'll be clear when the next move is decided. So I didn't do all the remodeling but only did the necessary parts. The next person to settle here will do the rest."

"By the way, bro. You have changed a lot."

"What?"

"You lost so much weight that you look like a different person, and you seem to have a different character. Your speech speed is very fast. And you talk a lot."

"Huh?"

"When you came here to recuperate last year, ···no, I met you for the first time 10 years ago at the hometown alumni and since then, you've always been a person who didn't talk nor show your inner thoughts and feelings. I had to ask a lot of questions to get to know your thought. In addition, I had to wait a few seconds for an answer, and you always gave me only short-answers. I had to ask you several more questions to know how you felt···. As a questioner, I lost a lot of energy and was exhausted. But now look at you. Even if no one asks you a question first, you notice it first and talks a lot, and does it at length. And your speech is also fast. Young-sik said that you were intelligent, smart, popular and spoke well when you were in your 20s··· I couldn't imagine that··· I think I know it a little bit now. I think you in your 20s might have been similar to you now."

"Have I changed a lot···?"

"The same goes for this apartment. It's refreshing to see the remodeled home. You said this home was old and gloomy in the past, but I can't imagine its previous look."

Yeon-woo looked around the remodeled apartment.

"Ah, you said before that you'd torn off the belly fat⋯. Are you still tearing it off? Seeing that you have become very slim, you must have torn off a lot of belly fat. Hahaha."

"No, my body lost weight on its own right now, so I don't have belly fat to get rid of. I haven't torn it off for months since I bought this home."

"Where is the belly fat you tore off earlier?"

"Come here."

Cheol-su grabbed Yeon-woo by the wrist and entered a room. There is a chest of drawers there. He carefully opened one of the drawers.

"These are the belly fats I have torn off so far. A gross lump of my abdomen fat. Now that I've seen it so many times, it looks covetous."

Yeon-woo looked into the drawer. It was empty and piled with gray dusts.

"What are you talking about? I can't see anything."

Cheol-su turned from Yeon-woo and looked into the open drawer. As Yeon-woo said, there was nothing there. What's going on here! Where did all the lumps of fat piled up like a mountain disappear? Cheol-su drew a line with his index finger in the empty space. There were only dusts on his finger.

"Bro, I took time to visit your apartment today because you said you bought a home. But I'm busy from now on, so I can't hang out with you. I'm busy running my pub every day, and when I have time, I go to seminars here and there with Hwa-young. There's a lot to learn to run my business better…." Yeon-woo left Cheol-su's apartment with these words.

Yeon-woo's girlfriend, Hwa-young, forbade him from meeting with Young-sik and Cheol-su. He had avoided meeting with them with plausible reasons without directly telling them that he could no longer hang out with them because of Hwa-young's objection. He was busy meeting new people, but Young-sik and Cheol-su kept trying to contact with him, so he couldn't help but get together with them. There was not only Hwa-young' opposition, but he also wanted to distance himself from them, whom he now had nothing to learn from. If Young-sik gets back to me, I will not meet him with an excuse for work…. Cheol-su is… he's changed. He looks like a completely different person because he bought a home and lost weight. I want to meet Cheol-su a little more, but Hwa-young opposes it, so I think I need to cut ties with him, too. And he still talks about the bullshit nonsense 'tearing off his belly fat'. As Hwa-young advised, I think it's time to sort things out with them. In fact, they don't look big anymore. I think I've now learned everything from them.

After Yeon-woo left, Cheol-su looked into the drawer once again. Where the hell did the huge abdominal fat, which existed until recently, go? Even though it was invisible to others, that mess of fat was visible to Cheol-su. Just then, at one corner of the drawer, he saw a small, milky-white skinned lump of fat. Just as a balloon got smaller and smaller in size when air was deflated, the milky-white lump of fat finely got smaller and smaller.

After graduating from college, negative emotions and thoughts such as stress, anger, frustration, inferiority, sadness, and resentment had accumulated in his abdomen in the form of abdominal obesity over the past 24 years. New negative emotions built up every day and grew larger with time. He couldn't throw away hardships and negative emotions of his past, which were built up every day. He held onto them until now. It was because if they disappeared, it seemed that his past and his present self would also disappear. He couldn't stand disappearance of his former existence that had spoken for himself, so he lived with those negative memories.

The pain and sufferings of his past could not leave him because they could not resolve their resentment just as it is said in traditional fairy tales that ghosts cannot leave this world because they have a lot of Han[29]. Cheol-su expressed his condolences and relieved his Han of his youth. He sent ghosts named Han to the place they needed to go. The lump of abdominal fat in the drawer continued to shrink like a deflated balloon. Now it became invisible with the naked eye. And it became a piece of dust, and disappeared forever from sight.

---

29 A complex emotion, which is unique to Koreans and is a mixture of various sorrowful emotions such as sorrow, pity, resentment, pain, regret, being oppressed, affection, hate and so on.

009

Fate in Time

Early June. Summer began. The rainy spell, which lasted for a few weeks, stopped for a while. Cheol-su walked out of his apartment. The sun was showing its face through clouds, giving a gift of summer sunshine. Feeling the sunshine for the first time in a long time, he walked down the road to the piano academy he hadn't walked in a while. He looked at himself in the mirror in front of the unmanned self-photo studio. A very strange man was standing in the mirror. It wasn't Cheol-su Kwon of the past. A man of normal weight was standing. He wasn't a fat pot-bellied old man. The same things as before were only his gray hair and thick glasses.

Walking a little further, there is a silk tree in front of a bank, that is, a cattle-rice-tree that cattle like. Cheol-su's animal year was the ox. His heart leaped at the thought of seeing the silk tree. Mysterious and beautiful deep pink flowers. Silk tree flowers that exudes a strong and beautiful fragrance.

Cheol-su approached the silk tree. The silk tree was starting to bloom. He picked up three or four fallen silk flowers and smelled the scent. He looked back to the first time he came to know these flowers. Exactly one year has passed. It has also been a year since I started learning how to play the piano because I started learning it when the silk tree started blooming. I want to see my piano teacher.

He walked straight to the academy with the silk tree flowers. The traffic light at the crosswalk immediately changed from red to green, and he crossed the crosswalk without waiting. From the crosswalk, he could hear the friendly piano sound of some children playing. Other children were seen entering the piano academy on the first floor one by one.

Cheol-su pulled the door of the academy open. The wind-bell hanging from the door made a transparent sound. At each booth, children were tapping on the piano keys with their fingers looking like maple leaves. He heard the voice of Miss Song teaching a child in a booth. Cheol-su entered the booth next to the director's office, where he always practiced. He put the silk tree flowers on top of the piano and played the piano. He made some mistakes because it had been a while since he stopped practicing it, but it was okay. When he was in the middle of practicing, Miss Song came in. She looked laid-back and behaved in a relaxed way.

"Mr. Kwon, you came."

"Oh, yes. I've been a little busy…."

"Are you starting again from today?"

"Yes. I've been under a lot of stress lately. remodeling my apartment. That's why I couldn't come."

He explained why he had not been able to come for the past two months. The underlying reason was hidden. She gave only polite greetings and showed no personal interest in him as always. Even though he had lost a lot of weight for the last two months and appeared in front of her with a completely different appearance, she did not ask him what had happened. He didn't expect her attention much, but he couldn't help but feel disappointed. In order to talk more with her, Cheol-su had to hold onto her with more talks about himself.

"I've been busy looking for right remodeling contractors."

"How much did it cost?"

"To cut cost, I didn't entrust everything to one remodeling contractor. I did the leg work, and made inquiries with each contractor. I remodeled each part separately."

"How much did it cost in total?"

She repeated the question 'how much did it cost?' twice. Her only interest was in money.

"It didn't cost that much. I lost a lot of weight due to stress. Don't you think I lost a lot of weight?"

Cheol-su kept asking questions to talk more with her. She didn't want any personal questions about herself, so he had to hold onto her with questions related to himself.

"You look pale."

"I consulted some remodeling stores, negotiate the costs, and ask for a cost reduction···. These processes were exhausting. I also hate seeing myself crunching some numbers."

"I see···."

She seemed to want to tell him something, but she left the booth without saying it. Cheol-su kept practicing the piano. After a while, she returned to the booth. She wanted to tell him something. He thought it was probably the tuition fee of a new month and started to float an idea first to ease her difficulties.

"Miss Song, I registered two months ago, but··· I attended only for a few days after registering, and I haven't been able to take lessons since then, so I want you to extend the period further."

"But, Mr. Kwon, even though you didn't take lessons, you

came a few times on the days you didn't take lessons and practiced."

Actually, it was that he deliberately avoided her. The day he
saw her boyfriend, after finding out that she was with her boyfriend in the director's office almost everyday, he wasn't sure if
he could confront her. He wanted to avoid her. But he couldn't
stop playing the piano, so he came and practiced with the elderly students for a while in her absence.

"Mr. Kwon, I'll extend your lesson period. But please don't ask
for an extension after you rest. From now on, let me know in
advance when you are taking a break."

How can I predict when I will be in pain and tell her that in
advance? Wasn't it all because of her that my fever went up to 39
degrees and I came back to life after almost dying? The day I
saw her boyfriend come out of the director's office, I realized
that the sound of the lecture played back at fast speed in the
director's office during past several months was not the one of
her studying, but the one played back whenever she was with
her boyfriend. I practiced the piano with my unrequited love,
not knowing that she was alone with him every day in her
office. I practiced the piano every day without knowing any-
thing···. I quit my job in court, bought a home here, and put my

efforts and expenses in remodeling the apartment in order to continue taking lessons from her.

Although all responsibility was on him for his unrequited love, which she did not know, he was disappointed and sad that she did not even have any affection toward him, who had learned how to play the piano from her for nearly a year. In the meantime, he was heart-broken, lost so much weight and showed up in front of her as a totally different-looking man. He finally showed up before her, after breaking through anxiety that weighed on him and defeating all the negative emotions that rushed to hurt him. He came running to only see her in the form of a shabby warrior who shed blood and sweats through all the adversity. But she had no affection for him, let alone personal interest. Her interest was only in tuition, whether to register now or not.

Her lesson didn't come into his head. He couldn't even look her in the face. He couldn't look at her with the same longing and complete joy as before. He couldn't go back to the old time when he learned how to play the piano without any worries. After a short lesson, she left the booth, leaving only businesslike words, "Practice." Cheol-su tried to practice a little more, but he had no internal motivation. He was so exhausted that he couldn' t practice any more. Cheol-su closed the piano cover and stood up. He picked up the silk tree flowers, which he had placed on the piano. He turned off the light of the booth, and came out of it. The academy was filled with the sound of children practicing with passion. The door of the director's office was tightly closed. The piano teacher was in the director's office⋯ with her boyfriend⋯. Cheol-su pushed the academy door closed and came out.

She may have been a fate in time for several months or a year, who was meant to help Cheol-su recover his health via music and communication during a period of his recuperation. She may have been a connection that was meant to last just a few months to a maximum of a year. He should have left when his five months of sick leave ended last year. Otherwise, he should have left here when his one-year sick leave ended early this year. He once again blamed himself for leading the connection of several months so far with his pure unrequited love.

It was past 8 p.m. But it was different from 8 p.m. in autumn, winter, and spring of the past year, when he finished piano practice after working at the convenience store. It was still bright, and not dark. He walked in a different direction from the direction of the silk tree. He headed home. On the way, darkness was falling little by little. He brought the silk tree flowers to his nose. Now the flowers lost some of their vitality but was still full of the scent.

010

Concerto

Mid-June. Yeong-sik came back after going into hiding for a few months. He repeated ghosting his acquaintances and then coming back to them like a submarine sinking and coming back up in the sea. It was a bit discouraging to be alone for so long after retreating to his cave. Now he wanted to meet his friends and have fun. Yeon-woo, that fellow, must be busy hanging out with Hwa-young while doing business, so he texted Cheol-su first. Yeon-woo got accustomed to my repeated ghosting and coming back, but Cheol-su must have been embarrassed because it was his first time experiencing it. But it's okay. Cheol-su is nice. Like Yeon-woo, he's going to welcome me back.

Cheol-su was delighted to receive Young-sik's call. As Yeong-sik thought, Cheol-su did not criticize his sudden disappearance and only talked about the present and the future.

'Bro, there is a concert at the Arts center here today. Would you like to go with me?'

Cheol-su, who used to see performance while receiving news from the Seoul Arts Center when he lived in city Desire, was also receiving news from his hometown Arts center after he returned home. He sent a text message to Young-sik with a poster for an orchestra performance at 7 p.m. on Friday.

'Cheol-su, invite Yeon-woo, too.'

'Sure.'

'Yeon-woo, there is a concert. Come out.'

Cheol-su also sent a text message to Yeon-woo. A reply came soon after.

'Good.'

They made an appointment to meet at the Arts Center at 6:30 p.m. Young-sik disappeared for a while, and Yeon-woo was busy with his business and dating Hwa-young, so the three of them had not met for several months. So Young-sik and Cheol-su expected that the three could unite again via this opportunity.

Yeong-sik and Cheol-su arrived first and stood in front of the Arts center waiting for Yeon-woo.

"After all, it's music. Music binds us. Yeon-woo plays the oboe, Cheol-su, you play the piano, and I play the violin."

"Hwa-young is coming too, but Yeon-woo says she's arriving a little late."

"Yeon-woo probably feels a bit empty after dating Hwa-young. She makes good money, but she's bad at music. So, when she got to know us, she made an effort to have interest in music. After a long time, the three of us, no, the four of us, are getting together again."

Soon, Yeon-woo walked into the Arts center with an unhappy face. Just as he was about to come in, the wind blew. The wind swept through Yeon-woo's stylish bangs, exposing his big and wide forehead.

'Was Yeon-woo's forehead that wide?'

Cheol-su and Yeong-sik were momentarily taken aback as they saw Yeon-woo's forehead as big and wide as his big ambition. Cheol-su also had a wide forehead, but Yeon-woo's forehead was no less than his. Yeon-woo's bangs were hiding his wide forehead, just as he hid his big ambitions.

"Bros, Hwa-young's arriving at 7 o'clock. Young-sik, you had better avoid Hwa-young today. Hwa-young is really angry right now. Whenever she met you and I together, she cared much about your financial situation, and she paid for alcohol, food, and coffee, but you described it as 'condescending'. It's not just once or twice, but every time we met, she treated us with her money⋯. Instead of saying 'thank you' after you ate for free, you said 'She's showing off' to other people behind her, so she's very upset right now. And did you borrow some money from her?"

"No, I didn't borrow it, but Hwa-young just sent it to my bank account. I didn't want to say anything regretful, but I unintentionally told her my financial problems, and she just sent money to my bank account."

"It's all because Hwa-young has a big heart and a desire to help those in need. Also, since you were my best friend, she didn't want anything from you in return. She must have felt a great sense of betrayal because you received help from her and said she was 'condescending' behind her back. She is disappointed and very angry with you these days, so I think it would be better for you not to see her for the time being."

"No, as you know she enjoys spending money. It's not because she has a big heart, nor likes helping. If she wants to spend money, she can just spend it, but she tries to be admired in return. It's enough to honor her once or twice. You don't know how difficult it is to admire her repeatedly. I don't want to do it anymore. You're completely smitten by her right now, and so praising her is like breathing for you. But we're not her lovers, or fans, or anything. Admiring her once or twice is enough. I'm tired of it.

"By the way, Yeon-woo, you always said you were busy, but what made you respond to our call today?" asked Cheol-su, who had been listening quietly.

"Actually, Hwa-young has been telling me to choose between her and you two bros. I told her to come out late because Young-sik, you don't know anything and you might be flustered if you run into her. I thought it would be very embarrassing because she is making plans. For now, you'd better avoid her."

"What? Are you saying that Hwa-young urged you to choose only one between her and us?" Yeong-sik, who had been quiet for a while, got angry.

"As you know, I'm busy with the business I've started recently⋯. I won't be able to see you for another few months." said Yeon-woo while looking at the entrance to the Arts center and Cheol-su and Yeong-sik in turn.

"Oh! There comes Hwa-young."

Yeon-woo, who was looking nervously at the entrance of the Arts center, shouted urgently. Cheol-su and Young-sik looked in the direction Yeon-woo was looking at. In the distance they saw a woman in her early forties in a flowy dress with long straight hair. At this time, Young-sik quickly disappeared somewhere as if he were avoiding a loan shark. He looked like a man running away from someone whom he was afraid of. At that time, Yeon-woo shouted again at the back of Young-sik, who was running away.

"Bro, let's not contact each other for a while."

He then spoke to Cheol-su, who was standing in front of him.

"Bro. I'll go to Hwa-young. I'm busy with work, so I don't think I'll be able to meet you for the time being."

Yeon-woo also disappeared into the crowd after leaving this comment. Cheol-su was left alone there. The two men disappeared with the appearance of Hwa-young. Young-sik, Yeon-woo, and Hwa-yeong···. They were not seen among the crowd of people. How long had it been. Cheol-su, who was standing there alone, called Young-sik.

"Where are you, bro?"

"Hiding in a nearby mart. Is Hwa-young gone?"

"I do not know. You are gone, and I don't know where Yeon-woo and Hwa-young are now. Come back. Let's see the music concert together."

Young-sik took a taxi back to the Arts center and they sat in their designated seats in the auditorium. They were watching the orchestra's performance, but their minds were wandering off among many thoughts away from the concert.

After the concert, they went into one of the beer bars lined up in front of Cheol-su's apartment. This time it wasn't what Cheol-su wanted. Yeong-sik asked Cheol-su to go in. Yeong-sik felt greatly disappointed and betrayed that Yeon-woo, who had shared many things with him for the last 10 years, said goodbye to him. He was shocked when he heard that Hwa-young, who was like a bully, had told Yeon-woo to choose only one between her and the two of them and urged Yeon-woo to cut all ties with him. Yeon-woo was the guy who always welcomed Young-sik warmly even after he suddenly ghosted Yeon-woo and then catch up with him again. Yeon-woo, who was nothing if not nice, met the old fox and became gradually estranged from him. Every time he contacted Yeon-woo, he said he was busy with work as an excuse and kept his distance. Now, when Yeon-woo even notified him not to contact him for a while, Young-sik felt a great sense of betrayal. It was a pity that Yeon-woo became as sneaky as Hwa-young Hong. But it couln't be helped. Yeon-woo was still young and needed to get married. Yeon-woo was too good for the dirty and rough guys like him. He thought it went well for Yeon-woo, but the feeling of being betrayed was inde-scribable. Young-sik kept drinking beer without saying a word.

"Cheol-su, please buy me another drink."

Yeong-sik gulped down the new beer that Cheol-su ordered again. He was the oldest, but He got always treated to food and drinks by younger friends, so he felt miserable and sorry for them. But that's okay. Cheol-su is a good younger friend. He is a very affectionate and kind-hearted. Yeong-sik finally began talking to Cheol-su after draining his beer glass for a while.

"Cheol-su, today is the last day."

"Are you saying you're disappearing again just a day after coming back?"

"I'd rather not see you anymore for you and for me."

"Yeon-woo left us··· and if even you leave me again, I feel lonely. I bought a home here···, how could I live alone?"

"I have a good gut feeling. I think you're going to get married soon. I think God made you buy a home to get you married."

"I've been single for 50 years. Will things happen when I get old like this that didn't happen when I was younger?"

"You are a diamond. What is a diamond? It is formed from pure carbon under extremely high heat and pressure in the crust layer 150 to 200 km underground. I still remember Cheol-su Kwon in his 20s. He was like a pure carbon lump. How oppressed and hurt you were in this storm-tossed world after graduating from college! How painful and lost the young Cheol-su was between ideals and reality! You had big dreams and ambitions at that time. How much you've studied over the past 24 years! While pursuing your dreams and ambitions, you also saved up money and bought a home. I made my parents pay an arm and a leg, pay a big fortune for my businesses. But you made it on your own. Now, you've lost all the weight and you are back to Cheol-su Kwon in your heyday. You've become a completely different person these days."

"Thank you. From now on, I will make a lot of friends here and live differently from the past."

"You've been telling me that you need to make more friends because you're lonely. There's something I'm upset about. Am I not your friend? Are you ignoring me? Am I just a drinking companion and meat companion that you meet when you want to drink and eat meat?"

"No, bro. You misunderstood. It was always you who drew the line first and notified me of the breakup, after meeting two or three times. You say goodbye every time we three meet. Then, you suddenly change your cell phone number, and make Yeon-woo and me confused. A few months later, you come back and contact us again and have fun with us for a while, then ghost us again, change your cell phone number, and disappear. I don't feel secure with you, bro. You keep disappearing, so I said I was lonely and wanted to make new friends. It was definitely not because I ignored you or something. Even today, you keep saying that today is your last day with me."

"It's because I am like a mayfly. I live only for a day, because I don't know about tomorrow…. God also tells us not to boast about tomorrow. God throws us a question, saying 'What if your soul is required of you this night?' when we pile up money and food in the barns and feel relieved that we will eat for the rest of our lives."

"Bro, you've been talking about God. Do you go to church?"

"Last time, when I lay low, I started attending, 'Cause I had no one to rely on. I lived the life of a prodigal son. I was the prodigal son who returned home after wasting my youth and my father's fortune in debauchery."

"You are not the only prodigal son. We are all prodigals in a way."

"Why you? You have lived a morally clean and socially diligent life."

"No matter how morally and diligently people have lived, if they have no fruits but only regrets, I think they have wasted their lives. I believe they are also prodigals in a way. I have struggled to succeed without knowing what's important in life⋯. I got old with time and my youth disappears before I knew it. Looking back, I also feel like a prodigal son who has wasted youth, money, and health on unimportant things."

"We're all living a life of mayflies. We don't know what happens tomorrow. Look, Yeon-woo that guy. He and I have been friends for 10 years. Yeon-woo and I have been best friends since we first met at the hometown alumni of law department of Seoul University. He has been my soul-mate. We met almost every day and talked about everything honestly, but today, one day later, he notified me of the breakup and told me not to contact him anymore, and left. I called Yeon-woo after I came out of my cave last night. We talked on the phone last night, but who would have thought that that guy would come today and say goodbye? Well, I'm sure the fox, Hwa-young, made him do it. He's grown a lot. He's grown so big that there's nothing I can do for him. That guy left us. Well, actually, what's the big deal about friendship? Love is more important because he is old enough to get marry. He's gone in pursuit of love⋯. No, he followed his ambition hidden in love. ⋯Actually, I don't want to⋯, either. ⋯I don't want to go into hiding. I'm older than you guys but ···no money. How can I have money? I live on the money that my elderly parents provide. I got treated at your own expenses, but too much of a good thing. I did go into hiding···, because I was sorry."

Young-sik paused for a moment. Cheol-su filled Yeong-sik's empty glass with more beer.

"Bro, I think there's something called a fate in time. Yeon-woo has been our friend for last 10 years, but··· now that he is leaving us, I guess he's done learning. Yeon-woo now needs Hwa-young, not us anymore."

"a fate in time···?"

"Another fate in time will come to us··· to learn from each other and grow."

"Yeon-woo took advantage of me and left. Are you going to use me and leave too?"

"Bro, what do you mean by taking advantage of you? We learn from each other. We grow together. If you don't leave me, I won' t leave you."

"Now that you've bought a home, go ahead and find your wife. Get married. I'll live by myself. Wait, come to think of it, you bought the home, and lost weight···, you have been preparing to get a wife. You're currently helping your brother with the convenience store business. You're learning well from your brother and soon set up your own business and become independent. You said you didn't want to do law-related work any more when you retired, but your legal knowledge will be useful for business. Good for you. You'll succeed. It's only a matter of time before you get a girl. Lucky you⋯."

Yeong-sik was now heavily drunk.

"Bro, you only say nice things to me today. Thank you."

"You regret buying a home in this area, but that home is the report card of your life. It's a report card showing that you have lived your life faithfully and not in vain."

"Thank you for saying that."

"You are fruitful. Your knowledge of the law, your home, your piano skills⋯. Men who play the piano are popular with women. And your appearance is back to your prime⋯."

When Cheol-su was told that he was fruitful in his life, tears welled up in his eyes.

"Sir!" said Yeong-sik to Cheol-su after pausing for a moment.

"You suddenly say 'Sir' to me. You're drunk."

"Because I respect you."

In an instant, Cheol-su's heart warmed. He felt like his past life, full of pain and suffering, had been healed and rewarded.

That night, before taking a taxi back home, Young-sik called Cheol-su 'Sir' again. Then he came home and sent Cheol-su a text message.

'Let's not get in touch anymore.'

Hwa-young Hong. She was 6 years older than Yeon-woo and liked to wear long and flowy dresses and loosen her long hair. She gave off the image of a weak woman, but her personality was different. Unlike Yeon-woo, who was not clear about relationship and always met up with others when they contacted him again no matter how they broke up, she was determined and firm. She was good at presenting herself and enjoyed spending money and being admired. As Young-sik said, even though she looked like a feeble woman but she was like a ringleader and had charisma. Yeon-woo liked the way Hwa-young presented herself wonderfully with her brilliant speech. She was always busy meeting many businessmen. Yeon-woo, who were younger and obedient, volunteered for her manager to follow her. He always drove for her. All the things he experienced while following her were a new world for him.

He was excited about building his personal connections through her. Every week, he attended various gatherings, and went camping or traveling with a lot of new connections. With the bros he would go to common barbecue restaurants, pubs, diners, convenience stores, and gugbabjib at best. However with her, he would go to fancy and expensive restaurants and wine bars. He also met new, wealthy people there. It was a completely different new world from when he hung out with Yeong-sik and Cheol-su. It was a world that even women at his age or younger could not give him. Yeon-woo couldn't miss her. It was okay that she was older. In any case, he was not popular with women at his age or younger. He was not good at improving his appearance and had even gained weight, so he did not look his age but looked at least ten years older, so he did not care about his looks. Also, because he always hung out with his middle-aged friends, people did not see him as in his 30s, but thought of him as being the same age as his middle-aged friends. Hwa-young told him to be sure whether he would choose her or his old friends.. He couldn't miss her. She was an opportunity for him. As he hung out with his old two bros for the past 10 years, he took advantage of them as a good reference, learned from their regrets, and made different choices from theirs. And now, he didn't have enough time to just meet new people he met through Hwa-young. He didn't want to let Hwa-young lose her temper due to his two old friends and miss out on her by constantly meeting them she disliked. He used to meet his two older friends without her noticing, but now he had to draw the line clearly.

011

A Man playing the Piano and
Silk Tree Flowers

In late July. The rain that had been falling all through July stopped for a while, and the sun peeked through clouds. After finishing his part-time job at the convenience store, Cheol-su headed to the place where the silk tree was located. The rainy season that continued throughout the summer made the air damp and humid.

He hadn't been here in a while. He could see the mysterious summer tree that blooms and bursts into strong fragrant scents every summer for three months from June to August. Last year, whenever he passed by this place in the heat, this place was filled with the scents of silk tree flowers, but this year there was no scent. It was because due to the rainy season that lasted for a few months. The silk tree flowers fell in the rain without showing off their beauty or emitting fragrance, and were swept away somewhere. The tree lost most of its flowers and was lush with green leaves. On the road, a few flowers that had fallen a long time ago were fading white and drying out. Cheol-su picked up some flowers which were still fresh. They were drooping in the rain. He brought them to the tip of his nose. It was still fragrant. He looked in the direction of the piano academy from where the silk tree was. Memories of this time last year came to his mind.

In February of last year, his life, which had been running nonstop, stopped in an instant, just as his car that had been running for him stopped. Physically, he was diagnosed with cerebral infarction, and mentally, he was suffering from depression, lethargy, emptiness, and regret about life, and he visited this city for recuperation.

On the first morning of June last year, he bumped into a piano academy. He still remembered the first time he saw his piano teacher. He didn't know at that time where the encounter would take him. In the hot summer, he walked on this road with excitement at the thought of seeing her. Starting at some point, whenever he walked down this road, he could smell subtle and mysterious scents. He always wondered where that scent came from. One day in mid-July, when the scent was exceptionally strong, he finally stopped and looked back. Where does this scent come from? He discovered a silk tree while following the scent. The mysterious and strong scent of silk tree flowers were added to the excitement that he could see his piano teacher soon after walking a little further, which made him feel like his heart was going to explode and made him so dizzy that he was going to faint. How happy he was then! How excited he was! How fragrant the road to the academy was! His heart was pounding and going pit-a-pat. It was like he was dreaming. In the end, at the time when the scents of the silk tree flowers were the most intense, he declined the demand for his reinstatement in August. And a year passed, and Cheol-su retired altogether and was standing under this silk tree again.

He wanted to walk this path again in the thrill of romance, smelling the scents as much as he did last year, but he coulnt anymore. In a way, human life may be like that of a mayfly as Young-sik said. We don't know what happens tomorrow. The predicted future may go wrong in an instant. He took the silk tree flowers to the tip of his nose. He breathed in the scents under the silk tree just like he did a year ago. This year, the scent was weak due to the rainy season, which caused a lot of flowers to fall, but the scents, excitement, thrill, and the feelings of this time last year still remained.

He was different from who he was a year ago. Now, a year later, he lost a lot of weight and had a normal weight and his stroke was cured. Depression and lethargy which had caused him emotional difficulties also disappeared.

Just then, he received a long text message from an unknown number. It was Young-sik.

'Cheol-su, how have you been? You still don't have a hard time drinking at home, do you? It was not Seoul, your dream city, where you bought your first home. But I think your dream to buy a home in Seoul has led you to buy one at least in this region. Don't be too disappointed that you were trying to draw a tiger but ended up drawing a cat. Who knows? This experience can serve as a stepping stone for you to buy a building and become a building owner, and buy land. Your apartment could be your first start. You don't know the future, so don't think too negatively. And I started working part-time as a cashier at a mart in front of my parents' apartment. I had to change myself too. It's my first time working for someone else, but it's fun. Now I can live like an older bro who can pay for me and you guys instead of just getting treated. I also paid back half of the money that Hwa-young lent me. I transferred it to Hwa-young's bank account. When I get my next paycheck, I'll transfer the rest of the money.'

Cheol-su called Young-sik right away with joy.

"Shall we have gukbap together for dinner?"

"That sounds great."

Young-sik came out by taxi right away. Cheol-su appeared with his left fingers holding up some of the flowers, which he picked up under the silk tree. Young-sik, who saw the flowers for the first time, asked.

"What are those?"

"Flowers."

"They don't look like flowers."

"Love that doesn't look like love, unrequited love is also love."

"What?"

"I picked them up on the street."

"No matter how pretty flowers are, don't pick them up. Pollen allergy symptoms may occur."

"Yes."

After saying that, Cheol-su once again held the flowers close to his nose and smelled their scents. Still fragrant. While they were having gugbabs, Young-sik's phone rang. Young-sik turned on the speaker and answered the phone. Yeon-woo's voice was heard over the receiver. After Yoeong-sik hung up the phone, Cheol-su asked.

"Do you keep in touch with Yeon-woo again?"

"Yes. When I sent you a text, I also sent another to Yeon-woo."

"Why didn't you invite him for dinner?"

"Other dinner plans."

"With Whom?"

"Hwa-young."

"The fact that he called you even though Hwa-young was with him probably means that Hwa-young has let go of her anger towards you."

"I paid back half of the money Hwa-young lent me. Where shall we go after eating?"

"Shall we go to my apartment?"

"That's good. If Yeon-woo were here, gukbap wouldn't taste good due to the strong smell of his cologne. But without him, it is delicious. Cologne doesn't suit gukbap restaurants. Hahaha. Let him eat spaghetti with Hwa-young at a fancy restaurant that women like, while giving off fragrance. Hahaha."

Cheol-su and Yeong-sik looked at each other and laughed heartily for the first time in a long time. The grains of rice they had eaten popped out of their mouths. They found it funny and laughed again. After finishing the meal, Cheol-su carefully picked up the flowers that was placed on their table and they left the restaurant.

"The flowers have withered now, right?"

"It's still okay."

"Give them to me."

Cheol-su handed the flowers to Yeong-sik. Yeong-sik smelled the scents of them.

"These smell good. The scents are still strong."

Cheol-su received the flowers back from Yeong-sik, picked them up again with his left fingers, and walked down the street. At that time, the back of someone's hand brushed and hit against the back of his hand holding the flowers, and passed quickly. In reaction, Cheol-su dropped the flowers.

"Huh!"

Cheol-su was embarrassed. His heart ached as he looked at the flowers scattered on the street. He felt uneasy. He got down on one knee reflexively and carefully picked up the fallen flowers one by one. The woman, who brushed against the back of Cheol-su's hand with hers as she passed by, realized she had made a mistake and immediately turned around.

She looked at Cheol-su, who was carefully picking up the

flowers one by one, with an apologetic attitude. She wanted to say sorry to Cheol-su, but Cheol-su was so embarrassed and preoccupied with picking up the flowers that she instead kept bowing and saying that she was sorry for that to Young-sik, who was standing next to Cheol-su.

"Hey, hey, now that they withered, throw them away. Throw them away!"

Young-sik, who was next to him, shouted at Cheol-su, but smiled generously and brightly at her and repeatedly said, "It's okay." Only then did she turn around and go her way. Cheol-su also stood up. Cheol-su and Young-sik started walking again.

"That woman said she was sorry. You were preoccupied with picking up the flowers, so she apologized to me instead." said Young-sik, looking at the back of her walking a few steps ahead.

"Okay."

The woman, who was walking ahead with quick steps, now disappeared from the sight of Cheol-su and Young-sik. They walked slowly. In the evening, the heat of the day abated and it was pleasantly cool.

"They say the summer rainy season is almost over."

"According to the weather forecast, we will see sunny days

often from now on."

While they were walking, talking about the weather, the woman who brushed and hit against the back of Cheol-su's hand was standing in front of a cafe talking to her friend. Yeong-sik and Cheolsu continued to walk slowly and gradually got closer to the women. As the distance between them gradually narrowed, Yeong-sik suddenly started making a fuss.

"Hey, isn't this the moment when we make something of our life? This is the moment when a novel is created. A man falls in love with a woman who accidentally smashes his flowers! A~ha!"

Young-sik's fuss was embarrassing and noisy, but Cheol-su burst into laughter because the expression 'smash the man's flowers' was funny. At that time, the woman standing in front of the cafe approached Cheol-su. Cheol-su and Young-sik stopped walking.

"I'm sorry earlier. I think they are precious to you, so you should be careful to keep them."

"No problem, It was my fault. I should have walked with flowers in front of me···."

"Ladies, if you're sorry, treat us to a cup of coffee. There's a cafe right here."intervened Young-sik, who was watching them next to Cheol-su. Yeong-sik liked those two women. It crossed his mind that either one of them, no, the woman who brushed against the back of Cheol-su's hand with hers would do well with Cheol-su and he hoped to get along with her friend. He didn' want to miss out on this opportunity, so he actively talked to them.

"No, it's on me. If you're sorry, please have a cup of coffee with us and leave." Yeong-sik smiled with his mouth open at them and spread his hands out toward the cafe. The ladies smiled back and entered the cafe ahead of them, and Cheol-su and Young-sik followed them cheerfully.

The Author's Words

One day in December, last winter, I went to the school library to take a breather after hectic days filled with creating questions for the final exam and doing exam-related works. Among bulky books on the bookshelves, a very small and thin book stood out. I found it was a short story and it was published with an English translation. It was also a work that a provincial cultural foundation selected and supported. At that time, I was encouraged by a friend to try out for the category of novels at Jeonnam Cultural Foundation, and the accidental encounter with that small book made me have the idea in mind that if I was selected for the National Culture and Arts Support System, I would also write and publish an Korean-English novel. And I was selected.

I set up a writing place to focus on writing. When I woke up in the morning, I went to my studio and a cafe and concentrated on writing and translating for 6 to 10 hours every day. Not to be distracted, I ate my first meal in the evening and took a break, only after I finished writing and translating for the day. Those were truly tough days. Now, the days have passed like a dream, and I am proud and happy to see the fruit of my efforts. And I give thanks to God. I also think that those hard days of mine may have looked shining in the eyes of God, who sees everything. Please read this book and share your impressions.

And I send my love and apologies to my beloved rabbits, Sarang(Love) and Hangbok(Happiness) in heaven, to their progeny, and to all of my past animal friends such as chicks, chickens, birds, hamsters, cats, puppies, dogs, rabbits, etc that have connected with me. May God bless their souls. And may God bless and care the progeny of Sarang and Hangbok that are still alive somewhere with his love and care.

November 2023, Autumn

Minju Jeong